"Adam and Stephanie P[...] prayer and the study of the word related to the [...] dynamics that believers will face at the end of this age. Left Alive, is an epic, well-written, fictional story that will thrust its readers into the reality and urgency of the days that are ahead for those who believe. It is a MUST READ!"

Jaye Thomas
Song of Hope Ministries, Inc.

"This apocalyptic novel will pull at your heart and leave you on the edge of your seat as you see biblical prophecy come to life. Definitely a must read for anyone wanting a captivating story or has an interest in the end-times."

Justin Rizzo
Worship Leader, Composer, Playwright

"The Parkers' research is astounding and profoundly comprehensive and will challenge the most dedicated believer and sophisticated intellectual to examine why we believe and do what we do in Christianity. His accurate portrayal of end-time events makes the reader see themselves in the stories and point them to Jesus. It won't take long before you grasp the Parker's deep seriousness, passion for combat, sly wordplay, and uncompromising love for God. This is truly a deeply satisfying read."

Charles Morris
Pastor, Author, RSI Ministry

LEFT ALIVE

AN END TIMES NOVEL

ADAM & STEPHANIE
PARKER

Parker Studios, LLC

Front cover design by Adam Parker

First printing edition 2022.

To my best friend in the whole world, my husband. Without teaching me your in-depth knowledge of the end times, this book would have been absolutely impossible. Thank you for always inspiring me.

To my wife, who is my best friend and the one who has always been there, supported me, and put up with me. You are my better half and I could not do this life without you.

FOREWORD

Why is a book like Adam and Stephanie Parker's on the end times so critical in this prophetic hour of human history? Because Jesus gave us numerous signs and teachings regarding the end times and we need to understand them. Today one of the least understood and probably least studied biblical doctrines is the doctrine of eschatology. Eschatology is simply the term that describes what the Bible teaches about the last days. When we mention the last days we actually mean the months and years directly preceding the second coming of Jesus to return for His church. But He comes not only for the church, He also comes to bring about the restoration of the earth through a series of judgments that is beautifully described throughout the book of revelation.

Along with Jesus, the Bible tells us of numerous writers that were inspired by the Holy Spirit to write down the insight that they received from God regarding the last days. The prophet Daniel, for example, describes the urgent need for believers in Christ to understand what God's word actually reveals for His people and the nations. The last days will produce a people that will be very familiar with the events that will confront those living on earth in that day and hour.

While Daniel was serving in the court of the Persian empire, he received insight from the Lord that the 70 years of Jeremiah's prophecy of Israel's time in exile in the land of Babylon was coming to an end. As a result, Daniel began to seek the Lord for greater clarification and what God's future had in store for his people. Daniel began to fast and pray and the Lord answered his prayer by giving Daniel very detailed information and specific events that revealed how God would deal with the nation of Israel and their place in the end times prior to the Lord's return. As Daniel pressed the issue and sought to receive a greater revelation of the events that would come about, the Lord instructed an angel to communicate to Daniel that the specific detailed information he was longing to receive, was actually reserved to be understood by those living in the end times.

In addition to Daniel, the apostle Paul also received great insight into the spiritual condition of society prior to the Lord's return. The Holy Spirit clearly showed Paul that massive deception and great immorality would be on the rise in the days leading up to Jesus' return.

The apostle John received a series of visions that revealed in great detail how the Lord will deal with the nations of the earth and how an end-time world leader will arise to lead many astray. This world leader will cause multitudes to reject the worship of the one true God an instead worship a man that will be known as the antichrist. John wrote all that he saw and entitled his prophetic revelation by calling it THE BOOK OF REVELATION.

Left Alive is necessary because it's a piece of prophetic fulfillment that promises us that God would release greater understanding to several of His servants about the last days. I believe you are holding this book, not by any mere chance or coincidence but because the Holy Spirit has directed you to purchase it or lead someone to give this book as a gift to you so that you would be one of those who will be better equipped to understand the doctrine of eschatology.

Take the time to prayerfully read this book and ask the Holy Spirit for insight and revelation. I am confident that the Lord will impart to you not only the necessary revelation that you will need as a believer with a better understanding of God's plan for the last days, but also to be one of His servants that He can equip and use to communicate with clarity and understanding God's plan for the church and the nations of the earth. May the Spirit of wisdom, revelation, knowledge, and understanding come upon you, flooding your heart and mind with great understanding of what He plans to do.

~ Carlos Sarmiento

Pastor Carlos Sarmiento is the Founder of the Orlando House of Prayer Missions Base, Forerunner Messenger Alliance, Author of Encountered By God, and has been preaching the Gospel for more than 25 years.

PREFACE

We believe we are living in the last days. We believe that either ourselves, our children or our grandchildren will be of those "left alive" when Jesus splits the sky, and we see Him coming on the clouds. If you are the least bit observant, you can look around the world today and see the signs Jesus' disciples were asking about in Matthew 24, when they said, "Tell us, when will these things be, and what will be the sign of your coming and of the end of the age?" There is a growing sense of urgency in believers we hear from to prepare for hard times, to prepare for persecution, and to prepare ourselves and our children to be ready for what is coming.

Isaiah prophesied about a people who would call evil good and good evil. The apostle Paul wrote that "in the last days perilous times will come: for men will be lovers of themselves... lovers of pleasure rather than lovers of God, having a form of godliness but denying its power. We are seeing a generation who are so confused about who they are. Many of the things our parents' and grandparents' generations knew as foundational, unmovable truths are being questioned and discarded by young people and trumpeted by those now in seats of influence.

In this novel we see some of the difficult times and persecution we know are coming. We take the position that believers will be here for the tribulation that Jesus talked about in Matthew 24:21. We do not see a secret rapture described in scripture, but a rapture that takes place at the last trumpet where every eye will see. I know and have great respect for many in the body of Christ who believe in a pre-tribulation rapture. However, I believe that it's possible this doctrine, if false, could be a stumbling block for many believers, especially in first world countries where Christians have not experienced persecution. Scripture is clear that the love of many will grow cold, people will be offended and there will be a great falling away from the faith. We do not want to be offended. We want to be prepared for what we know is coming upon the earth.

The knowledge of Jesus Christ has been and is still the answer for the Church today. This next generation is in need of a life-changing encounter with the person of Jesus. Men, women, and youth of all ages need to be pierced by the Holy Spirit to "count all things as loss for the excellence of the knowledge of Christ Jesus our Lord" (Phil. 3:8). We must declare to the world, that the only answer, the only solution, the only true peace is Jesus.

~ Adam & Stephanie Parker

CHAPTER ONE

"And I saw in the right hand of Him who sat on the throne a scroll written inside and on the back, sealed with seven seals"
- Revelation 5:1

Michael Hill looked on in horror as people, as far as the eye could see, were all walking in a trance toward a massive cliff. He yelled at the top of his lungs, "Stop! Turn around! You're going to fall off!" It was like he was yelling into the wind. Everyone he could see didn't even turn around at the sound of his voice. He wondered if they even heard him as they continued to walk forward, all the way up until the moment when they took their final step off the edge and plunged to their death.

As he continued to scream, he was able to see a few people turn their heads and stare quizzically at him before they turned back around and followed the crowd toward the cliff's rim. He had yelled until his voice felt like sandpaper, when he finally saw only three faceless people out of the thousands turn and look at him, and then walk away from the cliff.

It was a struggle for those three people. The crowd was

massive and their momentum going forward made it look like the people were fish in a river trying to swim upstream, but he was able to breathe a sigh of relief when they made it past the crowd and to safety far away from the cliff.

It was a steady stream of people heading to the edge. It seemed like a never-ending line of people emerged from behind him and began the death march to the cliff. The new arrivals were ignoring his desperate cries of warning as well. It was like they were all sleepwalking and completely oblivious to what they were heading straight towards. He yelled over and over, "Wake up! Wake Up! There's a cliff; you're going to die! Wake up!"

Suddenly he wasn't sure where he was anymore. Something or someone was shaking him and he heard an incessant 'beep, beep, beep' in the recesses of his mind.

"Wake up. Wake up. You're going to be late for work, Michael. Wake up!" His wife Sophia tried to nudge him awake not so gently as she pushed her foot against his shin. "I have another hour until I have to wake up. At least turn your alarm off."

The pieces were starting to make more sense in his mind. He had been sleeping. It was just a dream, but it felt so real. He reached over and turned off the persistent alarm clock when he realized he was drenched in sweat from the dream. He never used to even remember his dreams, but, this last week, he had experienced the same dream every night. He tried to shake off the feeling of urgency the dream left with him. It left him wanting to shout from the rooftops, but not knowing what he was supposed to say.

He had no idea who he was supposed to warn or what he

was supposed to warn them about, but as he began to get dressed he had a growing feeling that something big was coming. Maybe that was his pessimistic side taking over he thought to himself as he got ready for work that morning.

He was a normal guy in many ways. He was a muscular man of average height and his job as a police officer in Omaha, Nebraska made him keep his hair short and face clean-shaven. He hated the city and looked forward to returning home each night to his little town, Nebraska City, forty-five minutes south of Omaha.

He had a family and they were a rarity in this day and age in every way. They were mostly happy and they loved each other. They spent time playing board games, going on adventures together, and talking over dinner.

They weren't perfect, they had their fair share of arguments too, but you could always feel the love they had for one another even when they fought. Yes, in many ways Michael was a completely normal guy. In every way, but one. Lately, he started to have crazy dreams. They felt so real. It felt like he was watching a movie as he would see the dreams unfold in his mind.

Everyone dreams, but this felt different. His dreams would stay with him for days playing the scenes over and over in his mind. Maybe he was going crazy. Maybe it was his brain just trying to shut off the absurdity of the propaganda machine that all the news stations had become.

As he was getting ready for work this morning, shaving, and watching the television, he couldn't escape the fact that the news had become less and less about the facts and more and more about trying to sell the general population stories that would make them feel good and ignore the trouble all around them.

Maybe it was because he was a cop that he just couldn't make himself see through the rose-colored glasses everyone seemed to be wearing. Recently, even his youngest son, Miles, thought his old man had a few loose nuts. They used to be so close, but something happened when Miles had his twenty-first birthday. He started to change.

Michael remembered back when Miles was the tender-hearted little toddler that ran around the house. That little boy had once cared so deeply about what others felt, but Miles had allowed his strength of empathy to become his weakness. It was clear now that Miles had been slowly deceived by the common teaching that was all around them. Miles' desire to show love to everyone was warped into something ugly. He began to believe showing love to others required validation and support for their sin.

Michael wished he could go back in time and teach his son better. If he could do it over, he would instruct him that he should always show kindness, but that doesn't mean he should justify unGodly choices in the name of 'loving our neighbor.' Tolerating sin in the name of love was the mindset that led to a slippery slope of spiritual apathy in Miles. Once his son lost his convictions, it didn't take long before he lost his desire for a relationship with his family as well.

"Ouch!" Michael growled when his razor bit deep into his chin as his thoughts lingered on his unteachable son. Michael rinsed off his razor in the sink and decided he was done getting ready when his wife walked in.

His wife Sophia peeked her head in as she was walking by

the bathroom and teased him, "You know razors are sharp. Right?" She saw that he didn't appreciate her joke. She had known Michael her whole life and could tell his anger had a lot less to do with the cut on his chin and a lot more to do with something stirring inside of him. She stopped teasing and became compassionate, "Are you ok, Honey?"

Even after twenty-six years of marriage, she was still a spitball full of energy. She would complain to him that the children had left her body less than it was back in the early days of their marriage, but Michael didn't care. She was perfect for him. She sacrificed so much so that she could give life to two amazing boys.

But right now he could only think of one of their children, Miles.

"I'm great." Michael responded with just the right amount of cynicism and self-pity to make his wife put down the laundry in her hands and come over and give him a hug.

He inwardly scolded himself, "Great. Now I really feel like a schmuck. I can't even cut myself shaving without needing my wife to comfort me." All that anger seemed to dissipate as she wrapped her arms around him. She stood on her tiptoes to kiss his half-shaven face and rest her head with her auburn hair that smelled like pineapples on his shoulder. He marveled to himself as he felt all his worry dissipating, "How does she make me forget all my problems with one little touch."

He wrapped his arms around her, returned the hug, and enjoyed the embrace from the wife of his youth.

He married her when they were just kids. They met in high school and when they graduated they didn't want to wait another day to get married. So they didn't. Sounds like those typical rebellious teenagers, but it really wasn't. He loved her and she loved him, but more importantly, they felt like God was calling them together for something bigger than just themselves. He believed it like he believed he needed air to breathe. They were soul mates for a reason.

He had always thought that this calling from God was to be an amazing dad and husband and to love his family well. Maybe even it was to help others with his job as a cop. Now he wasn't so sure. Did he miss God's voice all those years ago? Was it just teenage lust that made him want to marry that beautiful cute little five-foot brunette girl and not God bringing them together?

The more he felt the rebellion from Miles the more he questioned everything he ever believed. His son still loved the Lord. He believed that, but he was pulling further and further away from the family. From him. Nothing good could come from that. He was an adult. He had a right to make his own decisions, but it was more than that. He was seeing Miles pull away from some of the values that accompanied his Christian walk.

Michael would try to tell him "Being a Christian means more than just Sunday morning church, you gotta walk it out!" It didn't go well when he did that though. The most recent spat ended with Miles yelling at him that Michael's version of Christianity was short-sighted and intolerant.

Sophia sensed where his thoughts had turned. "Our boy is going to be ok. He loves Jesus and loves you. Don't forget that," Sophia said as she pulled away from the hug and went back to putting away the laundry.

"How did she do that? How did she know exactly what

I'm thinking!" Michael wondered for about the millionth time in their marriage. But she was right. It didn't do any good worrying about Miles. He just needed to give it to God and move on. His older son, John, needed him. He couldn't let Miles consume all his thoughts.

John was recently engaged to a girl, Katie, from Kansas City which was about two hours south of them. She was a beautiful Christian girl; it was going to be a great match. Michael felt a sense of pride and accomplishment as a father when he reflected on John who was secure in his faith and had much love for his family. Even though his priorities were shifting, as they should, to put Katie first, Michael could still feel the love and affection from John whenever they spoke.

Katie Williams was a newer addition to their family. It was hard for Michael to think of her without tears coming to his eyes. Having had only boys, it was such a pleasure at the thought of soon having a daughter in the family. Adult children, their trials and successes, and now the world news... It seemed the weight of the world was on his shoulders this morning.

The news was applauding yet another great move in Europe towards peace and saying that America must follow suit. France had come out as the leader of social reformation and their leader, President Elyon, had reaped the rewards. His policies had virtually eliminated all violence in the entire country since his election. Other countries were taking notice and considering following suit.

Not only had France experienced unparalleled peace and prosperity as a nation, but they also led the way two years ago in accomplishing the impossible. They negotiated a peace treaty for Israel. France successfully brokered a treaty among the Arab nations surrounding Israel that called for an end to all hostility with their Jewish neighbors.

There had been attempts by many world leaders over the last two decades to enact a treaty that would end the conflict in the Middle East. It was the white whale of the political world and President Elyon was the first leader to actually succeed at it.

For two years the Middle East has experienced peace like it never had in history. The Jews and Palestinians lived in peace with one another and Elyon was declared a hero for bringing an end to the bloodshed that plagued the region for millennia.

Now, the news was saying that Elyon had the blueprint for peace and other nations should follow suit. The anchors were sharing the opinion of the American public that America should lead the way by following the example of France and take a similar course of action. They speculated that perhaps that way the United States could experience the same level of security and prosperity that France was enjoying.

Of course, Michael wanted peace and people to live in harmony with one another. He was a cop. Practically his entire job description was being a peacemaker. He just couldn't shake the feeling that something about the way it was going down across the ocean didn't sit right with him. He wished he could know more, but the news was only reporting the good and saying nothing of opposing points of view.

That was his first inclination that something wasn't right. Why are all the stories about the success in France one-sided? Where is the unbiased reporting? But it was more than that.

The news hadn't been unbiased in a while. There was just something that made the hairs on the back of his neck stick up whenever President Elyon's praises were sung by the news, but he couldn't quite put his finger on what it was.

Jacob Levi was the father of a traditional American Family. Sure, they were Jewish, but that's where their ethnicity ended. Judaism was just a last name to them, not a religion. Sarah and Jacob met and fell in love just like everyone else in the states. There was no arranged marriage, there was no being married under a chuppah or the bride carried on the chair or the groom stomping on the glass. There was a judge and city hall.

Their son, Benjamin, didn't go to Hebrew school or wear the prayer shawl like his devout and orthodox grandparents did. He played baseball and was lucky to make his math classes on time at the high school. Their daughter, Rachel, loved the violin and would play all day if her parents let her. She probably couldn't even tell you who Moses or the pharaoh was.

They hardly identified with their Jewish heritage, so why did it seem like everyone else only thought of them as Jewish? Everyone they came into contact with seemed to ignore that they were first and foremost American. That didn't matter. All that mattered was their last name, Levi.

It wasn't always like this. Sure, Jacob remembered stories his parents would tell of when it was like this back in Germany in WWII, but that was so long ago. To Jacob, that's all it ever was. Stories. Stories that would never happen again.

At least that's what he thought. He still hoped it would never happen again, but it did seem that things were different now than they used to be toward Jews.

It used to be that people would become outraged at any anti-Semitic comments made. Comedians would be ostracized if they crossed the line, and TV shows canceled if their jokes went too far. Now all that is different.

It had become the norm for Jews to be the punch line for others' amusement. It was nothing too terrible. It was mainly jabs about their physical appearance or greediness. Jacob had ignored all of that. It was after all just jokes.

Today it went further than cheap digs masquerading as anti-Semitic humor. At school, Benjamin refused to cheat for a boy who was failing math. Benjamin wasn't doing much better than failing himself, so it doesn't make sense why the boy wanted him to cheat for him on the test. Probably more Jewish stereotypes that all Jews are smart and successful.

When Benjamin refused to cheat, the boy became irate.

"Everything is handed to you on a silver platter, Jew. Show me your answers during the test or else!" The boy fumed at Benjamin with his hands clenched at his sides.

Benjamin responded, "I'm sorry, I just can't do that. You don't want to cheat off me anyway, like, I'm barely passing Algebra."

"Liar!" The boy yelled as he punched Benjamin square on the nose and walked away.

Benjamin stood stunned for a moment, then he began to process what had happened. Not only was prejudice evident in that boy, but he was surrounded by a crowd of students and even teachers all looking at him with what appeared to be disgust.

Benjamin went up to one of those teachers that had her arms crossed and was staring at him and said, "Did you see that? He punched me."

It was clear she had no intention of holding that boy accountable when she icily told Benjamin, "Boys will be boys, now return to your class."

Jacob still could not believe that the teacher did nothing. He went storming into the school after he heard the story. He broke every speeding law on the way in, slammed his car door, getting his coat stuck in the door in the process. He had to pause his indignant march into the office long enough to unlock the car and retrieve his uncooperative jacket before resuming his furious steps into the principal's office.

"Jacob Levi here to see Principal Strand," Jacob said before he was even fully inside the doorway.

The principal must have been looking for him out his office window. He was up from behind his desk in seconds and to the door ushering Jacob into the empty seat in front of the desk. As soon as Jacob sat down in the oversized chair that seemed to swallow him whole, he felt dwarfed and like the underdog in a wrestling match as the principal towered over him sitting in his large formal wing-back chair in front of him.

Jacob tried to speak up and inform the principal of the injustice that had happened earlier that day, but before he could say a single word he was cut off.

"I understand there was some unpleasantness this afternoon during school between your son and another boy." The principal continued, "Before you say anything I want you to know that we have decided to be lenient on Benjamin's behalf."

Jacob couldn't believe his ears. On Benjamin's behalf? Surely there must be some mistake. The principal must not have gotten all of his facts straight, so Jacob, as calmly as he could, relayed the facts of the day including the teacher dismissing the assault against his son.

When he was finished telling him of the prejudice and assault his son experienced on school grounds, he fully expected a different reaction from the principal this time. Jacob looked expectantly at the principal waiting for an apology and a list of punishments the other boy would receive.

That is not what happened though. Instead, Principal Stand stood up over the chair that Jacob was sitting in. It was clear he was trying to feel superior and intimidate Mr. Levi in the process.

"Let me be very clear," Principal Strand began with barely controlled rage. "Your son has instigated many arguments that, to be frank, deserved to be handled with a good punch to the nose. Today was the straw that broke the camel's back when he acted like he, a Jew, was morally superior. That boy showed restraint only punching him once and I personally commended him for that. You'd be wise to remind your boy of his place in the order of things and where he will always stand with a last name like 'Levi' and to conduct himself accordingly."

It was then that Jacob knew something drastic and dangerous had shifted in the world. It was no longer silly jokes aimed at his people, but something far more serious.

"I guess that's irony for you," he thought to himself. "I

haven't thought of the Jewish people as 'my people' since I was a boy at Saturday Sabbath meals."

Turning from his thoughts and momentary stunned silence, he took a deep breath and stood to face the principal. Whatever the outcome, he would not face it sitting down in that chair of forced compliance.

Jacob spoke strong and clear without breaking eye contact with his fists balled at his sides, "So is that your final answer? No punishment shall be given to the boy who attacked my son?"

The principal simply nodded and got up and opened the door clearly showing the meeting had come to an end.

Jacob took a deep breath and mustered all the strength he had to stay in control of his emotions. He released his balled-up fists and looked the principal square in the eyes as he passed by him and smiled as he said, "Shalom" and then left.

The principal looked as if he wanted to explode at the single Jewish word uttered in his presence. Principal Strand sneered as he said one final threat, "And if you're thinking about going above my head... don't. I have the full support of the school board in how I handled this." And with that, the principal slammed his office door in Jacob's face.

Jacob may have left the meeting defeated in spirit, but his head was held high. He refused to show any signs of the sadness and fear that he felt in his soul as he continued his walk out to his car.

Just a few moments earlier, he had been filled with purpose and with righteous indignation, and a list of punishments suitable for the offender. Now, he walked out with only questions.

Is this how things started back in Germany? First a few jokes, then sanctioned bullying, and then....worse? He wanted to think it would end here. After all, it's only a broken nose. There are worse things, right?

But then he felt that prickling fear at the back of his mind remind him that's what he thought about the jokes.

When his wife would complain or worry about the rise in anti-Semitic jokes he'd tell her "It's only a few jokes. There are worse things right?" He would remind her of all the strides the world had made to accept Jews. Elyon had done the impossible in Israel and had become a beacon of hope to his people that things were finally moving in the right direction for the Jews. Jacob would tell his wife that it was only a matter of time before Elyon was able to do the same thing and help Jews throughout the rest of the world.

As Jacob got to his car and sat down in it, he wondered for the first time, "What if I'm wrong? What if the worse things keep coming?" He realized at some point he would have to do something before it got any worse, but he wouldn't think about that now. First things first, tonight he will tend to his son's nose and they will spend an evening together. Tomorrow he will remove him from that school. After that? He honestly had no idea.

President Xander Elyon was the leader of what had become arguably the greatest nation in the world. It was only because of him that France had become such a strong nation and there was an end to all violence in Israel for the first time in history. France wasn't always the richest and most powerful nation. In fact, just recently, it was weak and riddled with turbulence and unrest, but then Elyon came onto the scene and everything changed.

Tall, with a muscular build and a face that looked like God himself, came down and sculpted it, he captured the hearts of his people instantly with his charm and charisma. The news outlets sang his praises as this unknown politician rose to power seemingly overnight.

He had never run for any political office prior to running for president and the media was astounded by his rise to fame. They loved him and their coverage of the months leading up to the election showed clearly who they favored and hoped would win.

He may not have been in the political world before he ran for president, but he was no stranger to power. His parents were some of the wealthiest people in all of Europe and spared no expense in making sure he was raised in the best boarding schools.

He always found it funny how some people felt sorry for him when they learned he grew up away from his family. He never understood why they felt that way as he never had a strong attachment to his parents or really anyone for that matter. All he cared about was himself and boarding school was a great place to make sure that he became the best version of himself possible.

It was when he was a senior at that boarding school that he learned how to tap into a power stronger than himself. He was in a private tutoring session with his math professor, Mr. Blackwood, when the teacher suddenly stopped talking about the homework which sat in front of them and said, "I have been watching you since you first arrived, Xander. You are capable of greatness."

Elyon remembered how he smiled smugly looking at the discarded math books on the table knowing he was well ahead of most of the kids in his class.

That's not what his teacher was talking about. Mr. Blackwood corrected Xander and shook his head, "No, I'm not talking about school work. Yes, you will use your education, but it's a much bigger thing I am talking about. First, I have to know if you're willing to tap into something bigger than yourself. Something supernatural."

Elyon remembered how he filled his free time in the years leading up to that moment with Mr. Blackwood. He loved anything supernatural. He spent hours playing with ouija boards, dungeon and dragon games, movies with witchcraft, and horoscopes. From a very young age, he loved anything that made him feel connected to things he couldn't see, so he didn't hesitate when he answered, "Of course! If it helps me to be the best, then I want it. What do I have to do?"

Elyon could see it like it was yesterday. Mr. Blackwood stood up from behind the desk and sat on the edge in front of him, "I need more than a quick answer that you didn't think through. I have access to power you can't imagine. You will become capable of things you hardly believed possible, but you need to know what you are agreeing to before you say yes."

He waited to make sure he had Elyon's full attention before he continued, "There is a dark spirit that has been speaking to me about you for many years, Xander. It wants you to give yourself to it fully." Mr. Blackwood closed his eyes and called out in an evil voice summoning something. Elyon didn't know what it was, but he had never felt anything like it before. All the windows were closed, yet there was a hot breeze that blew through the room.

Elyon remembered the cold feeling he felt in his stomach when Mr. Blackwood opened his eyes, "It's here with us, do you feel it, Xander?"

Even now thinking back, Elyon remembered the moment vividly. There was no denying Elyon felt it, he also felt fear, "Yes. What does it want?"

Mr. Blackwood had become agitated, "I told you. You! It wants you! If you are willing to completely surrender to it, it will give you every dream you have ever had. What do you want, Xander?"

Elyon stopped for a moment to think. His fear was completely forgotten, all he could think of was having his every desire satisfied. "I'm sick of being smarter than everyone yet being beneath everyone in status. I want power. I want to hold people's lives in my hands."

Mr. Blackwood nodded his head like Elyon was on the right track, "Are you willing to, of your own free will, accept the spirit into your life that will enable you for these things and more? Once you say yes, there is no turning back. You will be his, but he will make you great."

Elyon knew that was what he wanted more than anything. He wanted everyone to answer to him. He didn't care how it happened as long as he got what he wanted, "Yes, I accept it."

Instantly, Elyon felt something enter his body. His mind raced with thoughts he had never entertained before. He never felt affection for anyone, but now he felt hatred toward everyone. His body felt like it was on fire with the sensation of another being consuming him from the inside. He was still himself, but he felt as if there was something else pulling on the puppet strings of his soul.

Before he told the spirit he accepted it, he felt it in the room, but now it was more than that. He could hear it whisper into his ear. As it spoke, it drew out each syllable in a long breathy hiss that smelled of sulfur, "Youuuuuuuu're miiiiiiiiiiiine."

Mr. Blackwood reached over to his desk drawer. First, he took out a large dagger and laid it on the desk, then he took out a candle from his desk drawer and lit it before walking over to the wall and plunging the room into total darkness except for the single small flame. As he walked back to Elyon he grabbed the dagger and held it in his own hands as he faced Elyon,

"Acceptance of the spirit requires a blood sacrifice."

At that moment, he heard his new spirit guide whisper to him the name of a boy in his class that Elyon often made fun of for being a Christian. Elyon knew exactly what he needed to do. He grabbed the knife from Mr. Blackwood's hand and walked to the unsuspecting boy sleeping in the empty dorm room.

The memory of his first encounter with that spirit so many years ago was fresh in his mind four years ago when he heard that voice whisper to him yet again. This time it hissed into his ear a new word, "Preeeee-ssssssssssi- deeeeeeent"

He had learned early on to never disobey the voice. When he was in his twenties he tried to defy it one time. He recalled that as his rebellious thoughts took root his body started experiencing a new sensation. His skin felt like it was on fire and like a thousand ants were crawling all over him. He had tried to get up and shake off the feeling, but the sensation only got more intense.

Next, he felt like his head was going to explode as a ringing in his ears became deafening. He had fallen to his knees with his hands over his ears screaming that he submitted to the will of the voice.

Since then, he never went against what the dark spirit told him to do, so he announced his candidacy the next day and the rest is history. The voice had led him on a path to power. It was a meteoric rise to power unlike anything ever seen before. The voice was right. He was meant to become president.

Under his rule for the last few years, France went from a poor economy and the highest murder rate in the world to the richest and safest country in the world. Every leader in the world wanted to be like his country and share in the success he was experiencing. Leaders of nations came to him begging to be told what to do to experience the same prosperity and success. When he created a successful peace treaty in the Middle East his status as the most likable, successful, and powerful man in the world became complete.

Having power over an entire country and influence over the entire world was more exhilarating than he could have ever imagined.

As Elyon thought back to all the encounters he had with the voice inside of him, he had a feeling the voice wasn't done with him yet. He had a nagging thought that wouldn't leave him alone: there was more that he was supposed to do. He didn't need the voice to tell him this time; he wanted to do more. It didn't feel enough being the president of simply one nation, even if it was the greatest nation. He wanted more. He would make sure he had more.

CHAPTER TWO

"And I saw a mighty angel proclaiming in a loud voice, 'Who is worthy to break the seals and open the scroll? But no one in heaven or on earth or under the earth could open the scroll or even look inside it." - Revelation 5:2-3

Cardinal Benedetto Francis was a small man with few friends. As a boy, he never seemed to fit in with the other children. They teased him for his small stature and wiry glasses. He assumed he didn't fit in with them because he was called to become a servant of the church, but things didn't become any better even as he took his orders and dedicated his life to the ministry. It still seemed as though he didn't quite fit in with the other members of clergy either.

His ideas and interpretation of the Scripture were radically different from his peers. He was obsessed with rebuilding the destroyed Jewish temple because he believed whoever rebuilt it would bring peace to the world.

His fellow clergymen tried to counsel him to the error of his ways, but he argued if his ideas were so wrong why did God bless him with continual promotions? God must agree with his unorthodox theology because he continued to rise in authority and position within the Church.

He didn't know why thoughts about rebuilding the Temple to bring peace on the earth wouldn't give him any rest, all he knew is they made other people uncomfortable. In the end, he decided that he didn't care if it made them uncomfortable because felt like he would explode if he didn't do something about it.

One evening, as he was resting from his relentless research, he took a walk to clear his mind. As he walked down the alleyways of Rome he went down new pathways he had never taken before, completely lost in thought. Without realizing it, he had wandered miles away from the church and was in a strange part of town.

He found himself in a poorly lit alleyway that was once the heart of all Roman activity. He looked around at the cobblestone streets and imagined the horses that once carried Jewish captives into the city on these very streets almost two thousand years ago.

As he admired the history on the street he was walking, he noticed one stone that looked out of place. Surely his mind was playing tricks on him, but he decided to inspect it closer just in case. He bent down to one knee and, sure enough, one of the stones in the street had a small arrow carved on it.

He spoke aloud to himself, "That's weird. Why is there an arrow carved in a stone in the street?" He looked around to see if any others had the same arrow etched into them, but the one in front of him was the only one out of all the stones that had a carving in it. As he looked closer, he saw that it was pointing toward a building on the right of him.

There was a single cobblestone on the lower corner that matched the cobblestone in the street that had an arrow on it. Benedetto thought to himself, "Could it be a coincidence that there is only one stone in the street that doesn't match the others and it points to a building that has an identical, out-of-place stone? Surely that is more than a coincidence."

Cardinal Francis looked around to see if anyone else was watching him, but the very few people that were present in this poorly populated part of town were too occupied with their own affairs to pay him any attention.

Curiosity drew him to the stone in the building. As he inspected it, he tried to feign less interest than he felt. He wondered, "It's just a stone in a building, so why is my heart pounding; why am I excited about a stone?" But he knew why.

Just like he knew something had given him an obsession with the Jewish temple, he also knew something or someone had drawn him to this long-overlooked stone that stood ignored for almost two thousand years.

He ran his hand lightly across the stone on the building and was shocked to see the mortar begin to break away beneath his fingertips. He looked around one last time to see if anyone was watching before he began to chisel away in earnest at the mortar surrounding the stone. The mortar must have been extremely old because it came apart with ease and it didn't take long before the stone was removed revealing a small opening just big enough for a hand to fit through.

He paused for only a second at the thought of sticking his hand into a dark hole, but then curiosity overpowered his fear as he reached a fist into the hole to see what might be hidden in the dark space.

I'm sure many would hope for treasure or gold, but he knew when he felt a decaying piece of paper that he had found something more priceless than anything like the commonality that would come from hidden treasure.

With extreme care and gentleness, he pulled out the artifact and saw that the parchment was a papyrus manuscript and was ancient. Sections would disintegrate in his hand if he didn't handle it with care, so he carried it like a fragile infant back to his quarters where he could examine it with the precision needed to preserve the decomposing material from further decay.

When he got back to his home, he gently laid the ancient paper on his dining room table. He saw that portions were already crumbling, so he laid them all on a surface and used specialized tweezers to put the broken pieces together as they originally would have been. It was like trying to piece together a two-thousand-year-old puzzle that would disintegrate with the slightest wrong touch.

Once he got all the broken fragments in order and lined them up with the larger still intact manuscript, he gasped as he saw what he had uncovered. It was an ancient map of the city of Jerusalem before it had been destroyed by the Roman invasion of A.D. 70. On that death march to this Roman city, a Jew must have hidden this ancient scroll in one of the houses being built at that time where it remained untouched until today.

As Cardinal Francis poured over every detail of the map he sank to the chair behind his desk. This ancient artifact clearly showed everything everyone ever thought about the location of the Jewish temple was completely wrong. This map showed it was in a completely different location than everyone thought.

Rebuilding the temple was one of his odd dreams that made him an outcast his whole life. His interpretation of Scripture was so vastly different than everyone else. One belief he couldn't shake was that if he saw the temple rebuilt, he would, in his lifetime, see God on earth.

Now, the way to make that happen was right in front of him. It was in a location easily purchased. Rebuilding the temple was once again possible if the right person was in charge.

President Elyon's first act as president was to secure the hearts of the French people. Once he accomplished that, he wanted to secure the hearts of the people in the rest of the world. How he would do that was unclear until one summer morning when he was visited by Cardinal Francis of the catholic church.

Xander wanted nothing to do with organized religion and preferred to only pursue paths of spiritual enlightenment. So when his assistant told him that a clergyman was requesting a meeting, he refused.

"Tell him I'm a busy man and cannot meet with everyone who has a whim to see me," Elyon told his assistant, his usual charm wearing thin when it came to matters of religion.

His assistant relayed the message and tried to dissuade the cardinal from trying to meet with him, but the cardinal refused to give up. He called every day begging for an appointment.

The cardinal begged, "Tell him I have a matter of grave importance that I must speak with him about at once. I will not stop calling until he sees me."

Upon the last message, the president put aside his hatred for religion and decided to speak with the cardinal. It was not out of the graciousness of his own heart, but when his assistant relayed the message the last time he felt that familiar warm breeze and tingling sensation he would often feel when his spirit guide was pleased. If the message pleased the energy surrounding him, he guessed he could suffer through one meeting.

So he summoned the cardinal to meet him on his way to a dignitary luncheon. They could talk on the drive. He figured that way he wouldn't be trapped into a long meeting with a boring religious leader.

When Cardinal Francis got in the car, President Elyon almost laughed out loud. The man was a joke. A balding head with a single wisp of hair going across his forehead trying, unsuccessfully, to hide his receding hairline and glasses that refused to stay on his nose that he was constantly pushing up were just a few of the many features that first stood out to him.

More than his physical appearance, there was the air about him. Fumbling to hold too many things and dropping them all as he got in the limo, Elyon smirked enjoying the display of incompetence set before him.

When Benedetto finally got in, he wasted no time and immediately began sharing about the scroll he had discovered.

Elyon hated to admit it, but this ridiculous man had his attention. Elyon had been waiting for an opportunity to show the world how everyone could benefit from his leadership, and it seemed this little man was delivering the perfect medium to accomplish such a task.

As Francis explained the map to him and outlined the actual location of the Jewish temple, the president was eagerly leaning forward knowing this would unite multiple races and multiple nations around a common goal.

"So what is needed from me to rebuild the temple?" Elyon inquired when Francis was finished.

Cardinal Francis explained, "All that is needed is for someone to purchase the land. That will take money. It needs to be more than that though. It needs to be purchased by someone who has a vision to bring peace to that region. Bringing back the synagogue will endear to every Jewish heart the man that accomplishes this. It will also secure the allegiance of the Arab nations as the Dome of the rock location will no longer be a point of division among the two religions."

Elyon pondered all this for a moment before responding, "If done well, it will do more than unite those two groups of people. The whole world will be watching and will marvel at the man who was able to unite ancient enemies."

"You could be such a man," Cardinal Francis praised. "I have seen the way you have united your country. Everyone who follows you loves you. Many would even worship such a man."

President Elyon chuckled angrily, suddenly remembering his early disdain for all this man represented by organized religion, "Are you sure you should be speaking with me then?

Won't that go against the laws of your precious God?"

The cardinal shook his head emphatically 'no' as he responded, "I have been an outcast my whole life because I believe the Bible has been widely misinterpreted. Yes, I am a man of the cloth, but it has not been easy because I believe that the Bible says the opposite of what many teach. They teach that Jesus is to be worshiped above all else. Sure he was a good guy, but I believe one is coming who is far greater than Jesus ever was. He is who I have been searching for my whole life. If you can rebuild the temple, then I believe you are the man I have been looking for."

The president sat back with a satisfied expression on his face. Perhaps he had misjudged this little man, for he had just described what Elyon had believed about himself secretly his entire life. He was capable of great things and when the world saw what he was capable of, they would marvel at him and it would all begin with the rebuilding of the temple.

"I want you to quit your position in the clergy today. You are coming to work for me." The president said it as an order, not a request. You have the vision I want to see spread throughout the world. Our first order of business is for you to secure the purchase of the land. We must start the rebuilding of the synagogue immediately.

Jacob Levi's family were starting to feel some hope even though the world around them was crumbling. The attacks because of their lineage were increasing. Jacob pulled both Benjamin and Rachel from their schools and Sarah began to homeschool them.

At first, the kids protested. Benjamin begged to stay in and promised he would avoid that boy from now on and there would be no more fights. Rachel cried that she would miss her friends at her high school, but in the end, both children came around to the idea of homeschooling.

It had become easier to sell them to the idea of homeschooling because each time they went out in public the attacks against them increased. They lived in a small town and they were the only Jewish family in the whole town, so it wasn't hard to pick them out when they went to the store.

Sometimes it was small things like people avoiding talking to them, or refusing to serve them at restaurants. Other times it was bigger. More recently, Sarah took the kids with her grocery shopping and as they were loading up the minivan, someone began throwing eggs at them. They left the groceries and quickly got in the van and went home.

Now, Jacob has told them that none of them are to even leave the house unless Jacob is with them. It's not that he is some huge man that would draw fear in the hearts of any who see them, but hopefully, it would be at least a small deterrent to have a man there. If not, at least he could draw the attacks until his wife and children get to safety.

As bad as things were, there was hope on the horizon. Jacob beamed to Sarah one evening, "It's so exciting what Elyon is doing! He might be the best leader I've ever seen! I'm still in shock that he proved where the original location of the temple is, bought the land and has already begun construction!"

Sarah beamed at the news that construction had finally

begun on the temple! A year ago and it wouldn't have phased her. They never even went to the synagogue in their neighboring town. They were Jews in name only and never practiced the faith of Judaism, but as the attacks against their people increased it drew them back to God in many ways. They started to wonder if this was like the trials of the Israelites of old. Was God allowing them to suffer because the Jewish people had rejected Him? Not because God was mad at them, but because he wanted them to return to Him because He loved them.

The Levi family were like those Israelites of old. Their suffering had turned them back to the God of their ancestors. They began reading the Torah together. They still never went to the temple in their neighboring city, but that was more due to the danger of being seen together with a group of Jews. It was a risk they did not want to take with their family.

So they studied the prophets of old together in the evenings as a family. It was like a passion was reignited in all of them of the excitement of waiting for the Messiah. Maybe all these troubles were pointing to the coming of their long-awaited Messiah!

It seemed the rebuilding of the ancient temple was the first step in waiting for the messiah and it was all because of President Elyon!

"Maybe he is the Messiah and will save us from all the troubles we are facing!" Rachel said as she clapped her hands together in youthful excitement.

"Maybe children, maybe, but it's too soon to tell." Their father replied. "For now we continue to pray to God for our persecutions to end and for him to send the Messiah to deliver us."

Sarah replied, "Your father is right." She turned her attention toward Jacob and added, "but it does seem hopeful that things might soon change for the better for us now that the temple is being rebuilt doesn't it?"

He nodded in agreement and they all prepared for their sabbath meal thinking about the temple being rebuilt for the first time in almost two thousand years. A monumental task that would normally take years to do according to the original specifications of Solomon's temple. Somehow this miracle of a man, Elyon, had pooled all his financial resources and hired every available contractor in the entire region. It was said the whole project would take less than six months to complete.

Unfathomable! To discover the actual location of the temple, buy the land, and then rebuild it in such record time. This man was truly the first real friend to the Jewish people in a very long time.

CHAPTER THREE

"Now the Spirit expressly says that in later times some will depart from the faith by devoting themselves to deceitful spirits and teachings of demons, 2 through the insincerity of liars whose consciences are seared, 3 who forbid marriage and require abstinence from foods that God created to be received with thanksgiving by those who believe and know the truth. 4 For everything created by God is good, and nothing is to be rejected if it is received with thanksgiving, 5 for it is made holy by the word of God and prayer." - 1 Timothy 4:1-5

Michael couldn't believe his ears. He knew things were headed toward a dangerous path for a while now. As a cop, he daily saw the rise in anti-Semitic actions. He looked on with disbelief as Bible prophecy was starting to come to life with the temple being not only rebuilt, but rebuilt in record time. It was the largest, most historically accurate building ever constructed and it was weeks away from completion. Those two things alone would be enough to have his head spinning, but now there was more.

There had been a rise in false teachers over the last decade.

It seemed every year, a once-respected Bible leader would fall from grace in either some hidden scandal coming to light or, as was more common now, coming forward with a watered-down truth of the gospel.

False teachers were not new. What was new was the once head cardinal, Cardinal Francis, coming out and publicly proclaiming that the majority of Christians throughout history have been misinterpreting the Bible.

He called a press conference and said in that 'I'm smarter than you, so you better pay attention voice,' "A common false teaching is that Jesus is the only way to heaven. That is simply not accurate. There are many paths to truth. As a former leader of one of the largest Christian denominations in the world, I implore everyone to listen to the sound of my voice and to relinquish the intolerant and hateful parts of your faith. Only adhere to those elements of your beliefs that promote tolerance. "

Unfortunately, people listened to him and what was once a watered-down word became hardly recognizable as the Gospel anymore in most churches. People regularly claimed that Jesus was not the only way to heaven and that preaching sin was hate speech and should be punished. Free speech was no longer free if it was speaking about what the Bible calls sin.

As an officer, Michael saw the progression. It started with threats against people that spoke the truth about the Bible, but it quickly grew from there as more and more false teachers arose carrying the banner of the message of Cardinal Francis. It was like Christians who had been in church their whole lives no longer wanted to hear the truth. They sought out teachers who would tell them what they wanted to hear and threatened and berated the preachers who spoke of living a life like Christ lived and having a standard of holiness.

The screaming mobs' cries of "How dare you judge me," and "I have my truth and you have yours" did not stop there. Instead, it grew to demands for justice against the intolerant. They claimed that it was the hate of the extremist Christians that was leading to so much social unrest and they must be stopped at all costs.

The tides of the opinion of the masses had shifted. They blamed Christians who they deemed too fundamental as the reason for their suffering and they wanted them to pay the price. Christians who believed a full-gospel message were starting to meet together in houses secretly as that was becoming the only safe way to talk about everything in the Bible without retribution from the public.

Michael's job as a police officer was to be a peacemaker. To stop injustice and fight for the rights of all individuals, but that job was becoming harder and harder every day. Call after call would come into the precinct. The 'extremist' Church was vandalized and burned down. Fundamental Christians had their homes broken into and their possessions stolen. 'Haters' who preached salvation from sins were beaten.

The response from his captain was always the same, "Stand down. Do not respond to incidents of violence, theft, or destruction toward an extremist Christian group."

Michael saw lawlessness increasing daily. They didn't call it lawlessness. They called it fair play and that they were saving the court's time for cases of true injustice. Whenever Michael would question the fairness of it all, he was met with the same response. It's the Christians' fault. All they have to do is stop telling people the way they live their life is sinful and all the things they are enduring would end. Their unwillingness to stop shows just how extreme and dangerous their beliefs were and how important it was to send a message that they are stopped.

It was the worst where he worked in Omaha, but his little town south of there where he lived was not much better. His home of Nebraska City had less than eight thousand residents and was usually insulated from the craziness of big cities. That didn't seem to be the case anymore. Even his little city had a drastic rise in violence towards Jews and Christians.

It was not only here in the midwest. Michael was hearing reports like this from cities all over the country. It seemed that the higher-ups in every city were following a similar protocol. Laws were only applied to protect those who were not Christian or Jewish. If Christians didn't follow the teachings of Cardinal Francis they were deemed too extreme to deserve the protection of the law.

Michael came home from another day of not being allowed to help his fellow brothers and sisters in Christ. He waved to his sons, Miles and John, who sat on the couch watching TV and then threw down his badge and belt on the table as he complained to his wife, "What is the point of being a cop if I can't help anyone!"

She gave a sympathetic smile, but before she could offer him comforting words Miles paused his show and piped in, "I don't know what you're complaining about. It's their own fault that you can't help them."

Sophia looked at him unable to hide her surprise as she

heard her son describe the persecution Christians were under. "You're kidding, right? Please tell me you don't believe that. You're a Christian too. Your logic would mean dad shouldn't help you."

Miles responded, "I don't know that I'd classify myself like that anymore. I'm more spiritual than religious."

Michael couldn't believe his ears. Was his son rejecting everything he had ever been taught to be true? Surely he was misunderstanding his meaning, but the more Miles spoke the more Michael realized the truth; Miles had wandered away from the faith.

Miles couldn't leave it alone. He had to drive the point home of why he felt his parent's beliefs were so wrong. He peppered each word like bullets aimed for the heart of his parents as he continued, "I'm not so ignorant to believe only Christians go to heaven. I'm not intolerant and unloving like most of you are. I believe that people aren't sinning just because they make choices that are right for them."

Sophia became angry at the changes she saw in her son, "What happened to you? Have you lost all common sense?" She tried to stop herself, but sometimes her mouth ran away with her. She always struggled to know when she should hold her tongue and when she should speak her mind. "We raised you better than that. There is no morality apart from God."

Miles didn't respond in kindness or humility to his mom out of respect for her. He lashed out with what felt like years of pent-up hostility, "Who are you to say what is right to believe? You've done nothing short of brainwashing me all those years growing up making me go to church and telling me Jesus is the only way to heaven. Closed-minded people like this family are what is wrong with the world."

Up until that moment, Sophia had hoped that her son was only pulling away from the family, but that his core values had stayed strong. The more he spoke though, the more she realized he was pulling away from everything he was raised to believe.

She wanted to change the subject and try and redeem the evening, "Let's just have a nice night together, ok son? Dinner's ready. I made your favorite."

She smiled with more enthusiasm than she felt as she tried to muster up the strength for a happy family dinner. They all gathered around the table and Michael said grace. When he finished, the men sat at the table while Sophia went to the kitchen to bring in the dinner she was eager to surprise her son with.

As she carried the plate to the table, she remembered the many nights as a child when he would beg for Chicken Parmesian for dinner. It had always been one of his favorites, but she hadn't made it in years because the government had passed legislation stating that eating meat was banned and labeled as cruelty to animals.

As a child and young adult, she must have read the verses in 1 Timothy 4:1-5 a hundred times that said in the end times people would be commanded to abstain from foods which God deemed worthy to eat.

She had never thought anything of those verses. It seemed impossible to imagine her life could be regulated by the government regarding what foods she was allowed to eat.

Like everything that had changed in the world, it started small. It started with increased taxes on the ranchers and grocery stores that carried meat products. Over time those taxes grew to fines on the general population for consuming meat.

People found ways around the rules for a while. They'd buy meat from local farmers. Who would have thought there'd be a black market to eat a cheeseburger. It was laughable, but even that became cracked down on as of late.

Anyone could receive a fine for being caught in the possession of meat, but the harshest penalties were for those that performed the processing of meat for consumption. Those that butchered the animals would not only receive high fines, but all animals in their possession would be immediately confiscated and they would face a minimum of a year jail time for animal abuse.

Sophia always had chickens. When these laws came about, she was careful to follow them and not eat her chickens. She didn't agree, but it wasn't worth jail time to eat their favorite meals. She kept her chickens for their eggs and was grateful to at least have access to protein that way.

However, she saw her family splintering apart and she was desperate to bring them back together. A mom of adult sons has very few tools to capture her boys' hearts, so a good home-cooked meal was the first thing she thought of to bond them together again.

When she stood at the table, she proudly placed the steaming hot plate of Chicken Parmesan smothered in cheese on the table and beamed with anticipation of the joyful memories the meal would evoke in her youngest, wayward child.

The hope of new, sweet memories the dinner would create

was quickly erased as she saw Miles look at the meal in front of him and then up to her with eyes full of animosity and accusation.

Miles sneered as he asked her, "And what are we eating tonight?" He paused before finishing with hostility dripping from his voice, "Mother."

Sophia's smile instantly vanished. The pain mixed with love was palpable in each word she spoke, "I made it for you Miles. It's your favorite." She tried to remind him of better days and times when they had laughed around the table together as they shared this very meal, but he would have none of it.

Miles interrupted her stories of memories he didn't want to relive, "I knew your chickens weren't only for eggs. You claim to have the moral high ground as Christians, yet you break the law by abusing the animals in your care!"

John could see his mom becoming more hurt with each passing second and couldn't help but interject even if it made his brother mad, "Lay off of mom. She was trying to do something nice for you…. even though you've done nothing to deserve it!"

Miles shot his brother a look that would scare most men into submission, but not John. John just stared right back at him, not flinching or blinking. He would not back down when it came to protecting those he loved even if that meant protecting them from his over-eager brother.

Miles blinked first and looked away from John and back to his mother as he pushed the platter to the center of the table and away from him, "Well I won't be eating a meal that breaks the law. You're lucky I don't report you, mom!"

Sophia gasped at the sudden realization that her son seemed like he didn't even love her anymore. She didn't understand what she could have possibly done to make such a change in him. She looked at him with longing for the relationship she once had with him and wished she could have again. Her eyes began to fill up with tears.

She couldn't take another second and made up an excuse to leave the room, but all she was doing was trying to find a quiet place to cry and everyone knew it. She was crying for her son who was so lost and confused and also because she felt like a failure as a mother. Maybe if she was able to respond with soft words and more kindness in her tone he wouldn't have turned away from God. She wondered if his waywardness was really her fault.

Miles rolled his eyes as she left and his dad exploded in anger, "Have you no love for us or gratefulness for all we have done for you? You show no compassion to your mother in her pain? What is wrong with you?"

"Nothing is wrong with me! You're the one who is blind!" Miles yelled as he stood up from the table.

Michael realized he was letting anger control him and raised his hands in surrender and said, "We will talk later. Please Miles, remember who we raised you to be." And with that, he walked out of the room to comfort his wife.

John Hill was left to pick up the pieces of yet another family fight. It didn't use to be like this. They all used to get along so well. One big happy family they would often joke about together. Somewhere, all that changed. It seemed Miles found the wrong friends who started to introduce him to dangerous ideas. They didn't call it dangerous. They called it free thinking, but Miles didn't see how it slowly changed him into something so much uglier than he used to be.

He used to be the kindest and most generous guy ever. He'd give up all he had to make someone else happy. He lived for the Lord and his heart broke when he made mistakes. Somewhere with his new friends, all that changed. He started attending their church that preached tolerance to all beliefs.

John had, with his parents, tried to tell his younger brother that it wasn't intolerant to simply say something was a sin, but that you still loved that person despite their sin. Miles wouldn't hear of it. He was starting to buy into the ideology that he was surrounding himself with. If anyone dared to say anything was wrong he called them hate-filled.

Calmly, John tried once again to win his brother's ever-hardening heart over to the truth, "Where does it end Miles? If there is no right and wrong, where is the moral line? You can't believe that you are like God and can decide what is right and wrong do you?"

Miles, still full of anger, had venom in his words as he spoke, "Yes! My truth is my own. I don't need you or the Bible to tell me what's right or wrong. I'll decide that for myself and until you accept me for who I am I want no part of any of you!"

With those last words, he turned and left the room and slammed the door behind himself. John sighed with a heavy heart knowing that whatever pain he felt his parents felt ten times more. As he went to sit alone on the living room sofa, he could hear his mom crying in the bedroom saying it felt like death losing their child to the world.

Their pain was something more and more Christians were experiencing. It seemed every day more Christians were being enticed into Cardinal Francis' religion of acceptance of all beliefs and lifestyles and those who refused to follow were left picking up the pieces of broken relationships.

Christians were leaving churches that taught the Bible as the actual word of God in droves. Though young and still in his early twenties, John had never seen anything like it in his lifetime. How could so many people be drawn away by preachers speaking only what they wanted to hear and not speaking the truth? How could his brother be drawn away by such lies?

They had both grown up in the same house and were taught the same things. They went to church every Sunday and grew up knowing right from wrong, but somewhere Miles hardened his heart and in the process broke his parents' hearts.

In all the pain of the day, John decided to call and check on his fiance, Katie, before checking on his parents. He was so eager for the day when he would marry her and could comfort her daily, face to face and not over the phone.

Of course, weddings looked different now than they used to. The government no longer referred to the union of a couple as a marriage. The consensus among the general public was that marriage was a traditional, Biblical, and archaic institution.

Marriage was deemed a failed experiment. Those in favor of doing away with marriage stated the examples throughout history that they believed proved marriage as a dangerous practice.

They would claim that in the 1950's it was racist because it only allowed people of the same race to marry. In the early 2000's they said it was homophobic and wouldn't allow the homosexual community to create an equal union. Every time the government would get involved and try to legalize change to marriage there would be another crisis to regulate.

To the majority of the world, the word marriage had become a hate word implying exclusivity and superiority. Marriage pointed to outdated traditions instead of the enlightened agenda of the current political ideologies.

Instead of trying to redefine marriage yet again, the government simply did away with validating traditional marriage in any way. There were no longer tax breaks for the married or a recognition of rights to property or the ability to share in a spouse's health benefits. Every financial incentive to marry was done away with and applied to a new concept called commitment contracts.

Commitment contracts were an agreement of intimate partnership for a specific length of time. It could be a contract with two people or with ten. It didn't matter how many, who or what was in the commitment contract. Anyone in the contract was entitled to large tax breaks for their relationship as well as recognition from the government that their relationship was legitimate.

Large ceremonies that looked like traditional weddings still took place, but the outcome was different. Now the end result was a short term contract that entitled those named in the contract to legal recourse for finances, property and other such rights once applicable only to married couples.

At the end of the contract term, those in the relationship could choose to renew the contract for another set of predetermined years or they could dissolve the contract with ease. Divorce was no longer a major legal hassle that took years to complete with fights in the courtroom. All you had to do was wait till the end of the contract and follow the plan laid out in writing. Every contract had a section for the dissolution and non renewal of the relationship. Divorce was built into the relationship as an inevitability.

1 Timothy 4:1-5 was coming to life before their eyes where the Bible prophesied that in the end times people would be forbidden to marry. It now made more logical sense to complete a commitment contract than it did to marry.

Christians had a choice to make. Would they take the financial and legal benefits of a commitment contract, but as a result have to plan for their eventual divorce? Or would they follow the traditional path of marriage that was created by God and not a man-made institution?

Many believers initially participated in commitment contracts. They vowed that they would stay strong in their beliefs and when the time came to renew, they would renew for the rest of their lives. However, that rarely happened. Relationships are hard and when the 'out' is already built in and planned for in advance the temptation to take the easy way is extremely hard to resist, no matter how good their intentions were.

Over time, Christian leaders started openly preaching to avoid the commitment contracts at all cost and have a traditional marriage. Marriage had become nothing more than a ceremony provided by a pastor. There were no longer wedding certificates or legal incentives to getting married. It wasn't even possible to take a husband's name anymore legally.

The marriage ceremony that the world deemed antiquated was significant for those that chose that path. It was a statement that the couple was choosing to have their relationship be modeled after what the Bible deemed good and not after what the world deemed expedient and beneficial. It was a choice to deny themselves the privileges the government offered to those in a commitment contract and instead say that there was no end date in mind. It was a lifelong vow before God.

John was looking forward to his marriage, not just his commitment to Katie. So they planned a big ceremony. He wanted her to feel loved and adored and to know marrying her was the most important thing in the world, even as they were surrounded by so much chaos.

She wouldn't be legally allowed to take his name, but she told him that the government couldn't stop her from having all her family and friends call her by her new name. She said that on the day they would be married she would no longer be called Katie Willaims. To those who love her, she would forever become Katie Hill.

John lived in the country on a big piece of land with his parents and she lived in Kansas City. Her home was about two hours away southeast of him. Not terribly far, but in this crazy world sometimes it seemed like a lifetime away. Whatever problems he and his family were facing here as Christians were nothing compared to what Katie faced living in a big city. Things were so much more violent there and the police force was practically powerless to combat the rising lawlessness. He worried so much for her so far away.

Their wedding was still nine months away, but the more the unrest seemed to build in society, the more he thought maybe it was better to do the wedding sooner than later. That way, whatever they faced, at least it would be together. His parents didn't agree, but that was probably because they worried for him. The plan was to move to the city once they got married so she could be close to her family and that scared his parents.

Scared or not, John was becoming more confident daily that it was his duty to protect Katie and that they needed to be married. John looked at the bedroom where he heard his mother weeping and decided he could wait till another day to tell his mom that.

Michael spent hours comforting his wife, well, trying to at least. He seemed at a loss of what to say to her. He was hurting too and just wanted to scream or throw something, but he couldn't do that right now. He had to be strong for her.

So he said all the things he thought might help. He told her that it wasn't her fault, that she was a good mom, and that Miles would come back around. He was just spreading his wings. Michael hoped he was right and Miles would come back around.

Sophia cried herself to sleep in Michael's arms and as he stroked her hair waiting for her to fall asleep he began to doze. That is when the dream began.

Michael was standing on a tall cliff similar to the one in his previous dream that everyone walked off of, but it was different this time. There was a single cottage nestled comfortably in the tree line with a stone fireplace reaching above the roof. Out of it came a plume of smoke from the fire inside the home and a strip of wood hung above their front door that read, "Patterson Family."

Michael noticed the lush grass dotted with wildflowers surrounding the front of the home and a beautiful blue sky that seemed to stretch on forever. He felt such peace as he looked around him. As he took a few steps closer to the cottage and looked through the window by the dining room table and noticed a family inside. They looked so happy. A mom cooking at the stove and a father sitting at the table reading the Bible while a little girl no more than six years old and her baby brother sat on the floor in front of the fire playing with dolls.

It was such a beautiful picture, Michael wanted it to never end. It was a perfect family enjoying a perfect day together, but something was not quite right. Michael couldn't figure out what it was at first, but as he looked closer all around the cabin, he noticed a shadow lurking in the tree line just beyond their home. It didn't move like the rest of the shadows that bent in the proper direction according to the movement of the sun. Instead, it moved as if it had a mind of its own like it was alive, but it didn't have the form of either a man or a beast.

Michael had lost the safe feeling he felt just a few moments earlier, but it didn't matter. He had to figure out what he was seeing. The shadow glided back and forth as if it was pacing the length of the cabin eager to pounce on it. Michael approached it. He could see it, but it didn't seem to be able to see him. At first, it looked as if it was faceless, but the closer he got the more that Michael could see it did indeed have a face. It was grotesque and disfigured and looked more like a beast than a human shrouded in a veil of black.

Michael shuddered and wanted to run away, but he knew he must stay and see what happened to the family inside the cottage who remained completely unaware of the evil that lurked just outside.

As the shadow left the woods and crept closer to the cottage, Michael could see clearly that instead of teeth it had sharp fangs and those fangs were dripping with blood like it had recently killed and eaten its prey. It looked hungry as it got closer to the little family.

Michael saw the mother set the dinner at the table and sit down. The kids came running and sat down too and they all joined hands and bowed their heads and prayed before they ate their meal.

The shadow sent a shriek into the air that brought with it many more shadows. They were all intent, it seemed, on harming this little family who felt safe in their hidden home and who had done nothing more than pray.

The home became surrounded by shadows and Michael knew death was just moments away for the residents inside. He tried to scream, but no sound came out. He tried to run to help them, but his feet stayed in place like they were cemented to the ground below him.

The little six year old girl inside the cabin suddenly turned from her meal and looked directly at him through the front window. She looked at him with eyes that seemed to bore into Michael's soul and with her voice she called out to him with a strength and volume she should not have possessed and cried out, "Warn them!"

With that, Michael woke up with the words, "Warn them!" echoing in his mind.

He couldn't sleep after that and decided since his shift at work was only an hour away, he would go in early and get a head start on the day. When he came to his office to see the items to complete for the day, his eye caught on the top sheet. It was an order to raid and detain a family suspected of preaching hate. Their name was Patterson.

CHAPTER FOUR

*"So I wept much, because no one was found worthy to open
and read the scroll, or to look at it. But one of the elders said to
me, 'Do not weep. Behold, the Lion of the tribe of Judah, the
Root of David, has prevailed to open the scroll and to loose its
seven seals."* - Revelations 5:4-5

Benedetto Francis was happier than he had ever been as a
cardinal. He felt like he was finally fulfilling his life's mission.
President Elyon had tasked him with uniting the religions of
the world together in an effort to bring peace to the world and
it was working!

All of his life, those above him told him uniting the
religions was a lost cause and dangerous. Well, he was
showing them how wrong they were now. Dangerous? Things
had never been more peaceful.

It took a little time to make the world see the truth, but as
of this week, each religion had its own expression of this
world religion. No one had to give up their faith entirely to
join the new global religion. They were able to keep all the
same practices and beliefs they always had as long as they did

away with any intolerant views. It was a fully sanctioned government-run church and it was present in every country.

In Iran, they had a unity Islamic mosque that had removed all teachings promoting intolerance called the Global Religion of Islam. They still taught Allah as God, prayed three times a day, and women still wore their head coverings. What was different was that the Qur'an had controversial verses removed. Verses that said, "fight against those who do not believe in Allah nor in the Last day and who do not consider unlawful what Allah and His messenger have made unlawful and who do not adopt the religion of truth" were no longer part of the Global religion of Islam.

In Israel, unity synagogues were established and their governments called them the Global Religion of Judaism. They still can practice observing the sabbath, eating kosher and they even have resumed animal sacrifices in their newly built synagogue thanks to Elyon. However, they must use the revised state-sanctioned scriptures that remove verses like the one in Hosea 13:4 that says "Yet I am the Lord thy God from the land of Egypt, and thou shalt know no god but me; for there is no savior beside me."

There was a newly established Global Religion of Christianity too. It claimed people could still sing their worship songs and wear their crosses. The only difference was it had removed portions of the Bible deemed hateful. Many Christians embraced this change to the original Christian church because they wanted a message that made them feel good and they were more interested in tolerance than in truth.

Most religions seemed to merge seamlessly with the unity global religions, but Christianity struggled to join fully as others had. Even though many fell into the trap of the Global Religion of Christianity, there were still many Christians believing that Jesus was the only way to heaven. This teaching was incompatible with the new unity global religion and drove the true church underground.

Those that continued to teach what quickly became called the 'full Gospel' met secretly in people's homes to worship because in the newly state-sanctioned churches everything was different. There were no longer preachers provoking people to what was considered intolerant views regarding sin and repentance. You would never hear from a unity pulpit "I am the way and the truth and the life. No one comes to the Father except through me."

Each religion in the world has embraced this new global religion with open arms. The religion that Francis helped establish did not obliterate the traditions of each religion, but instead, he believed, improved them to include only the best parts of their faiths and leave out the parts that have been a detriment to society.

Cultures all around the world were having improved peace among previously warring factions. The Jews and Arabs of the middle east were getting along for the first time, not only because the Jews now had a place to worship without infringing upon the rights of the Palestinians thanks to Elyon, but also because of the improvements to their religion which gave them language to live in peace with one another.

With peace comes safety. Things that were once commonplace had now become virtually a thing of the past. Bombings between opposing religions and jihadist extremism were all eliminated.

There were, of course, some who were reluctant to join. They were often members of the old ways of faith in each religion. Francis thought how amazing it was how each person's superstitions could run so deep. They couldn't let go of their traditions when they could clearly see that things done in a new way produced better results!

He comforted himself with the knowledge that those dissenters wouldn't last long before joining the Global Religion of their particular faith. Many had gone underground and began worshiping in secret. Almost every government in the world criminalized worshiping in the old ways and mandated state-sanctioned churches only as acceptable places to gather together.

Those that didn't want to be a part of this typically met secretly in their homes and worshiped together. The freedom to conduct secret meetings in houses wouldn't last long though because the general public saw the "good" that came from the Global Religion. They saw the peace and safety that came from letting go of the intolerant views of religion and they had had enough. They were quick to report large gatherings or frequent traffic at their neighbors' houses. This always led to prompt investigations where the Global Religion enforcers would find contraband materials of the unedited dangerous versions of their scripture which would immediately be destroyed and everyone in attendance rounded up to attend reeducation camps.

Benedetto was very pleased with the work he had done in regards to promoting a religion that was good for all the faiths of the world and the peace that came as a result. He was sure when he presented the positive changes to the president that

Elyon would be pleased as well. He didn't know why, but the more time he spent around Elyon the more he felt a growing desire to please him. The president was quickly becoming the most important thing in Benedetto's life and making him happy was what Benedetto wanted more than anything in the world.

John kept replaying the conversation over and over in his head. His parents begged him not to leave, but he hugged them and told them he must go to the city and marry Katie. They just didn't get the urgency he felt.

They kept asking "Why not wait till things settle down?"

Deep down John knew that his parents knew why he couldn't wait. Things weren't going back to normal. His parents didn't say that outright. They said there were signs that this was the end that was prophesied, but there was no proof yet that it had begun for sure. There've been bad times in history before, maybe this was just one of those bad times in history and things would return to normal. They wanted him to wait until it was safer to marry. They wanted him to stay close where they could protect him.

John knew differently. He didn't know how he knew with such certainty, but he felt it. This was the beginning of the end and if he was right that means he only had a short time left on this earth and he wanted every second he had left to be with Katie.

He wanted to protect her from what was coming and comfort her when it got hard and he couldn't do that from a phone call two hours away.

He spent the drive lost in thought. He tried to take his mind off of his troubles with the radio, but that only worked for thirty minutes. Then he tried to distract himself by looking at the changing landscape. He saw the scenery start as a lush landscape filled with farmland as far as the eye could see with the occasional trees scattered throughout. Most of the land was filled with crops growing tall and flocks of birds that dove in a uniform pattern around the open land. The further into his drive he got the more he saw the landscape change. The flat farmland gradually became replaced by concrete and the trees were replaced by buildings. "I already miss the country," he thought, but he knew it was worth it as he thought of spending the rest of his days with Katie.

He spent the remainder of the drive through the traffic and smog of the city thinking about what their life would be. He was so caught up in his own thoughts that he didn't even comprehend he had finished his whole drive until he saw that he was pulling into her driveway.

She wasn't expecting him and he didn't know if she would be happy or mad at the surprises he had in store for her. He got out of his car and walked up to the front door of their split-level midwestern home and knocked a little less confidently than normal.

Katie opened the door and she squealed with delight, "John!" Katie's eyes shone with a brightness that only young love could give. "I thought you weren't coming until next week for a visit."

He wrapped his arms around her and picked her up off the ground spinning in a circle with her. "I couldn't wait another second." Putting her down he looked into her eyes, "Katie, marry me today. This minute."

Shocked, she took a step back, tears starting to fill her eyes, "John, what about the hall we booked, the money we paid the caterers" she paused. "My dress isn't even ready, it's still being altered!"

John reached a hand up and started to stroke his thumb against her cheek as she looked up at him with water-filled eyes, "Honey, I know all those things are so important, but what's more important is that we are together."

He bent down and, on her forehead, gave her a soft, tender kiss. He was filled with love and compassion for her knowing that all the changes in their world meant changes in their hopes and dreams for their future. "Things are getting worse, not better. Your pastor was sent to a reeducation camp just last week for preaching the full gospel. I don't know how much time we have left on this earth, but I do know I want to spend every second of it with you."

Katie wiped away her tears, "I guess you're right. Our life is going to look different now than we thought it would."

John interrupted her trying to evoke a smile, "But at least it will be our life, together."

Katie smiled up at her soon to be husband as excitement at the thought of pushing up their timeline began to build inside of her, "Let's go tell mom and dad!"

Her parents were not hard to win over. The Williams' saw the way John cared for their daughter and knew he was what she needed right now. Katie and her mom spent the day running around town picking up as many things as they could to make the ceremony special.

Katie picked up her dress, even though it wasn't done being altered, "So what if it's a little big in the waist," She said to her mom as she carefully laid it across the back seat. They went to a local florist and picked out a bouquet for her. Her mom told her to not look at the price tag of anything that day. It was about making her day special. Katie looked at her mom with such appreciation, "Mom, I'm getting married because I want a marriage, not because I have to have a beautiful wedding. I won't let you spend too much on me."

Her mom, like moms often do, won though and in the end, Katie had the most beautiful bouquet of pink roses and baby's breath to hold as she walked down the aisle that evening. All Katie cared about was that all the people that she loved would be there, but her mom made a few more last-minute stops to make sure the day felt as perfect as possible.

The mother and daughter laughed together as she had her hair and make-up done, then stopped for coffee on the way to get a manicure. It was a perfect day for Katie. Not because of all the stuff they had bought and planned, but because it was a day spent with her mom leading up to an evening spent with the man of her dreams.

When she was dressed and ready to go, Katie felt a sudden wash of sadness for John. Everyone she loved would be there, but John's parents weren't going to be able to attend. With the civil unrest toward full gospel Christians and Jews, John's dad couldn't get away from his work and didn't want Sophia driving alone through a big city. Things were so different now than they were even just a year ago, it was too dangerous for his mom to come alone.

Never could she have imagined John's mom not being safe

driving to a big city just because she was a woman and a Christian, but she understood. If anyone found out you were a full gospel Christian and not a member of the Global Religion of Christianity you were immediately targeted for hate crimes by the general public and for detainment to reeducation camps by government officials.

All these thoughts were swirling in her mind as she stood outside the door that led to the backyard of her house. With marriages not being recognized anymore, she couldn't go to a courtroom and with Christians being targeted she couldn't go to a church.

She peeked out the door and saw a deacon from her church waiting to officiate and John standing next to him looking eagerly at the door that Katie was about to exit. She hugged her mom one final time as her unmarried daughter. When she opened the doors and saw John smile at her, every worry fled from her mind. She knew that John loved his parents so very much, but their absence didn't seem to be what he was thinking about during their wedding. As she walked into the grass toward him standing under the tree, he couldn't seem to take his eyes off of her and all she saw on his face was joy.

As he looked at her wisps of curls surrounding her face, his eyes filled with tears of joy that he couldn't hide. He reached a hand up to wipe them away and the smile that she fell in love with spread across his face making her completely confident. They were made for each other and she couldn't be happier that they weren't waiting another day to get married.

It was a simple ceremony with a church leader officiating and Katie in her slightly too big wedding dress. When the ceremony was over, John leaned down and whispered in her ear, "It's you and me against the world from here on out." Katie closed her eyes with his forehead resting against hers and then was startled when she heard music begin to play.

Katie looked around the yard confused, "Where did my family go?"

John smiled mischievously, "I talked to everyone ahead of time and asked when the ceremony was over to give us privacy for a few moments. I also set my Bluetooth speaker on the picnic table." He grinned playfully, took her hand, and spun her around in time with the music, "Now if we are done asking questions, I'd like to dance with my new bride."

They danced together as the song sang about enduring love that would never end, both just as happy as if they would have had the most elaborate ceremony that cost thousands of dollars. Happier probably, because it was just the two of them.

Katie smiled up at John as the song ended, "You and me against the world."

President Elyon was seeing major progress from his rebuilding of the temple in Israel. Though Jews were still facing widespread persecution, they looked to him as a savior and hope from the persecution. It was him alone that brought peace to a region that had been plagued by wars for millennia.

Not only did the Jews sing his praises everywhere they went, but the world as a whole seemed to be falling more in love with him everyday. The news outlets spent large portions of their coverage saying all the good he had done for the global economy and peace relations worldwide. It seemed he could do no wrong.

The more Xander thought of his many accomplishments, the more he grew in his confidence that there had never been another leader like him. One so loved and so powerful.

As he thought of his power and influence a hot breeze blew in the room and his hairs on the back of his neck raised to attention and his spirit guide whispered, "It's not enough."

How had Elyon not realized it wasn't enough? How had he let himself become satisfied with what he had? The spirit was right, it wasn't enough. People must do more than revere him, they must all serve him!

It was then the idea came to him that he must unite the nations of the earth into one global economy and one worldwide government. He already had three of the largest nations that did his bidding whenever he asked. France, Iran, and Russia all fully embraced the global government that Elyon promoted. They practically worshiped him. They would have no problem joining his Alliance of Nations. He could think of at least three others, that with the right charm and subtlety, could be easily convinced and manipulated to join his ranks.

"Not enough," the voice whispered again. "There must be ten."

Ten nations. He would make at least ten nations join his cause of creating a one-world global government. He decided then he would conquer these nations without ever lifting a finger in battle. He would gain most of his Alliance of Nations through his practically supernatural charm.

For those he couldn't win over with his words, he would see to it that his followers created havoc behind the scenes. He would use his secret accounts to flood money to local groups that he knew prided themselves on looting, rioting, and anarchy. For governments that refused to join, he would tell his men to flood the internet with reports about those nation's leaders with accusations that would make it impossible for them to lead.

He knew what the result of all this would be. Leaders facing a myriad of accusations, though baseless, would become handicapped from leading effectively. They would have to resign and could then be replaced with leaders sympathetic to the cause of Elyon. Other nations that didn't join him would face so much inner turmoil and unrest and riots in the streets that they would come begging him to join his Alliance of Nations. They would beg for him to take over and bring peace and safety to their troubled land as he did for the countries that followed his leadership.

CHAPTER FIVE

"Now I saw when the Lamb opened one of the seals; and I heard one of the four living creatures saying with a voice like thunder, 'Come and see.' And I looked, and behold, a white horse. He who sat on it had a bow; and a crown was given to him, and he went out conquering and to conquer." - Revelation 6:1-2

President Elyon had won the hearts of three additional nations to his own by first aligning with them to create a Middle East peace treaty several years earlier. Once he had joined with them to accomplish the goal of peace in the Middle East, it wasn't hard to later convince them to join him in the Alliance of Nations. The nations all had a similar ideology to Xander and his country. This combined with a few well-timed compliments and strategic promises of aid and, without any bloodshed or threats of force, three world leaders- Iran, Russia, and China - all fell into line. With ease, he had three countries that eagerly joined France in the Alliance of Nations with him as their leader.

The other nations were not coming so willingly. Elyon had

scheduled a secret meeting of ambassadors and leaders from the three nations who had already joined him as well as from the additional nations that he wanted as part of his alliance. In the week leading up to the meeting, each county sent in a security team to sweep the building they would be meeting in for bombs and bugs.

On the day of the meeting, the countries' security teams did a final sweep of the building and then all stood guard outside of the perimeter of the building making sure the building stayed safe. When the leaders arrived, they walked past the guards which stood outside each of the entrances to the unoccupied building and they walked up to the empty office room.

It was a typical office room with wainscoting on the walls and double doors that were left open that led to the hallway. They were all sitting in the room with him now around a large rectangular table with Elyon sitting at the head.

Elyon laid out his plan for global unity stating that for the world to truly experience peace first it had to join together as one and not be divided into so many factions. He referenced the peace treaty he had formulated with Israel and how much good he brought to the region and that he wanted to do for the whole world what he had done in the Middle East.

The United States president nodded his head in agreement and stood to speak, "President Elyon, many of the leaders of my nation are on your side. They want to join with you in whatever you propose, but you know we are a nation ruled by politics. Our nation is divided. If I have any hope of winning reelection next year, I simply can't join you. I'm sorry." He sat back down in his chair on his final words with a loud thump as if he was accentuating his point that there was no room for debate on this matter.

It was Elyon's turn to rise. He slowly pushed back his chair and began to stand, never breaking eye contact with the American president. As he stood, he leaned over the table onto both of his hands which were on the table palms down. He leaned toward the man who had just defied him, glaring at him as he spoke, "Martin" He addressed him by his first name to show the president of the United States he was not in charge and was not the most powerful person in the room, "You think, as the leader of a superpower, that you are invincible, but I assure you that is not the case. You will learn to make your people ok with joining my Alliance. If you don't, you might not like the natural consequences of your delayed allegiance."

The U.S. President was shaken by the clear threat he had just received from Elyon, but he tried to hide it as best he could and appear strong. "That sounds like you just threatened the leader of the world's most powerful country. I have nothing left to say to you." He stood to leave and walked toward the open double doors that led to the hallway.

As he did so Elyon straightened his back standing up fully. Then he stretched out his hands and closed his eyes in what looked like an act of worship to something. The windows were closed, but everyone in the room felt a hot breeze blow in and all around them. The room seemed to come alive with something that made the air thick with fear and, suddenly, the double doors slammed shut all on their own. President Martin turned slowly back around to face Elyon with his eyes wide with a fear he could no longer hide. The doors had just closed on their own. No, not on their own. Something had closed them when Elyon prayed.

The whole room was speechless as Elyon spoke again, "I can either be your greatest asset or your greatest enemy." He looked around the room at the eyes that looked at him with a mixture of awe and fear, "All of you have already joined together in the treaty that brought peace to Israel. I want to bring it to the next step and bring peace to the entire world and not just one small nation. For those that join with me willingly I promise you to aid in the biggest economic boom your country has ever seen. You will see the end to violence with the lowest crime rates in your nation's history. All that you have seen me accomplish in France, I will bring to your country."

He stepped out from behind the table and slowly walked over to the leader of the Western world. He stopped when he stood right in front of him. Elyon was a tall man and he towered over Martin. He intimidatingly stared down at him, like a lion about to pounce on its prey, and his words came out like ice, "For those nations that don't willingly follow me they will pay the ultimate price. I have secret followers in every corner of the globe in the highest positions. I have an army of followers ready to do my bidding. You will suddenly see food becoming more scarce as your farms and factories mysteriously burn to the ground and your delivery systems become disabled.

As the people starve in your streets, the riots will begin. I will make sure of it. I will plant insurgents in every city and they will claim they represent the Christians and the Jews as they murder innocent civilians en mass. The people will rise up against you, the Jews, and the Christians as the cause for all their problems.

That's when the civil wars will start. I will cause such unrest that your nation will fight against itself. Your people will beg to join me to bring an end to all the problems they are having. They will crave peace and safety and they know I can give it to them because they will see other countries experiencing what they do not have. There will be wars in the street and as your people die on your doorstep fighting one another, then you will join me willingly."

President Martin stood unflinching before Elyon. His body language showed defiance and courage, but his eyes portrayed his fear. Elyon turned away from the man and walked back to the table, "President Martin, your presence is no longer needed in our meeting. You may leave as we have matters to discuss."

The leader of the free world stood still shocked with his mouth agape before slowly turning back to the now closed double doors. As he left, he looked back and saw the room all staring at him not daring to speak up against Elyon. He left there feeling defeated knowing there had been a major shift in power in that room that evening and he didn't know what to do to get back the upper hand.

After he had left the room, Elyon turned to look at the remaining leaders seated around the table all staring at him. "America has become a cancer upon our world. I knew Martin wouldn't do what needed to be done to help the world. He's too caught up in his own reelection campaign.

Most of you here would probably agree with me that something needs to be done about the United States. They are too powerful and they promote ideas that are contrary to global unity. They oppose the socialist beliefs that have made many of our nations so unified and impose their capitalist and nationally independent ideologies on weaker nations by enacting regime changes. They have to be stopped if the world as a whole is going to join together.

My nation alone is not strong enough to crush them. I need all of you to join me and, if you do, I assure you that you won't be sorry. I have the power and influence that will make your nation flourish under your rule and your people will be in awe of the peace and prosperity you have brought to your land.

The choice is yours. Do you join me now of your own accord, or do you need me to show you how powerful I really am?"

The Levi family loved the Global Religion of Judaism. They even began attending the temple in their neighboring town and observing the Sabbath. Things had never been better and it was all because of President Elyon. Jacob believed him to be a savior of his people. There was still some prejudice they experienced, but not as bad as before Elyon came onto the scene and started promoting the Global Religion.

There were dissenters in every religion that made things difficult. Jacob thought about the devout orthodox Jews that were rounded up last week and sent to the reeducation camps. He wished things could be different for them, but thought that it really was their fault. "All they had to do was make a few small concessions and they could live in the same peace he and his family were experiencing," he said to himself.

The temple in Israel had been rebuilt and was open for people to come. They had even begun to reinstitute animal sacrifices to God. It was a strange and foreign concept to him. Especially because he couldn't even eat meat in America without risking massive fines and penalties. But if he went over the sea to Israel, he could slaughter a goat as an act of worship to God.

Much of the persecution his family still experienced was a direct result of the animal sacrifices. Americans viewed animals as having equal rights to humans and the fact that the Jewish people in Israel were killing animals for sacrifice infuriated many. They took out their anger on the Jews in America who had never participated in the rituals.

Jacob would never speak it outloud for fear of retribution, but it brought him comfort knowing that he could offer a sacrifice to God for his family to bring them closer to God. He began to wonder what it would be like if he did take part in an animal sacrifice in Israel. In fact, the more he thought about it the more he wanted to experience it for himself. "What would it be like to hear the scripture read aloud in the same place the priests of old would have read them?" he wondered.

As the days wore on, the thought of seeing the temple in person consumed him. As a Jewish studies professor at an ivy league institution he had been offered VIP seats for the anniversary service at the temple next week, which he accepted. He rarely got any perks from his Job anymore because of his ethnicity, but no gentile was interested in visiting the temple, so he was given the tickets. He wasn't sure, initially, if he was going to use them.

President Elyon was set to make an appearance at the temple next week for the special anniversary ceremony. It had been one year since the temple was reopened and began to reinstitute the practice of making sacrifices to God after almost two thousand years without it. It was a momentous anniversary and Elyon himself, the reason why it was all possible, was scheduled to appear in order to officially dedicate the temple to God and to the people of Israel.

The more he thought about the upcoming momentous occasion, the more excited he got at the thought of being a part of it. It was a chance of a lifetime. He told his wife and children that they were going on a family trip to see the temple and they could all barely contain their excitement. How great would it be to see the temple in person, offer sacrifices and get to see the man that miraculously brought peace to his people? He could hardly wait!

Michael sat straight up in bed panting as if he had just run a marathon. He had another dream telling him to "Warn them!" Sometimes it was very clear who he was supposed to warn, like that first time when he dreamt about the Patterson's and then the very next day saw their name on an order for detention and interrogation. Other times, he didn't know who he was supposed to warn or about what.

Things had gotten so bad in the world. There have been several mass killings recently in the name of Christianity. No real Christian would ever do that, but the general public bought the narrative that full-gospel Christians were dangerous and had to be stopped. Every bad thing that happened in his county seemed to be blamed on either Christians or Jews lately. It was like the country was becoming a kindling box ready to ignite.

Michael was determined to get that dream out of his mind and think about something else. Anything else. He got up and saw his wife was already awake and in the living room folding the laundry. He sat on the couch next to her and put on a comedy to try and take his mind off of how serious life had become these last couple of years. She joined him on the couch and while they waited for the movie to start he thought how strangely quiet the house seemed now that all their children had moved out in what felt like overnight.

He tried to watch the movie and laugh and pretend like everything was ok, but as they cuddled on the couch watching a movie, Michael's thoughts kept turning to his children. John was living with his new bride in Kansas City and Sophia worried about them both so much. She begged them to come live with them. They had so much land, they could build their own private little house, but John refused.

"There are people that need to be reached for Christ in the city," John was always thinking about others. "I promise, when things get too dangerous we will come, but for now Katie and I feel called here."

Sophia worried about John, but Michael couldn't help but feel a sense of pride thinking about his oldest son. He only wished he had the same feelings about his other son, Miles. He used to think Miles was just like himself. He even followed in his footsteps and recently had finished the police academy. It wasn't that long ago that the similarities went deeper than that. They loved the same Christian songs on the radio, they both had the same favorite Bible verses, and they could sit in pleasant silence for hours fishing together.

All of that changed as full gospel Christians started to become increasingly persecuted. Miles loved being a Christian his whole life and all it stood for, but when being a Christian became hard and became looked down on, it was like it suddenly wasn't worth it to him. Miles was offered an easy way out of Christianity because from every news outlet and every street corner were people preaching the Global Religion of Christianity. You could still be a Christian, all you had to do was leave out certain portions that were deemed hate-filled.

"How did he raise a child who had fallen away from his faith," Michael wondered as he half-heartedly continued to watch a movie with his wife. Michael used his position on the force to warn Christians who still preached the full gospel when a raid was about to happen. It felt a little wrong at times, hiding that he too was a full gospel believer, but it was how he was able to still make a difference and help his brothers and sisters in Christ.

Miles was a completely different story in how he handled the police raids against Christians. He seemed to enjoy busting into their homes and finding them in active prayer meetings or with an open unaltered Bible. He would put their handcuffs on too tightly or purposefully bang their head on the side of the police car as he loaded them up on their way to the reeducation camp.

Michael remembered an incident that happened just the day before. They both got called to the same disturbance; a destruction of Christian property. Miles had arrived first. Someone was vandalizing their neighbor's house. The husband of the victim's house had been recently arrested for preaching the full-gospel. With the wife and children alone inside, the neighbor began throwing rocks through the window, painting hateful messages across the garage door and smashing the car with a baseball bat. Michael pulled around the corner taking all of this in, while also seeing his son, Miles, leaning against his police car, arms crossed with a smirk across his face watching it happen and doing nothing to stop it.

As Michael exited his patrol car, the woman came out of the house, leaving her crying kids inside. She was a small African American woman no more than five feet. She looked strong like she was used to dealing with unkind people, but also the lines of worry were evident on her face as she walked cautiously toward her neighbor. The violent neighbor, undeterred by the police presence, walked right up to her and punched her in the face calling her a hate-filled religious fanatic.

Michael heard his son laughing as Michael ran to the woman and pulled the man off of her as he tried to land another blow. "Enough! You've had your say. It's time to go home" Michael was furious he was powerless to do more than that under the current laws.

As the man sulked away to his own house next door, Michael got the woman to safety in her home and comforted the children that there was nothing to be afraid of. They were safe.

There were no laws against physical assaults against full-gospel Christians property or person, so there was nothing he could do to give this woman justice. All he could do was help her get to safety and give her some advice to avoid future confrontations. Never did he think the laws would be in favor of violence to believers.

Michael left the woman's house and headed back for his patrol car. On the way there, he couldn't help but think that it was like the whole world was upside down and right was wrong and wrong was right. When he told John recently about the uptick in violence against real Christians, John told him he believed that was because the restrainer talked about in the book of Thessalonians had been removed piece by piece. John said the restrainer was the law.

Michael remembered being taught as a kid that the restrainer mentioned in the Bible was the Holy Spirit, but John told him the other day, that if that was true, then nobody could be saved in the Great Tribulation. That is because it takes the work of the Holy Spirit moving on an unbeliever's heart in order for salvation to occur. Michael marveled at the spiritual maturity of his son. When had the roles shifted to where he was the one learning and his son was the one teaching.

What John was saying made far more sense to Michael. He said that, in the Bible, Paul taught that the power of the state was appointed by God to restrain evil and to enact just laws. God, it seemed, had removed his protective hand that had previously kept men from fulfilling the evil that was in their hearts.

Michael didn't know what to think about that. In some ways, John was right. It seemed as if every righteous law had been taken away, and only laws that promoted evil remained, but Michael wasn't ready to buy into what John was saying fully yet. If John was right, that would mean they had entered into the end times, and Michael just didn't want to believe that was true. He wanted to believe he had more time. More time to make good memories, but most of all he wanted more time for Miles sake. If it was really the end, he was terrified of where Mile's ever hardening of his heart could lead.

As Michael neared his police car, he saw that Miles hadn't left yet. Michael should have held his tongue, but his anger got the better of him at that moment and he stormed over to his son, "You could have done something. I can't believe you sat there and laughed!"

Angry that his dad corrected him, Miles' smile left his face, "Don't lecture me, old man. It served her right." Then he got in his car without any expression of even the least amount of sorrow or embarrassment for his actions and sped off tires squealing on the asphalt as he left.

It was then that Michael knew his son had allowed something very dark to fill his soul in place of the love of Christ that was once there. He still loved Miles dearly, but he had become ashamed to call him his son. He hoped that would change one day. He and Sophia prayed for him daily to have his eyes opened to the truth and to return to Christ. Michael would just have to pray harder that Miles wouldn't be disillusioned with God; that he would know God is still good even when things are hard.

Michael looked over realizing Sophia was staring at him, "The movie has been over for five minutes and you have been staring at the screen like it was the most interesting thing in the world" Sophia playfully nudged him back from his thoughts.

"I was thinking about Miles" the sadness etched in Michaels eyes as he spoke.

Compassion and understanding filled Sophia's face. "It's not too late for him. God can still soften his heart."

"I don't know how much longer I can work side by side with him and see his cruelty and hatred for God" Michael got up and started pacing the floor. "Every time I see him, it seems like he's lost a little more of the man he used to be. I miss my son!"

Sophia nodded in agreement, "I miss him too. He was my baby, but you have to be strong." She stood up and stopped him from pacing and looked at him with fierce fire in her eyes. "God placed you in this job for a reason. He has blinded the eyes of your coworkers to the fact that you are a full-gospel Christian. You were able to warn 3 families last week alone of an impending raid and save them from being rounded up. For as long as God allows, you must continue to help our brothers and sisters... Even though it hurts to see our son slipping further and further away."

Michael knew she was right. He had to be strong. He had to help everyone he could until things got back to normal.

Emma Johnson couldn't believe her neighbor had just punched her and that cop had sat back and laughed. Thank God the other officer showed up and stopped her neighbor from landing another blow. She could hardly believe it. Her husband had once called that neighbor a close friend.

Her two little boys stood crying by her bedside as she

frantically flung a suitcase onto the bed and started throwing clothes into it haphazardly. "It's ok boys. We're just going to Nana's house in the city." Her mom had recently passed away and left them a house in Kansas City. They had planned to sell it and use the money to pay down their own mortgage, but now she was glad they hadn't listed it for sale yet.

The youngest boy was barely four and wiped his nose with the back of his hand as he sniffed and stuck out his bottom lip, "But I don't want to go! How will Daddy find us!"

Emma took a break from her packing and took a deep breath realizing her children were terrified. She bent down before her youngest boy who had just spoken, "We are going to leave a note for daddy so he will know where we went. He can call us when he gets back too. I will have my phone, but we can't stay here. All our neighbors hate us. It's not safe."

Her older son who normally felt very mature at the ripe old age of eight years old was now filled with questions and uncertainty, "Why did they take Daddy? Is Daddy bad?"

Emma realized her kids didn't understand anything going on around them and she had to slow down and make time to help them. She sat on the floor and brought both of her boys onto her lap and gave them a big hug, "Daddy did nothing wrong boys. All he did was tell our neighbors that Jesus died for their sins."

Her littlest boy did not understand, "Why did they take him away for that? That's not bad."

Emma let out a long sigh, "You're right honey, It wasn't bad. People are just very confused right now." She gave each boy a kiss on their head and lifted them off of her lap and began packing, but this time a little calmer. "It's going to be ok boys. You'll see. We will go to Nana's and Daddy will join us there soon. You have nothing to worry about"

Even as she spoke she realized she didn't believe the words she was saying. She didn't know if everything was going to be ok. Her husband told her to trust God no matter what happened, but that was becoming harder and harder to do. She couldn't think about that right now. She couldn't think about what was happening to her husband in the reeducation camp. All she could think about were her sweet boys and protecting them. She had to leave this neighborhood before something worse happened than today.

She glanced into the mirror above her dresser and saw the golden brown skin around her eye becoming discolored by the darkening bruise. There was no time or desire to try and hide it with make-up. She picked up her suitcase and with her two boys in tow, they loaded into the car and drove the two hours to the city that she hoped would treat her better than this little town had.

CHAPTER SIX

"But when you see the abomination of desolation standing where it should not be (let the reader understand), then those who are in Judea must flee to the mountains. The one who is on the housetop must not go down, or go in to get anything out of his house; And the one who is in the field must not turn back to get his coat." - Mark 13:14

Emma's husband, Jerry, was returned home from the reeducation camp after a week. He had gone to their home in Omaha and seen her note and hopped in their second car and drove to the city to find her. When she opened the door she gasped at how much he had changed in a week.

He had always been a fit, strong man, but it looked like he hadn't eaten in the entire week he was gone as his face was sunken in. His dark skin has always made it hard to see bruises, but there was no mistaking the blackened skin surrounding both his eyes. Those eyes that she loved to look into could now barely open. They had become two small slits that looked to be fighting a losing battle to stay open.

"Jerry, oh my goodness, come sit down!" She tried to help

him over to the couch to rest. He carefully laid himself down. It looked like each movement sent pain coursing through his body. "Oh honey, what did they do to you?"

Jerry tried his best to open his eyes wide enough to look her in the eyes for the first time, "I don't ever want to talk about what happened there." He reached up and tenderly touched her eyes that shared a lesser version of the same telling marks of abuse. "Oh Emma! Who did this to you? I'm so sorry I wasn't there to protect you."

Tears streamed down her face at her husband's care for her even when he was in so much obvious pain, "It's nothing. I'm fine." She angrily swiped away her tears and stood up pacing the couch in front of him, "How could God do this? You have only ever done good and He punishes you? Punishes us?"

Jerry tried to sit up, but when the pain made him wince he laid back down, "Emma, God didn't do this to me. Men did. You can't lose faith. God is still good."

She knelt back next to her husband and hugged him as gently as she could. She marveled at his strength. Not just his strength of body that he endured what looked like must have been torture, but that his spirit remained strong despite it all. That he still trusted in God. She wished she could be more like him.

Jacob, Sarah, Benjamin and Rachel were all crammed into the sanctuary of the new Jewish synagogue in Israel. They could hardly contain their excitement at being in the Holy Land on such a momentous occasion. They looked around at the massive columns, ornate paintings on the ceiling, and the stone pews that filled the room facing toward the front of the room.

"I can't believe we're here," Rachel said in awe as she took in her surroundings.

"I can't believe we are actually sitting in the temple in Israel," beamed Benjamin

"Hush children!" Jacob was impatiently waiting for President Elyon to enter and address the crowd. Even though the temple had been open for a year to the priests and open for several months now to the general public, today was the day of the formal inauguration of the historic building. Jacob had increased in his belief that Elyon might be the long-awaited Jewish messiah as he saw that he brought peace like the world had never known.

He and his family had all marveled as now six nations - France, Iran, Russia, China, Turkey, and England - had all willingly joined together under Elyon's leadership. It was deemed the Alliance of Nations and they willingly came under him as their supreme leader. Never has there been a man that has conquered land and brought peace all without the loss of a single life. Surely this man might be the savior they were looking for.

He only wished his own country would follow the example of the other six nations. His country was riddled with violence. There were bombings every day from extremists. Almost everyone wanted to join Elyon, so the senate presented a bill to join the Alliance of Nations and it passed. Jacob had hoped that congress would soon get on board and they would finally have peace. But the process was too slow and, now, it didn't matter. A civil war had begun within the borders of America. Rebels were fighting in the streets. The National Guard tried to respond by instituting martial law. There was chaos in the cities of his nation.

Rebels said the government no longer represented them and they were going to form their own county. President Martin tried to bring peace to his warring country but it seemed to Jacob that nothing the president tried seemed to work. Every attempt at peace and reconciliation was met by sabotage by either a Christian, Jew or rebel.

Jacob reflected that he was glad he was here in Israel for a little while and away from the troubles of his homeland. His thoughts and the excited hum of the room was all silenced as Cardinal Francis of the Global Religion took the stage. He was announcing all the accomplishments that had happened in the last several years since Elyon had risen to prominence and all that people could expect to continue with him at the helm of leadership. It was all things everyone in that room already knew, but still they were on the edge waiting. They knew everything Francis was saying was all leading up to Elyon taking the stage.

After what seemed like forever, Francis finally finished the introduction and invited Elyon to the stage. A thunderous standing ovation began the second he entered the stage. This monumental building with intricate designs seemed to pale in comparison to the man walking to the podium. The clapping and cheering was almost deafening, but Elyon just stood behind the podium patiently waiting for it to die down to allow him to speak.

When the last of the applause had ended everyone crammed back into the stone pews and took a seat. There was an energy that was palpable in the room as they waited for that first word to emerge from his lips.

Elyon stood with a confidence and determination that Jacob had not seen before. He truly admired this man. Elyon spoke of the six nations that had joined his cause and all the good that those nations were now experiencing. They all had a decrease in violent crimes and an increase in economic prosperity. "Everyone should petition their leaders to join the Alliance of Nations, with me as your leader, you will never want for anything again. I will see that all nations that join me will experience the same benefits the first six nations have experienced!"

As his voice echoed throughout the room, cheers rang out. It seemed everyone agreed that with Elyon as the leader, everyone would be better off, but then Jacob thought he heard a single voice of descent ring out. He must be mistaken. Who wouldn't want the peace and prosperity Elyon was offering?

Sure enough in the aisle opposite his own, but almost on the same row as him a single man stood up and began to yell loud enough for everyone to hear, "Those who would give up essential liberty, to purchase a little temporary safety, deserve neither liberty nor safety."

"Great, another rebel" Jacob thought to himself. There was one naysayer in every group, but it irked Jacob that someone would quote Benjamin Franklin in defiance of Elyon who had done so much good. This man clearly didn't understand and he saw the security guards coming down the aisle to remove him from the congregation, so Jacob began to turn his attention back to Elyon, but before he did he turned to take one last look at the man just a few feet away from him. He thought he saw something shiny in the man's hand being lifted.

He looked more closely at the irate man and saw that he had lifted a gun and was pointing it straight at Elyon. The security guards all began to pull their weapons to neutralize the threat. Jacob heard the sound of guns firing and, not knowing if the bullets were coming toward him, he bent down in front of the pew laying over his family trying to hide them from the spray of bullets that might be flying in his direction. Once things quieted down, Jacob peeked out and glanced at where Elyon stood moments earlier. He was no longer standing, but laying on the ground, dead with a hole in the center of his head.

The screams that filled the room when the first shots were fired grew when people realized Elyon lay dead only a few feet away. Jacob was pretty sure he heard screams from his wife and daughter as well on either side of him, but he was paralyzed by the scene in front of him and couldn't comfort them. Elyon, with a hole in the middle of his forehead, lay on the ground in a pool of his own blood. Lifeless. The man who just across the way from him had assassinated the most powerful man on the planet also lay lifeless on the floor.

The room was in chaos. EMT's surrounded Elyon trying to see if there was anything that could be done to save him. It quickly became clear to everyone watching the first responders that there was nothing that they could do. Elyon was no more. Women were trying to run out of the building for safety, but security had closed all exits to make sure the gunman was working alone and there were no other conspirators that could get away. News cameras were flashing furiously not wanting to miss a single thing.

Jacob sat stoically holding his wife and daughter who were both crying on his shoulder. So many hopes and dreams suddenly lie dead on the floor in front of him. He was not surprised when he heard a doctor who had rushed up to aid the EMT's, shout in despair as she wept on the stage, "He's dead. He has no pulse."

Minutes turned into hours as the security wouldn't let anyone leave until they had interviewed every last person in that room. As Jacob waited for his turn to be interviewed he didn't understand why they didn't remove the body. A single sheet had covered the body for an hour now and Jacob grew with anger at the disrespect being shown to Elyon. "Security, surely you can at least release a first responder so that they can bring Elyon's body to a more respectful place to rest."

The security ignored him at first, but as Jacob persisted in his questions the security officer gruffly responded, "My orders are no one in or out. Now sit down!"

The guard was cut off by a commotion at the front of the room. The body was alone on the stage and had been for over an hour, but the sheet that covered it began to move.

The shrill scared voices in the room slowly began to quiet as the room became more aware that something was happening on the stage. It wasn't long before the room was completely silent and every eye transfixed on the body on the stage. The cameras for the news stations were rolling and catching everything in real-time and broadcasting it to the world, but even the news anchors at their desks in their home city had stopped reporting and were silent and just watching the scene unfold.

The same question was on everyone's mind, "Why was the sheet beginning to move?"

The room of thousands gasped as one when the white sheet completely fell off of Elyon and his hand began to twitch. First one finger and then the next all tapping the floor as if they had a life of their own. Jacob felt Sarah squeeze his hand tightly as Elyon's fingers moving morphed into his whole arms pushing down on the floor as if to give strength and leverage and sure enough Elyon began to sit up. Slowly at first he sat as though being raised up by an invisible pillow gently and slowly lifting his still closed eyes and the wound still clearly visible on his forehead.

He could sense the fear all around him including the beating of his own heart that seemed to want to pound right out of his chest as the body continued to be lifted by some unseen force until it was standing in a fully upright position facing out toward all of them.

Jacob whispered to Sarah "What is lifting his body?" It was clear he was still dead as his eyes were still closed, there was still a bloody open wound on his head and his face was still ashen and devoid of life.

Just as the last words left his mouth Elyon's eyes shot open and he looked at every person in the room. Jacob felt like he was about to lose his lunch when he saw the color return to Elyon's face and the wound on his head began to close. During the minutes that the wound was closing the room sat in stunned silence as Elyon stared at them.

When the wound was fully closed, you couldn't even see a mark where it had once been. It was then that Elyon spoke. His voice was different. He always sounded confident and powerful, but now, Jacob couldn't put his finger on it, but there was something in his voice that sent chills down his spine. "I was dead, but now I am alive. I am not surprised by today's events. I knew they must unfold precisely this way. I wanted it to happen so that you could see, so the world could see" he said looking directly at the cameras "exactly who I am."

Jacob felt uneasy and looked to both sides of him and saw his wife. She looked white as a ghost, his son looked strong and unmoved, and his daughter was shaking like a leaf." They all felt it. Something was coming with what Elyon was saying that none of them wanted to hear.

Elyon continued speaking to the room, "I allowed myself to be killed, so that everyone would know who I am. To erase any doubt. You all witnessed something miraculous here today with your own eyes. Who could raise themselves from the dead? Only one person. God himself. I am god!"

Jacob knew at that moment he had to get his family out of there and to safety as quickly as possible. This man was claiming to be God? In the temple no less? It was an abomination to all that was holy. He felt as if his eyes had been opened instantaneously and realized how blind he had really been about so many things. He leaned over to his family and whispered, "I don't know what's going to happen, but we have to get out of here. Now. Watch me closely and do as I say."

They all nodded their heads eager to leave this room that felt suddenly alive with evil each time Elyon spoke. His eyes dark behind the podium he continued, "Even my name, Elyon, means 'most high god.' I am no longer president of a single country or leader of the Alliance of Nations. I am the Supreme ruler of the world. This temple was built for the Jewish sacrifices, but since this is the location of my greatest miracle, it is now holy ground to me alone. All will worship me here."

Jacob saw an opening. Most in the room were enthralled with the supernatural power before them. They had never seen anything like it and were eager to worship someone who could come back to life. Even the security guards had left their posts and began to make their way forward to bow before Elyon.

As the guard closest to them walked past them toward the stage, he grabbed his wife's hand and whispered to them all, "Now, we must go now!" and as quietly as they could they started to move. They pretended like they were wanting to go to the front to worship as well, but were being kind and letting others go in front of them. Each time they would let someone cut ahead of them, they inched their way back to the rear exits. They saw a handful of other families doing the same at other exits.

When they got to the door they looked to the front and saw thousands of people worshiping this man that claimed to be God. Some were laying face down on the ground before him, others were pushing their way to touch him and kiss his feet. All were saying over and over "I love you Elyon; I serve you Elyon."

Jacob's wife and children were through the door, only Jacob still was left to leave. Before he stepped through the door he looked back one final time, but this time he made eye contact with the supreme ruler as everyone in the room had begun chanting. He saw hatred and death in his eyes that seemed inhuman. It was as if he was looking into evil personified.

As quickly as he could he took the final step through the door and with his wife and children ran to the hills behind the temple. He didn't want to waste a single second going to town for supplies or even going to the parking lot for his car to drive further away. Something deep in his soul was telling him he had just looked at the very face of the devil and he had to run. Run fast and run hard to the mountains and hide. His family's life depended on it.

Michael had tried to stay awake to see the inauguration of the Israelite temple, but there was a ten hour time difference and around two-thirty am he fell asleep on the couch with the news still playing, waiting for the imminent arrival of Elyon.

He immediately knew he was in another of his dreams, but this one was different. It wasn't modern time anymore. He was back in the days of the Bible. Everyone around him was wearing long brown robes and sandals. There were people riding on camels and living in tents all around him. The women all had long hair with scarves that covered their head. He saw women going to the well to get water and carry it in jugs on their shoulders. He was trying to get his bearings when he heard a man shouting in the distance, "You have all become corrupt in God's sight. You have filled the earth with violence and do harm to the children. You must repent!"

A man right next to Michael began to laugh as he pushed his child down into the ground to get closer to the man preaching repentance. "Noah, go back to building your ark you crazy old man. Leave us to live our own lives as we see fit! Who are you to judge me for my choices!"

Michael took several steps closer to the preacher. "So this was Noah!" He marveled. He was staring at Noah! He was shorter than he expected.

Noah began to pick up a hammer and hit the wood of the ark in its beginning stages behind him. "With each hammer blow I strike and each nail I drive into the wood, let it be a call to repentance. Judgment is coming. Turn, while there is still time!" And with that Noah turned back and began to hammer in the next board onto the boat in front of him.

Michael turned from Noah and looked around him. The scene was very different than he first perceived it. At first he saw only the woman getting the water at the well, he didn't see the task masker behind her whipping her if she slowed. At first he only saw the camel carrying a child upon it, he didn't see that the child was headed toward being offered up as a sacrifice to an idol. At first he only saw the men walking around in long robes and tents peppering the hillside, he didn't see them all headed toward choices of immorality within those tents.

It was a world full of evil. The people were calling evil good and were calling the good message of repentance evil. As he looked around he saw a shepherd leaning against a large stone with a rod in his hand. The shepherd was looking around at the scene in front of him with sadness written across his face.

The world shifted and Michael was no longer with Noah at the ark, but was in his hometown. He saw the abortion clinics, drug houses, victims of human trafficking, husbands beating their wives, mothers abandoning their children and so much more wickedness.

The shepherd that had been on the rock was now looking away from Michael and toward the people doing such horrible deeds in his city when he heard him say, "Just as it was in the days of Noah, so also will it be in the days of the Son of Man. People were eating, drinking, marrying and being given in marriage up to the day Noah entered the ark. Then the flood came and destroyed them all"

The shepherd slowly turned his head away from the people before him and looked at Michael. A single tear slid down his cheek "The time is here. Warn them!"

Michael awoke with a start and no longer had any doubt what 'warn them' meant as he watched the news unfold that Elyon had raised himself from the dead.

There was safety in numbers now, so John made the decision to move in with Katie's parents, Robert and Beverly Williams, in the city. When they first got engaged, they imagined a month-long honeymoon in Paris and then finding a cute little apartment downtown that they could make a home and maybe even kids within a year or two. Now, all that was different. They didn't know how much worse things would get or how quickly, but at least they had each other.

John sat his new bride down the morning after the incident at the temple and explained to her exactly what had happened and what that would mean for Christians everywhere. After what happened in the temple, there was no longer any doubt that they were in the end times. The end had begun and there was no more than three and a half years left before the return of Christ.

"I believe you John, but I just don't understand." A look of confusion etched on her face as her parents listened intently to what John was sharing. "The Bible says no man can know the day or the hour of Christ's return. So how can you say that you know it's three and a half years."

John kissed her endearingly on her forehead. "That is an amazing question. One I'm sure you will be forced to answer many times in the coming months. The Bible says no man can know the day or the hour, but that does not mean we can't know the season.

We don't know the exact day winter will happen, but when we see the leaves begin to turn colors and fall off the trees, we know that it is coming very soon. The same for the return of Christ. We don't know the exact day or exact hour, but we know the countdown has begun."

Katie's parents began to emphatically shake their heads trying to control their disbelief. "It's just not possible. This just must be something similar to what the Bible prophesied, but not the actual abomination of desolation. We are still here. Our pastor taught every Sunday we would be raptured before that happened, so you see he just can't be the antichrist!"

John looked at his new parents with compassion, "You're not the only one that is shocked. I'm sure most of the western world is shocked that they are being called to live through the end times, unfortunately. You must remember that God is still good. We are called to fellowship in his sufferings. It is not normal how easy Christian life has been up until the changes in the last several years. For most of history, Christians have suffered. We must remember this isn't our home. Heaven is."

Robert spoke up, eager to refute the claims that John was making and explain away what he was seeing on the news. "What about the verse that says two men working in a field one was taken and one left. That clearly shows we will be raptured... right?"

"Look at the word 'taken' in context to other places it's used in the Bible. In one excerpt it said, "They did not understand and the flood came and took them all away, so will the coming of the son of man be." John saw that he had Katie and her parent's full attention and he prayed they were able to receive what he was saying. "When people were taken in the Bible it means killed. Not escaping tribulation."

"No!" Katie's dad jumped up from the couch interjecting. "I do not serve a God who delivers wrath on people who love him and serve him."

John calmly stood up as well and placed a comforting hand on his shoulder, "You're right we don't serve a God like that. The wrath of God that will be poured out will be on unbelievers and followers of the antichrist. We will be spared his wrath, but you have seen it these last several years. We are not always spared from the wrath of the evil men of the earth."

Robert sat down understanding dawning on his face, but still struggling to rethink everything he had ever thought regarding end time prophecy and struggling to remain hopeful amid such a drastic shift in the world overnight. "So that's it then? We are just going to suffer the next three and a half years? Some life!"

Understanding lit Katie's face for the first time really getting what her husband had been trying to tell her all those months they were dating and engaged. "Daddy, no. I get it now. Yes, there will be more suffering, but true Christians will walk in more supernatural power than they ever have before! We are going to see miracles like they used to see in Jesus' days!"

John felt such pride that he married a woman with such wisdom and strength. He took her hand, "Don't forget that we are called to have joy when we can participate in the suffering of Christ. What better way to die than to die a martyr's death and to be counted worthy to join in the suffering with Christ."

Hope started to play at the corners of Robert's lips as he listened to his daughter talk, "We will see God move in ways that can't be explained away by men. Think of all the things you taught me about Revelation...we get to see it first hand!"

Beverly spoke up for the first time. She had a look like she was lost in her thoughts and more speaking to herself than anyone else as she recited her favorite quote, "Never feel sorry for raising dragon-slayers in a time when there are actual dragons." She pulled herself out of her daydream and looked at her husband, "We have raised a dragon-slayer dear."

Robert smiled proudly at his daughter, "That we did. That we did." He looked with purpose over to John. "I think you're right. I think this is the beginning of the end. That means we have to tell as many as we can about the antichrist and what must be done to be saved."

John nodded knowing he was right. It had already started. As thousands worshiped Elyon yesterday he imprinted a mark, seemingly supernaturally, of a name on those that worshiped Him either on their hand or forehead. It seemed the mark of the beast was already at play and they must warn as many as possible before it was too late for them.

Elyon was wasting no time and neither would John. "Elyon," he thought. John was disgusted that he had turned a beautiful name of God and made it into something vile. He vowed to only call him by his true name from that moment on, the beast.

CHAPTER SEVEN

"When He opened the second seal, I heard the second living creature saying, "Come and see." Another horse, fiery red, went out. And it was granted to the one who sat on it to take peace from the earth, and that people should kill one another; and there was given to him a great sword." - Revelation 6:3-4

Elyon always knew he hated the Jews. Having to pretend to be their savior was like vomit in his mouth, but he didn't know how much he hated them until he saw that one man sneak out of the very temple where he raised himself from the dead.

Since that day, thousands of Jews every day have been fleeing to the mountains surrounding Israel and in other countries going into hiding there as well. "How dare they after all he had done to bring peace to their land after centuries of unrest!" He thought to himself that he would see that every last one of them paid for it.

"Francis" he bellowed throughout the hall of his mansion.

Quickly Benedetto Francis came running around the corner and went to his knees before him bowing low, "How may I serve you, my Lord." Elyon vacillated between loving the power of having someone bow before him in worship and also detesting the weakness of humankind. He didn't know how he went from dead to alive. When the bullet was sailing toward him, he had felt anger and indignation that this wasn't the way it was supposed to end. Unlike what he told the onlookers, he was surprised the second before he died.

Then everything went black and cold, but in what felt like the next second he was standing before the podium in the temple looking out at the mass of people with a strength that made him feel invincible. Ever since then, he had felt like a god. He didn't need to sleep, he didn't need to eat and everyone around him disgusted him.

He felt like he was immortal. "Rise, Francis. We have two problems that I need you to deal with. The first is the Jews."

Benedetto shook his head furiously, "Yes, I can't believe how they have betrayed your kindness by abandoning you just when you show yourself in your greatest splendor."

Elyon stood with his arms crossed in front of him, "You are the founder of our great Global Religion. What do you suggest we do?"

Benedetto mulled it over for a moment before coming to a conclusion. "We were only rounding up to reeducate the extremists in all the religions. After all, there are many roads that lead to you as god, but I believe we have reached a crossroads. First, I believe reeducation camps are a thing of the past. Everyone in the world has seen your power. It is time for them to make a choice. Either they choose to worship you or they choose to die."

Elyon was clearly pleased by this recommendation so

Francis continued to expound on everyone who deserved death. Since the day that Elyon was healed from his fatal head wound, a group of Christian extremists had begun to refer to him as a beast and some even called him the antichrist. It infuriated Francis and he wanted something done about it, "Continue to round up not only those that preach the full gospel but the parameters should be expanded. Anyone that dares to utter the vile words of anti-christ or beast should be immediately arrested and demanded to pledge their allegiance to you or face death. Lastly, there should be no leniency for Jews. Every Jew on the face of the planet should be exterminated without a chance for repentance."

The supreme ruler of the earth knew then that he had picked the right man to be his prophet in the coming days. As he looked at the man in front of him, he started to feel something that was starting to become an increasingly familiar sensation since the day of his resurrection. Something took over his person.

He felt himself hovering above his body watching himself down below him lay his hands upon the small bald man's head. Then he heard himself say to Francis, "You shall be known as Prophet Francis from this day forward and I will give you the power to do signs and wonders in my name." Then Elyon breathed on Prophet Francis and the man seemed to stand taller and straighter and a strange, crooked smile spread across his face as he looked upon his god who had just breathed life into him.

The Levi Family ran for days into the wilderness that

surrounded the Judean mountains. They couldn't explain the feeling they had to run and hide, but they knew it deep in their soul. They couldn't return home, they must hide.

Rachel regretted her choice of wearing heels within the first hour of their hike and threw them into the woods. She would just have to walk barefoot from that point forward. As night crept upon them, the air became colder and the fancy clothes that they had worn to the inauguration proved vastly insufficient to protect them from the elements.

Evidence of spring was all around them with the flower blossoms blooming on each bush they passed. They were grateful for the warmth during the day and that they weren't making this escape during the winter. However, the nights were still cold.

That night they huddled together for warmth. It was Benjamin and not their father, Jacob, that led his family in a prayer, before they went to sleep for the night, that God would protect them and guide them. The next morning as they woke up to continue their trek into the mountains, they looked up and saw an abandoned cabin in the woods. Jacob whispered to his family, "That's odd, I don't remember seeing that last night. Must have just been too dark."

They walked carefully and quietly up to the dwelling to make sure it was indeed empty. Once they were confident they weren't going to stumble upon an owner of the home, they went inside and looked around for anything that might help aid their escape. Rachel clapped her hands, jumped in the air and squealed with delight as she looked in the closet of the bedroom. "Shoes!"

Never did she think she'd be so happy to see a pair of ugly

brown sneakers. The house must have been a vacation home only rarely used because it had everything they needed. Shoes for Rachel, a coat for Jacob and Sarah and even food. They gathered everything they could carry and continued on their journey.

The sun had almost set on the second evening when they began to hear talking in the forest just a little west of them. Benjamin immediately put his finger to his lips and motioned to his family to get down. They all quietly and quickly dropped to their knees just as a bright beam from a flashlight shown above their heads. As they stayed crouched low, they began to see more beams of lights all around them. It was Elyon's men searching the woods for defectors from the cause. Benjamin pointed toward a thick cluster of bushes and they all crawled over and tried to surround themselves inside the brush as best they could while they laid flat on the ground.

They heard footfalls all around them throughout the night and it wasn't until first light that the last of Elyon's men had moved the search to a different area. They waited in the brush hours longer than the last sound they heard just to be sure they truly were alone and wouldn't emerge to a slew of men waiting to arrest them.

They slowly rose from the cover of the bushes to set out again to find a hiding place among the mountains and by the time they did, it was already midmorning.

They walked slower each day than they had the day before, but they continued on. Finally on the seventh day of their hike they came upon a mountain that seemed so far removed from the cities. They looked up at it and it seemed like it was impossible to climb. That is what made it clear to

Benjamin that it was the perfect mountain for them to hide on. If it looked impossible to him, it would look impossible to others as well. They could be safe staying there.

So they climbed for a full day straight. It felt like climbing a ninety degree vertical to their inexperienced legs, but really it was just a steep hillside. He had no idea how they would eat or drink or survive in such an inhospitable and hard to navigate location, but he knew he had to get his family to safety. He'd figure out the rest later.

He was lost in his thoughts as he brought up the rear of their climb making sure everyone ahead of them made it ok. On the long walk to safety this last week, he had a lot of time to think about many things. He thought about how easily blinded he was by Elyon. He realized he was so eager for him to be the Messiah of his people, that he didn't even check to see if he fulfilled the more than five hundred prophecies of old about the coming Messiah.

That got him thinking about the prophecies he had started learning about the last couple of years as he got in touch with his Jewish heritage. He thought of all the prophecies Elyon didn't fulfill. He wasn't from the lineage of David, he wasn't born in Bethlehem, he wasn't born of a virgin, and he didn't come into Jerusalem riding on a donkey. Elyon didn't fulfill any of those prophecies.

As he thought of that, he had a sudden realization that the Jesus of the Christians did fulfill all of those prophecies. What if the messiah had already come and he had been blind to it just like he had been blind by thinking Elyon was going to save his people?

The more he thought it over the more he began to believe

in Jesus as the Messiah, but he didn't even know where to begin. He had never even read a New Testament scripture. At only eighteen, there was so much he had never done. He had never even had a girlfriend, he thought to himself as he had almost reached a stopping point on the climb where all his family were waiting.

They had stopped in front of the mouth of a cave thinking that was a good place to at least camp for the night, but they all stared at him as if he had grown a horn on top of his head. He looked around at the open mouths of his family surrounding him, "What are you staring at?"

His sister cleared her throat and swallowed, "Um, you have this strange mark on your forehead. It's blue and it looks almost like a shield. You know, like the shields the knights in the middle ages used to use with a family crest on it?"

"What?" Benjamin didn't believe her. It was probably another one of her silly pranks, but with no mirrors around he couldn't check to see if there was actually something on his head.

His mother sprang into action and spit on her two fingers "It's just a little dirt, let me get it off." She began scrubbing with her wet fingers as hard as she could on his forehead like only a mother could while his sister giggled in the background at her brother being treated like a little boy with his mommy cleaning his face.

Benjamin rolled his eyes and looked at his mom, "Well, did it work?" She shook her head no; nothing had happened. It didn't come off. There was a permanent mark in the shape of a shield on his forehead. What in the world was happening?

* * *

Michael realized now that his dreams were more than dreams. God himself was speaking to him through his dreams. At first Sophia thought he was crazy when he told her this, but later that day as she was praying, a verse came to her mind about old men dreaming dreams and young men seeing visions in the end times.

She excitedly ran and told Michael about the verse and how she believed that God was speaking to him through his dreams. He laughed as he tickled her, "Woman, are you calling me old?" They laughed together and it felt like old times. There was joy in their house again.

After his wife had her fill of teasing him about his gray hairs. She told him "Even God is calling you old since He chose to give you dreams and not visions."

Michael laughed. She was right. He guessed that meant he was old. When their laughter died down he got serious "So what's next? How do we help people to learn the truth, when speaking the truth gets you killed?"

Sophia thought long and hard before answering, "I don't know. All I know is that I need you with me, so don't do anything stupid!"

Michael tried to laugh off her comment, "Me? Do something stupid? Never!"

Sophia smiled a little at that, "I'm serious Michael. Don't go being a hero. It's bad enough you can die just doing your job as a cop, but now just speaking about Jesus can get you killed. Don't take unnecessary risks. Promise me."

Michael saw her worry and he promised her that he would be careful, "You can trust me, Sophia. There's a way we can still help people. We will pray. We may not be able to shout on a street corner holding a cardboard sign that the end is here, but we can pray for God to bring us the right people at the right time to share his truth with."

Sophia seemed to visibly relax that he wasn't planning some huge evangelism outreach and that his plan was a safe one.

Michael continued, "It seems we still have a little bit of time where I can keep my job too and continue to help Christians and Jews at risk." Michael knew the signs were everywhere that he didn't have long before he would have to flee his job and go into hiding. That was not just because it was becoming harder to hide that he was a true Christian, but because he could tell the time was close when it would become mandatory that everyone take the mark of the beast.

He had studied many times in the Bible where it prophesied that no one would be able to buy or sell anything unless they had a mark on either their forehead or hand. It would be a mark specific to the antichrist and for anyone that took it, it would be a sign of their devotion to the antichrist. "We know the mark of the beast is coming and everyone will have to take it, but it will take time to implement it. Right now, people are voluntarily worshiping Elyon, but they have to make a trip to Israel and see Elyon in person. And, praise God, Elyon hasn't spoken of any mark yet. We still have time."

Sophia lowered her voice as if they might be overheard in the privacy of their own home, " How long do we have until then?"

"I don't know, but we have to try and save everyone we can until then," Michael said as he grabbed Sophia's hands and rested his head against hers.

———————————————

Elyon was glad that America was no longer an independent nation. The death toll from so many civil insurgencies pressured the president to finally concede to Elyon's demands. He made an executive order and officially joined the Alliance of Nations as did three other nations. Elyon smirked as he reveled in the thought that he was seeing his vision for the future come to pass.

There were now ten nations joined together ruling the world, but those ten nations did not yet have peace. His happiness was short-lived as he thought of those that still fought the idea of one government of the world ruled by him.

He watched the news on the tv on his wall. It spoke of civil wars and a rapidly rising death toll. His anger boiled to the surface and he growled as he threw a vase at the tv smashing the picture turning it black, "Those stupid people led by stupid leaders. It had been the leaders of the four nations that were slow to join him that had caused all this. If they would have joined him right away, the people would not have revolted like they did."

The result of those four nations fighting against him for so long before finally joining, had dire consequences. Elyon had been forced to take drastic measures to make those rulers lose credibility among their people and it worked. They eventually joined and the world proclaimed him as a king who conquered the world without ever shedding any blood. He was hailed as a hero.

However, the rebels of the world did not accept him as

their leader and continued to fight everything that represented the one world government. The whole world was fighting.

It had turned into a third world war, but it looked different than any war in the past had ever looked. In America, three states had organized together against the federal government's attempts to join Elyon's Alliance. Texas, Florida and Missouri all organized their own military force and refused entrance to any of Elyon officials into their states' borders.

These three states made formal declarations declaring themselves independent nations no longer a part of the United States of America. Any intrusion by the federal government was seen as an act of war and was met with force.

Civil war had broken out on America's shores yet again and they weren't the only country like that. Countries all around the world were facing similar problems as their officials attempted to join Elyon's world government.

The Alliance was fighting in almost every country trying to squelch the rebellions and the rebellions were fighting the Alliance army and their own governments as well.

Elyon paced the floor as he thought to himself, "I must end the rebellion and end it decisively and quickly. And when I end the uprisings I will be hailed as a hero yet again for stopping the civil wars that I created." He laughed out loud at the blind stupidity of the people around him.

Miles Hill saw the way certain Christians seemed to escape his raids. He was no idiot. He knew his dad had something to do with that, but he had no idea how. The names were kept a secret from everyone but those that were confirmed loyal to the cause of Elyon. Still, somehow Christians were warned and avoided raids much of the time.

Despite his suspicions, he had no proof, so he turned a blind eye to his dad's sabotage of the new world government and tried to make sure his dad didn't catch wind of any raids he had in the works. As angry as he was at his father, he wasn't so mad that he wanted to see him arrested.

The raids were increasing daily. It wasn't just the Christians and Jews he was rounding up, but those that were trying to evade Elyon's draft. Elyon boasted of the ten nations that joined together to lead the whole world and that they would lead by stopping the uprisings that were erupting around the world.

Miles' brother called him the other day and told him the war that was spreading around the world was actually the second seal prophesied in the book of Revelation. Miles' had become so angry he hung up on John not wanting to hear more of his speculations.

He thought to himself how ridiculous his family's beliefs were. There had been wars for centuries and none of them were fulfillment of prophecy, but of course his superstitious family thought this time it was different.

His family might have got it wrong thinking that the war was a sign of the end times, but it wasn't surprising they were fooled because the third world war was so different than what everyone expected it would look like. Instead of a few superpowers fighting each other and plunging the world into a nuclear holocaust, it was all the superpowers joining together and fighting to stop the civil wars that had begun in each county.

It didn't take long in the war for the death toll to rise at an alarming rate. Never had so many people died so quickly in a war. Soon, to have enough soldiers to stop the rebellions, every country would have to reinstate the draft, not just America. The United States draft included both men and women from ages sixteen to forty-five. It was then that people started hiding themselves and their children from their orders to report for duty. It seemed everyone wanted the greatness that could be had by aligning with Elyon, but no one wanted to pay the price.

Nations warring within themselves, young men and women trying to avoid the draft, religious zealots preaching a full-gospel heresy. Miles' job as a police officer was at times more than he bargained for.

Miles often thought to himself that at least he didn't have to respond to any calls made by people listed as Christian or Jews anymore. Other than raiding their homes and detaining them, they were on their own and that made his life easier. He remembered how, at first, people just committed acts of vandalism and assault against them. That changed when everyone saw Elyon do the impossible. Miles saw how followers of Elyon became increasingly infuriated as the extremists still defied him. Their defiance set many over the edge to enact change. Their refusal to capitulate to Elyon was the straw that broke the camel's back.

Laws were set forth and approved at the federal level that made it legal to steal from or kill someone you could prove to be a full-gospel believer or Jew. Not everyone agreed with those laws right away and hardly anyone acted on them. However, the bombings and mass killings continued daily. The news was reporting it to be all from the hands of the Jews and the Christians. As a result, people slowly began to embrace and love the new laws of the land to legalize the murder of the extremists in those two religions.

Miles believed it was a step in the right direction and things had been better off since that change. His philosophy was if you eradicate the people causing so much turmoil, then things could go back to how peaceful they were not long ago.

He saw what looked like Elyon raising himself from the dead on the tv just like everyone else. He just wasn't sure if he believed it. "It's much easier to believe that there isn't a God than to believe some man wearing a pinstripe suit was God," he thought to himself as he patrolled the streets of the city in the middle of the night. He continued to think it over trying to keep himself awake as the late hours of his shift pulled at his eyelids, "Who else could do what Elyon did? Maybe he wasn't God. Maybe he was a superhero who had invincibility, like Superman, and he would save America from the villains of the world. What did it matter who he was? He was special and deserved to be followed."

He didn't care one way or the other if people thought he was God, Superman or an alien from outer space. All Miles knew was that he liked what he was doing for the world. Before the world broke out into war, things had never been so peaceful. Everything was perfect when everyone just followed Elyon. Miles slammed the steering wheel in frustration, "God or not, why can't people see that. Why can't my family see that?!"

Katie sulked on the walk home from church, "John, I hate going to that place. They are literally preaching that we are doing a service to the world if we kill Christians who preach the full-gospel."

John wrapped his arm around her shoulders as they continued to walk, "I know sweetie, but it's a great way to keep suspicion off of us a little longer while we try and seek out those eager for the truth."

Katie sighed, "I know." She stopped suddenly and discretely pointed up ahead. There was a girl, no more than sixteen, sitting on the park bench with her head down crying quietly. "John, I think we just had an answer to our prayers. Look there's someone who needs to hear the truth." She subtly nodded her head in the direction of the young girl crying, "Go home, so we don't raise any red flags. I'm going to go sit with her and see if I can help."

He kissed her on the temple of her head. It was a kiss filled with love and concern knowing that she was about to risk her life like they both did now on a daily basis. "There's no way I'm going home and leaving you here, but I will go stand in the shadow behind the building across the street. That way I can watch you to make sure you're safe and it's not a trap. Be careful. I'll be praying."

He walked across the street to the other side of the road and stood in a shadow that completely hid him. He watched his wife's every move praying the whole time that she would be ok.

Katie continued on to the teenager who was clearly in

distress and sat down beside her. "What's your name?"

The girl, startled, sat up and wiped her eyes. "Beth," she said as more of a question than an answer.

Katie smiled, "Beth, that's a beautiful name. I saw you crying and thought you might like a friend. I'm Katie and I'm a newlywed. Can you tell me a little bit about yourself? Why are you crying on this beautiful sunny day?"

Beth looked around at the sky around her like she was noticing it for the first time in a while, "Everyone I know is dead or gone. My brother got drafted into the war and died. I haven't seen my dad since I was a little girl when he and my mom split. My mom was caught helping a Jew escape to safety and was killed on the spot in front of me."

She paused as she relived the memory looking down at her shoes as she told it, "Jews had been coming to our home in the middle of the night for months. I was told to never tell anyone about it and I didn't. Until one day at school, my friend asked me why I was always so tired and she started making fun of me for failing my test. I got so mad I told her that it wasn't my fault we have company over all hours of the night keeping me up."

The young girl paused before continuing her story with a voice laced with sadness, "I knew I made a mistake the moment the words left my mouth. My friend's eyes grew big and a smile spread across her face. She suspected it was more than just company. She had always been jealous of me and I guess she thought this was the perfect opportunity to get me. I hoped I was wrong, so I went home feeling guilty about my big mouth and ate dinner."

Beth looked up from her hands to Katie's eyes as if she

was pleading for her to understand, "I was trying to build up my courage and tell my mom what I had done. I had planned to tell her before bed, but I didn't get the chance. Before I finished my dinner, I heard a loud knock on the door. My mom could hear the knock was not a knock of a friend and told me to run out the back of the house and I did. I didn't leave though; I hid in a tree in the backyard. I could see inside from many of the windows from my vantage point.

I saw my mom went to answer it and it was Elyon's police force. They didn't ask to come in, they just barged in. They tore up the house ripping cushions, tearing apart the walls. Then they found it. They found the secret room behind the kitchen cabinet where we would hide Jews until a safe house could be located for them.

We didn't have any Jews in our house that night, but there were clothes and food, and personal articles from the family that had left the night before. There was no trial for my mom. She stood in the middle of the kitchen, the officer walked right up to her, put the gun to her forehead, and pulled the trigger."

Beth ended her story and looked up at Katie, "I'm all alone."

Katie's heart broke for Beth. Dressed in the latest styles and still so small and petite, Katie guessed she was still just in high school. So young and already in so much pain. She wasn't the only one with a story like this. The death toll was rising everyday around the entire world. Martyrdom increasing as Christians were being killed for their faith daily, the war was producing more deaths than any war in the history of mankind, and there was a new strange disease she heard about that was just starting to also affect the global population.

Katie reached around and gave Beth a quick hug. She said a quick prayer asking for wisdom if this was the right time and the right person to share the gospel with; just that moment she saw a white dove fly right above them both. She wasn't superstitious. She wouldn't say for sure that was a sign of God telling her it would be safe, but it was close enough. She decided to risk it.

"I think your mom was very brave to do that," Katie whispered. Beth was shocked that this stranger would speak so openly in favor of her mom. Her mom was a criminal whose activities led to her death. The fear of someone overhearing them made Beth look around in fear. She looked at the shadows of trees as if they might report this conversation to the police.

Undeterred, Katie continued, "One of my favorite pastors said, 'The only answer to a bold lie is a bold truth.' What everyone is reporting about the Jews is a lie. They are not evil and deserve to live in peace. Your mom was a hero for seeing that and doing something about it."

Beth could no longer hide her emotion and cried freely while trying at the same time to not draw attention to them sitting so vulnerably out in the open, "Thank you for saying that. All my friends have treated me like a criminal, just for being her daughter. I've been so confused. I'm being told that everything I've always thought was a lie. I used to think…"

Beth stopped mid-sentence once again looking afraid to speak what was on her mind, so Katie finished for her, "Maybe I can give words to what you're feeling. It feels wrong to hurt people. It feels wrong to say you are not free to speak what is on your mind. Something feels off about this new leader everyone seems so in love with."

Beth looked at Katie with her mouth agape, speechless before she finally answered in a stunned, "Yes. Exactly."

Katie noticed someone across the way staring at them, so she stood up and motioned for Beth to join her hoping walking would deter attention from their intense conversation. "You probably heard about Jesus your whole life, but never paid much attention. I want to tell you now is the time to pay attention. All the things you're seeing? A world war, a man calling himself God and saying he raised himself from the dead even though it was actually God who granted Satan the power to raise a man from the dead. Not to mention Christians and Jews being rounded up around the world and slaughtered. All of this was written in the Bible over two thousand years ago. None of it is a surprise."

Katie had a feeling they were being followed, so she quickened her step. "We need to separate. They are watching us. Take time to pray tonight! Ask Jesus to forgive your sins. We will meet again and when we do I will tell you what will happen next. Remember all of this was foretold a long time ago. I'll be praying for you, Beth!"

And with that, Katie left a stunned Beth on the sidewalk and quickly walked down a side path toward the alley where her husband was waiting. Once they were together and sure they weren't followed they headed home together and away from the prying eyes that seemed to be everywhere nowadays.

CHAPTER EIGHT

"When He opened the third seal, I heard the third living creature say, 'Come and see.' So I looked, and behold, a black horse, and he who sat on it had a pair of scales in his hand. And I heard a voice in the midst of the four living creatures saying, "A quart of wheat for a denarius, and three quarts of barley for a denarius; and do not harm the oil and the wine." -
Revelation 6:5-6

Michael knew he was dreaming as he found himself walking around a cute little park in Kansas City. There were trees lining the sidewalk with park benches every so often and a moving stream across the way from the sidewalk. Ducks waddled lazily into the stream and people were walking the sidewalks of the park at a leisurely pace enjoying the day.

Michael decided he would enjoy the day too and began to walk on the sidewalk taking in all the sights of nature. As he walked, he noticed a strange man hiding behind a tree staring at two women talking on a park bench. This man did not look like an official officer of Elyon. He looked like a nosey neighbor that wanted to earn a reward for turning in a suspected Christian extremist or maybe an undercover cop. Michael averted his attention from the man and looked closer at the women and saw that one of them was John's new wife, Katie.

Michael wondered, "Why was that man staring at them?" The man started to creep closer each time hiding behind another tree watching the women as they seemed engrossed in conversation, Katie's young friend was crying.

Katie looked up and saw the man staring at her. He tried to pretend like he wasn't when he made eye contact with her. He pretended like he was just resting against the tree staring off into the distance the minute Katie looked his way.

John breathed a sigh of relief as he saw Katie and her friend rise from the bench and begin to walk away from the park and from the man. It was clear that Katie still felt uneasy because she kept looking behind her as she spoke with her friend. Michael looked for the man in the tree and saw he was gone. He was initially glad he was no longer there until he saw the man following the ladies at a distance behind them.

Katie looked back behind her one more time and quickened her step, said a final few words to her friend, and then ran off in the other direction. At first, her friend stood still, like a deer in headlights, watching Katie run off. Then she continued to leisurely walk toward her home completely unaware of the man that still followed her.

Michael followed them both and saw her turn onto her street and into her house locking the door behind her. He turned his attention then to the man who had been trailing her the entire time and saw him pull out a cell phone as he stared at the house she had just entered.

Michael was able to hear every word of the man's phone conversion, "I just saw her walk into her house. She had a very suspicious meeting at a park this evening. Gather a team and meet me at 546 Washington Street tomorrow evening. We will arrest her then and find out who the woman was that she was with on the park bench.

He hung up the phone, pulled out a cigarette, and leaned against a tree still staring at the house the woman had entered.

Suddenly he saw Michael standing there. Michael almost ran to hide, but what good would it do, he was caught. The man threw down his cigarette on the ground and stomped out any embers and walked over to Michael, "We are coming for Beth."

Michael sat straight up in bed panting and drenched in sweat. This dream wasn't about some obscure family he had never met or faceless people, this was about his family. He had to call John and Katie and tell them his dream!

Katie was shocked when she heard Michael's dream. He described exactly the park she was at yesterday and the girl she had met. She felt like she was being followed, but now she knew for certain. She had to go back and warn Beth not to return home.

At first, John said it was too dangerous, but then she reminded him that they were placed here on this earth for such a time as this. God wanted her to help. John agreed she was meant to help, but he wasn't letting her go alone.

John went with her and scoped out the park looking for

what may be secret police canvassing the area. He planned out possible escape routes for them and then they stood out of sight of all passersby for what seemed like hours. He wondered if it was all for nothing and Beth would not even come, but Katie remained confident, "She will come."

No sooner had the words left her mouth, did he see a young girl walking down the street and sitting on the same park bench that his wife had pointed out as the one they shared together yesterday.

He looked at his wife with a look that suggested there was no room for argument, "Stay here," and with that, he was walking toward the scared teenager. As he walked by her, he pretended to ignore her and be interested in the trees around him. When he was right in front of her he made brief eye contact before looking away, then he bent down to tie his shoe, but discreetly placed a piece of paper that was folded very small next to her foot. Then he stood up and he continued past her walking like nothing had transpired.

She waited a few moments, then slowly bent down like she was brushing a piece of dirt off of her shoe, but in one swift quick motion picked up the folded paper and kept it hidden in her hands. She let a few minutes pass and then she looked around her to make sure no one was watching before she opened the paper and read its contents.

I am the husband of Katie who you met yesterday. She is with me. You are in danger. Take a walk around the park, so we can check if you're being followed. If you aren't being followed, you will hear an owl hoot three times. If you hear that walk to the beginning of the trailhead. If you are being followed, you will hear a whistling cat call as you walk by. If you hear this run as if your life depends on it, because it does. Lose your tail, come back tomorrow and we will try again with the same codes. Destroy this letter immediately before you begin walking.

John and Katie saw Beth reading the letter and then rip it up into tiny shreds, her hand shaking as she did so. She then wandered over to the stream, took off her sandal, dipped a toe in, and then sat next to the bank and put a hand in the water letting it rush over her hand. When John looked closer he saw that it wasn't just her hand in the water, but that tiny white specks were being let go from between her fingers and floating away as they disintegrated in the water.

"The letter," John whispered to Katie from their hiding place as she nodded her head in agreement. They watched as Beth slowly got up from the water and began walking around the path of the park. They inspected with eagle eyes every shadow and every hidden crevice if there was anyone following her or watching from a distance, but there was no one but them interested in what Beth was doing at the park.

As she came closer to them, John let out three hoots like an owl. "Good. She's coming to the trailhead," he held out a hand to Katie to help her up from their hiding place and they both also walked to the meeting spot.

When they got there, Katie gave Beth a hug, "I'm so sorry for all the secrecy, but we had to be sure it was safe to talk to you. You have been targeted. Your home will be raided tonight."

Beth took a sharp inhale of air, "How can you know that? I haven't done anything wrong. It was my mom who helped the Jews, not me."

Katie took her hand and began the walk down the secluded trail, "My dad had a dream."

Beth laughed out loud before she looked at her new friend and realized she wasn't joking.

"I'm serious," Katie described the dream in detail including a description of the house and the man smoking a cigarette outside of it.

It was clear Beth believed her and her voice quivered when she spoke, "I saw the cigarette bud outside my house this morning on the way here. My mom had made me do yard work just last week and I was annoyed that someone littered so close to my house." She paused, "What am I going to do?"

Katie looked at John for reassurance and he gave a comforting nod of the head, "You're coming home with us. You will be safe there for now.

Beth stiffened and moved away. "I hardly know you. Maybe you're with the people that killed my mom and are just trying to trap me."

Katie realized she was coming on too strong and the young girl beside her was scared, "You don't have to trust me, but I hope you will. I really do want to help."

Beth turned away trying to hide the tears in her eyes, "I know I can trust you. I just don't want any of this to be real. I want my old life back. I would do so many things differently."

Katie nodded understanding that feeling as she felt it many times herself.

Katie tried to build trust with Beth by showing her she

cared, "Tell me more about yourself Beth."

Beth paused before answering. It was clear she had a lot on her mind that she wanted to share, "I was raised in church, but when everything started to get hard for Christians, I just didn't want anything to do with it anymore. I broke my mom's heart. I could hear her crying at night in her bathroom as she would pray for me. I wish she could have lived to see that her prayers worked." She paused and looked right at Katie, "I did what you said and prayed last night."

Katie couldn't hide her excitement and jumped up and tried to hide her squeal, "That's the best news. And rest assured your mom does know. She's watching from heaven and rejoicing with you!"

Beth couldn't hide her smile, but John broke into their special moment, "I'm so glad for you Beth, but we really need to be getting home before we draw attention to ourselves. Katie, you walk home with Beth and I will trail behind you."

So the three of them exited the trail behind the park and began their walk home. Beth peppered Katie with questions about what happens next the whole way. John was smiling behind them as he watched his wife come alive talking about the role Christians got to play in the coming days.

"We are winning the war," Elyon boasted proudly to his prophet, Francis. "Nine countries have joined the Alliance of Nations and the tenth is completely overwhelmed by their civil war. Their leader has recently come to me begging me to come help them. Now that I have their leader's invitation, I can send my forces in and squash the rebellion. It won't be long before I have a unified ten-nation alliance!"

Francis beamed at the greatness of Elyon, "Once the Alliance is complete there will be no stopping your total global dominion!"

Elyon nodded his head solemnly, "It's time to make sure everyone worships me. Not everyone can make the pilgrimage to Israel, so start setting up the worship and mark stations in every district."

Francis grinned, "And for those that refuse?" He asked, already knowing the answer, but wanting to hear it again.

Relishing each word as it came out of his mouth, "Kill them. In fact, once the allegiance stations are set up, make it a law across the world that you cannot buy or sell unless you have taken a mark of allegiance to my cause. Starve out anyone who is resisting my reign."

"With pleasure, my Lord" Francis sneered as he walked out of the room.

Elyon, left alone once again, waited a few minutes until he was sure he was alone. "Come to me oh great spirit." Instantly his body filled up with some unseen force filling him with power and ridding him of any fatigue he had previously felt.

The hot wind blew across his back and he heard his beloved serpent's voice hissing in his ear, "As they will worship you, so you must worship me." And so he kneeled and worshiped his god.

Benjamin Levi and his family tried to get settled as best

they could in the large cave that they had stumbled across. They gathered firewood from the trees that engulfed the mountainside and had a fire to keep warm for the cool nights. They made sure to go deep into the cave whenever they had a fire, just in case anyone with evil intent might be passing by and see their flame.

That's why they were surprised one evening as they all sat around the campfire when another group walked up to them. It was a group that looked not too different from them. There were two young men and a girl and they looked like they had traveled very far on foot.

Their faces were covered with dirt, except for the girl. On her, the dirt made a clean path from her eyes down to the bottom of her cheeks showing the evidence that she had been crying. Their clothes were ripped and there were twigs stuck in their hair. When the girl saw the campfire, she collapsed from what appeared to be exhaustion.

Any fear that these strangers were a threat set on harming them vanished as she fell to the stone floor. All the men sprang into action to carry her to a comfortable place around the fire while Sarah prepared a bowl of stew for her. Rachel began to drop spoonfuls of water into her mouth.

She slowly woke up to one of her brothers, Jonathan, telling his story, "Things have been bad for our family for a very long time. We never joined the Global Religion of Judaism. My brother, Zeke, my sister, Leah, and I were all raised devout Hasidic Jews. We have been hidden by Christian friends for over a year as things have become increasingly dangerous for us. We watched the news as Elyon appeared in the Temple. One second he was dead, and the next he was alive and saying he was God.

It was like a light went on in each of our eyes the second he said that. He was not God, and the man who our friends had been telling us about, Jesus, was actually the Messiah we had been looking for."

Leah began to sit up as she regained her strength and felt suddenly famished, so she fed herself the stew in front of her. Zeke looked lovingly at his little sister, who was no more than 14, as he continued Jonathan's story, "Our friends had been telling us about Jesus the whole year we lived with them. We didn't want to listen. They didn't just tell us about Jesus, but they started showing us a book of their Bible we had not read...Revelation. Have you heard of it?" He looked to the Levi family as he asked that question to which the whole Levi family shook their heads that they had not.

Zeke took a little Bible out of his back pocket and flipped to the end of the book, "They told us all things were going to happen before they happened. They knew Elyon was evil before any of us did. They said he was going to call himself God. They said a world war would begin. They said..."

Jonathan interrupted his eager brother by putting a hand on his knee, "Let's not overwhelm these gracious hosts with too much at once." He looked at all of the Levi family one by one, but then his gaze stopped at Benjamin who seemed dumbfounded, staring at them all.

Benjamin was not scared by their sudden appearance, or by their story that they knew ahead of time what was going to happen. Benjamin was in shock because each one of them had the same blue shield on their forehead that he had, "Your head. You each have a blue shield on your head!"

Jonathan smiled, "Yes. The day Elyon declared himself to be God, we knew everything our friends had been saying was true. If they were right about what was going to happen next, they were also right that Jesus was the son of God. My parents and us all prayed with them right there in the living room in front of the muted TV that was showing an evil man being worshiped by thousands. When we opened our eyes, each of us had this seal upon our head"

At the word, 'parents' Leah began to weep softly, "We knew we had to get out of the city. Our friends were so kind and offered to let us stay with them to the very end, but something deep inside us told us to get out."

Benjamin marveled at everything he was hearing, "It was the same for us. We just knew to run to the mountains."

Leah shook her head in agreement, "It was a hard journey and our parents were old. We went slow so that we could care for them, but they fell behind one day. When we realized they weren't with us, we traced back our steps. It wasn't very far. They..."

Leah erupted into fresh sobs and Rachel took her into her arms like they had been sisters all along. Jonathan looked as sad as Leah sounded, "As she said, it wasn't far at all. Maybe only a hundred paces they had fallen behind, but it was filled with so many trees you couldn't see three paces in front of you. When we had almost caught up to where we last saw them, we saw them surrounded by Elyon's men. They were on their knees with their hands raised, but the soldiers didn't care that they surrendered. They raised their guns...."

Leah covered her eyes at the memory, "When we heard the shots we ran as fast as we could and we didn't stop for an entire day. I have never felt such exhaustion, but we knew we couldn't be captured. There were no more 'reeducation' camps. There is only death for being a Jew."

Rachel released her arm which was around Leah's shoulder and instead held her hand, "I am so sorry for everything you've gone through. You're safe now. We are in the middle of nowhere."

Jacob had been mulling over everything that was being said. He looked at the new arrivals and the mark on each of their foreheads. Then he looked at his own family and saw the mark only on Benjamin's forehead. He looked at the newcomers, "So, you are saying you were marked after you said a prayer accepting Jesus as the Messiah?"

Zeke comprehended first what their acknowledgment meant for their new friend Benjamin. He looked with compassion toward Benjamin at what he was about to say, but then looked back at Jacob with purpose in his eyes, "Yes. We are the one hundred forty-four thousand Jews that are sealed by God."

Tom was a country boy through and through. He lived in the southern region of the Ozark mountains in a little town called Jasper, Arkansas which had less than a thousand people in the city. He lived on a dirt road filled with potholes in a small trailer his granddaddy had left to him. He never went anywhere without his cowboy hat and a pickup truck. He'd been around on this earth long enough to see the signs well before most people that things were getting worse and not going to get better.

That's when he started prepping. He started with storing food. At first, it started as just picking up a couple of extra cans of vegetables each time he went to the store, but it quickly amped up from there. By the time the fiasco at the Israelite temple happened a few months ago, he had stored enough food to last three people a couple of years. Not only that, but he had a water catchment system in rain barrels on the side of his house and an underground bunker safely hidden away under his pole barn in the far pasture.

He remembered how his ex-wife had called him crazy for spending all that money, but he refused to stop. He thought back to the day that she had left him as he sat in his fading oversized reclining chair that was full of holes. She had taken his son and daughter.

She left after she found out that one night with too much to drink he had found himself in the arms of a stranger. When his wife found out what he had done, instantly, his whole world had fallen apart. The last time he saw his kids was when his daughter was six and his son was nine. He missed them, but it was too complicated.

He sent them a card every year for their birthdays, but they never wrote back. So, he tried to forget them and throw himself even more into prepping for disasters. He leaned over the armrest of the chair to pet his mangy dog, Jack, "We don't care though do we boy? Seems we were right all along."

Tom always believed in less government power, not more, and since Elyon came into the picture, he believed the government had gotten way out of control. He didn't believe the nonsense that Elyon was God.

Tom got up from his comfortable chair growing angry at

his own thoughts, "How could he be God, there is no God!"

Jack followed eagerly behind him as Tom left their little home and went outside into the garden to tend to his vegetables. Tom was completely self-sufficient and had no need for grocery stores any more and it was a good thing too.

Food had become incredibly scarce everywhere. He went to the grocery store two months ago because he just didn't feel like cooking and wanted a frozen pizza. It had been months since he had been and he was shocked at the empty shelves everywhere. There had been times in the past when one item was out of stock in the store, but this was almost every shelf. He had never seen anything like it.

He remembered how he started to wander around the store out of curiosity, the frozen pizza he came for completely forgotten. He wanted to see what items the store still had. He found a single loaf of bread on the bread aisle but did a triple-take when he saw the price tag underneath. It was $100 for a loaf of bread! "That's a mistake," he thought to himself, bringing up the loaf to the cashier so she could tell him the actual price to appease his curiosity. He thought to himself, "There's no way it's a hundred dollars. That is almost what a minimum wage worker would make in a single day. There's no way people have to work for a whole day just to get a loaf of bread."

As he made his way to the checkout counter he realized the store was not only empty of most products but also customers. There was only one woman in the store shopping with her young child. It was feeling more and more strange as he looked around. He handed the cashier the loaf of bread to ring up waiting impatiently for the correct total.

The cashier didn't ring it up but was staring at him like she was waiting for something. She finally and impatiently told him what she was waiting for, "Sir, I need your ration passport before you can buy this bread."

Tom was shocked, "ration passport, what the heck are you talking about? I just want to buy this here loaf of bread," he said with his typical country accent.

The woman looked like she had given the same speech a thousand times that week. "I'm sorry, but you can only buy your week's worth of allotted food and it must be tracked on your ration passport to make sure you aren't buying more than your fair share. Now, would you please back out of the line while you look for your ration passport?" She said as she motioned to the young mother who Tom had failed to notice walk up and stood behind him.

Tom remembered how he had gotten out of line, shocked at how much the world had changed in such a short amount of time. As he was lost in his thoughts he overheard the young woman talking to the cashier, "I'd like to buy this gallon of milk, but I also need bread and you didn't have any. My ration book says I am allotted a loaf."

It was clear the cashier was becoming increasingly impatient with customers who didn't seem to know the rules, "Look lady, I don't know what to tell you. Yes, you're allotted a loaf of bread for the week, but if there's no bread on the shelves, then there's no bread."

Tom saw the woman try to hold back tears as she looked sadly at her little child sitting contentedly in the shopping cart oblivious to what was happening around her. Tom couldn't help thinking about his little girl at that moment, wondering if she was ok and if she had enough to eat. She was a teenager now, probably almost an adult, but it was hard to think of her all grown up. He kept picturing her as the little girl he would push on the swing each Saturday.

Frustrated at how his thoughts kept turning to his family lately, he shoved the loaf of bread into the mother's hands, "I forgot my ration passport at home anyway. You have it."

As he left the store, the cashier yelled after him, "There is a bread delivery scheduled for Saturday. Come back then, but make sure to get here early before it's gone."

Tom didn't come back. He had enough food at home, but he could only imagine the line of people eager to get their bread that cost a day's wages. It was like they were back in the days of the depression he thought to himself as he walked out of the store empty-handed.

Tom shook himself from the memory of that day to return to the task at hand. All of his preps had been for a hypothetical situation. The realization that he now actually needed them made him work even harder in the garden which used to be just a hobby but was now part of his survival ritual.

As he weeded around his growing plants, he realized something. If people were starving, they would become desperate for food. He had food. He had to take measures to make sure people didn't know he had food and to keep it safe from anyone that might want to steal it.

Emma's husband, Jerry, was healing more every day from the torture he endured. He was able to move around and even sit on the floor and play board games with their boys on the floor. He was not able to work anymore though. Even though he wanted to get a job, he had been labeled an extremist, and no one would hire him. Every day he went out and begged people around the city for work. He was willing to do any job for a few dollars. People could sense his desperation and often paid him far less for tasks he completed than they were worth.

Thank God Emma's mother's house was paid off. They didn't have to worry about monthly mortgage payments as their finances became tighter and tighter. Even still, It didn't take long at all to burn through their savings just to pay the monthly bills. They hadn't had electricity in a while, but that didn't bother the boys. They thought it was an adventure having candlelight each night to read by and build forts next to. It felt like a long camp out in the living room to them.

Emma was worried though. Their savings was gone, their credit cards were maxed out and they couldn't get work. If that wasn't bad enough, food had become so expensive. They had been issued a ration book for their family, but, lately, they didn't have enough money to even get all of their weekly rations.

All of them were losing weight rapidly. Her little boys were starving before her eyes. They were always complaining about being hungry, but she did everything she could to keep their minds off of it. They built forts and played board games, and she read them stories. Her goal was to keep them distracted.

Her husband, Jerry, came home that evening weary and worn out with barely enough money for a loaf of bread. Her boys ran up to him, "Daddy!" and gave him a giant hug. They looked up at him with sweet trusting eyes, "Did you get enough money for food today daddy?"

He tousled their hair, "I sure did. God has been so good to us by allowing us to be together in hard times. And tomorrow He will bless us with bread!"

The kids cheered as they were sent to bed by their dad who followed after them to sing them to sleep. Emma watched as they all walked to the bedroom. Her husband's devotion to God never seemed to waver. Being tortured and now watching his babies' bellies swell with hunger didn't make him turn against God. Why couldn't she be like that?

Every day it got a little harder to not be angry at God. Her babies were suffering and God should stop it! Her husband saw her heart becoming angry at God and tried to remind her that when things got hard to keep her focus on Jesus and eternity with him. He'd remind her that there'd be no more suffering there.

She would feel better for a little while every time he encouraged her in the right way to view their suffering, but as soon as she heard her little boy's belly growl, her doubt returned.

Jerry tried to tell her that he thought the high cost of food coupled with a world war was more than a coincidence. He was convinced that it was a sign they were in the third seal of Revelation, but she didn't want to believe it. Her brain knew he was right. She knew it the second she saw Elyon raise himself from the dead on the television, but her heart didn't want to believe it.

Whenever he would try to tell her what to expect and that she should prepare her heart for hard times ahead, she would yell at him, "You're wrong! Our preacher told us we would be gone before the end. Things are going to get better. You'll see!"

CHAPTER NINE

*"And you will hear of wars and rumors of wars. See that you
are not alarmed, for this must take place, but the end is not yet.
For nation will rise against nation, and kingdom against
kingdom, and there will be famines and earthquakes in various
places." - Matthew 24:6-7*

John was standing in the pouring rain in a food line with
his ration passport, glad that the weather was warm from the
heat of the start of summer. Everything had gotten drastically
worse after the antichrist had declared himself to be God a
little over a year ago. Now, not only was food ridiculously
expensive but there also wasn't enough of it anymore.

He looked behind him and saw the line now wrapped to
the end of the block and around the corner. He couldn't even
see the end. He had been waiting since seven in the morning.
It was almost nine and he still had ten people in front of him
before he was served.

It wasn't just food that there were shortages of. It seemed
like everything was in short supply. In part, it was because
there was a lack of workers. After all, so many of them were

drafted. John was one of the lucky ones to avoid the draft. He was legally blind in his right eye, due to a childhood injury. It never bothered John. He was able to see fine out of his left eye, but not having full use of his right eye disqualified him from active service.

He was glad because it meant he was able to stay home and keep Katie safe. As the food line slowly inched forward he noticed a police officer, detaining the man at the register. The officer spoke into the police radio velcroed to his shoulder, "We have another person trying to use a fraudulent ration passport. I'm bringing him into the station now for questioning."

As John was one person closer to the front of the line, he watched the man in handcuffs, who was arrested over a loaf of bread and carton of eggs, walk past him.

Every week in the food lines it was the same story. Someone trying to fake a ration book, or trying to go in line a second time even though it was already stamped. He saw the woman in front of him had two young sons with her that barely looked strong enough to hold up their heads. John could see that they were all malnourished and his heart went out to them.

The woman's weekly rations were based on the size of her family and her rations were also based on if she had everyone in her family present at the time of disbursement. She had herself and her two children with her, so she would be rationed triple what John would receive as a single person in line.

She had stood in the line in the pouring rain with John, then made it inside the store and, finally, she had reached the front of the line. She walked to the counter with her emaciated children where she gathered her allotted food and paid. As she walked out the door holding her bag of groceries in one arm and the hands of both of her kids in her other hand, she slipped on a puddle and the groceries went flying in the air landing with a crash in the rain. Half of them were destroyed by the impact and the water.

She slowly stood and started to pick up the scattered food, but before she could, several people from the end of the line sprinted over to where she was. At first, John didn't move to help because he thought they were going to help and he didn't want to lose his place in the front of the line, but then he realized they weren't helping at all. They grabbed her unspoiled food and ran off with it. She was powerless to stop them and it all happened so fast John just stood stunned as he watched it all unfold.

As they ran off with her food, John heard her cry of desperation, "Wait! Stop! We need that!" The woman limped her way back to the front of the line. No one minded her cutting, everyone had seen it happen including the Ration Passport authenticators that distributed the food. He was shocked that those in charge showed her no compassion. They didn't care that her food was destroyed and stolen as they responded without emotion, "Sorry ma'am. You've received your weekly allotment. You will not receive more until the following week. Now please get out of the line and make room for the gentleman behind you."

John thought to himself, "That poor woman had probably spent all the money she had on that food and is going home empty-handed. Her sons look like they wouldn't make it without that food." He called out to her as she turned to leave, "You can have my weekly portion."

She was so grateful, but John knew his portion wouldn't come close to being enough food for her family for the week. At least he was able to do something. He had known food shortages were coming months ago and he still had lots of oatmeal stored away that he had bought when things started getting bad. It would just be an oatmeal kind of week he guessed.

The Passport authenticator shouted, "Next!" It was his turn. He paid for his weekly allotment of bread and eggs and walked the woman and her boys out to her car making sure she, the children, and the food were all safely inside before he started walking back to his car. On the way to his car, he wondered how he would be able to contribute money toward rent for Katie's parents when all his money was going toward food.

As he reached the door handle of his car in the parking lot, he looked at the line of people still in line who stared at him enviously for the small weekly rations that he had just given away.

He saw what seemed like a flash of light and, instantly, the scene changed. It was like a light had flashed before his eyes and what he was seeing was suddenly different. He was looking at the same line of people, but their eyes were transformed, they were dark and devoid of any of the emotions that make us human. They looked hopeless as they stood waiting for the scraps of food to be handed out to them. He wondered to himself, "Why do they look so different than they did a moment ago?"

He took his attention off of the people and looked around and saw that the landscape looked much different too. When he first stepped out of the store a minute ago there were cars in the parking lot and driving on the street. Now it has drastically changed. Instead of cars, John saw that there were bodies piled everywhere. "What is happening?" The stench was unbearable. It seemed like the dead surrounded them, but the people in the line didn't even seem to care or notice. "Why are there dead bodies everywhere?" John was so confused and he couldn't take his eyes off of the scene in front of him.

John saw rats weaving their way in between the bodies that were stacked in disorganized piles and some vultures circling above and then swooping down and landing and taking a bite while others fought over each scrap of human flesh. John wanted to throw up, so he tried to turn away from the scene before him and look instead to the tree line in the distance.

There he saw bears and mountain lions that were skin and bones leaving the safety of the forest and roaming about the city desperate for food. The people at the back of the line waiting for food were attacked by wild animals in broad daylight. Those around them ran and scattered, but the people in the front of the line seemed unfazed and determined to not lose their place in line.

There was something different about the line, John realized. He saw that none of the people had ration passports and many of them looked ill. "How are you going to pay?" he questioned the people in front of him. They didn't answer him or even look at him, but just coughed a violent hacking cough that John noticed produced a little bit of blood. It was as if he wasn't there. "How are you going to pay?" He asked the next person but again received no response.

He decided to leave the line and walk into the store where he saw the shelves were still bare and there would not be enough food to feed everyone that was waiting in the line. He saw there were no ration passport authenticators when the person at the front of the line walked up with their weekly allotment of food.

John waited for them to take out their wallet and pay, but it didn't happen like that. Instead, they placed their right hand on top of the barcode scanner and John heard the unmistakable sound of a "beep" that a scanner makes when it's scanning an item of food.

He watched as person after person, all with dead and hopeless eyes, walked up to the scanner and scanned a part of their body as they received their food. Some scanned their hands and some scanned their forehead. John didn't see anything on their hand or forehead, but every time he heard the sound of a 'beep' and knew there was some kind of mark on them that he could not see.

He felt evil all around him and wanted to run and hide. He ran out of the doors of the store and into the parking lot amid all the decaying bodies and saw someone working to try and clear away the bodies, loading them onto a dump truck as if they were mere trash. As the man leaned down to pick up another body, he first looked at John and said, "Get out of the city!"

Instantly, John saw another flash of light and was back in the present day. The sky was sunny, there were no bodies littering the street, and, while there was a food line, they had ration passports and money to pay for their items. The people were sad and scared, but you could still see hope and life behind their eyes.

"What had just happened?" He said aloud and the person next to him looked at him like he was crazy for talking to himself. "Sorry," he said to the onlooker as he walked quickly to his car and got in, and sat down, locking the doors as fast as he could.

"Was that what it was like to have a vision?" he thought to himself. He didn't know. He only knew he had to get Katie, her parents, and himself out of the city. Tonight.

Emma came home with her boys. They were all soaking wet and defeated. She had to bring her children with her to get all the food she was allotted, but they were starving. They hadn't eaten anything in three weeks and very little before that. The trip to the store drained them of what little energy they had remaining. The little games of keeping them distracted from their hunger stopped working weeks ago. They didn't complain anymore, but her heart ached as she knew her babies were hurting and she couldn't help them.

She wished she could just whisk them away to the hospital as she would have a few years ago. It wasn't an option anymore. With so many dead and dying, the hospitals were being overrun with patients. Also, she couldn't risk her sons getting this strange new disease so many were getting by going to the hospital where it was so prevalent. She took great care to keep them away from their father at home, so he didn't spread it to them.

They slowly walked past the couch where their dad was sleeping to the chairs on the other side of the room. Her husband was burning up with a fever. She saw the tissues on the table in front of him that he coughed into all had specks of blood on them. There had been a strange illness that she had heard about, but she didn't know much about it. Could that be what her husband had? She looked at the single loaf of bread and dozen eggs that were supposed to feed her family of four for the next week and laughed to herself.

She knew she had to do something or they were all going to die there. She carried her boys, who were too weak to walk anymore that day, to the backseat of the car. She went back into the house and roused her husband from sleep and helped him stand to his feet and she supported his weight while they walked to the car. It wasn't as hard as it would have been even a month ago as he was considerably lighter than he had ever been.

He mumbled incoherently to her, but she didn't even try to understand what he was saying. She just had to get him to the car. She decided that she was going back to their old home. She had a little food in the pantry. If no one had broken in and stolen it, she could feed her children with that. More than that, she had medicine. Lots of medicine. She was powerless to help her husband with his mysterious illness in this empty house and she didn't have the money to go out and buy more medicine.

She had to risk going back to her house in Omaha. She hated the idea of her neighbors seeing her, or God forbid, them seeing her husband who they hated now. She had to get her family to where she had supplies. As her family slept in the car, she cried at how she feared she was about to lose everything that was most precious to her as she pulled out of the driveway and drove out of the city. "Do Something!" She screamed to the sky at God.

Then she looked at her husband and the boys next to her. They didn't even stir at her sudden outburst. She knew it was a race against the clock to save her family.

"Now that so many people show me the reverence I deserve, it's time to put some policies in place that will weed out any resistors who are slow to get in line" Elyon paced the floor as he dictated a new list of procedures to his second in command, Francis. "So far people have had to make a pilgrimage to Israel if they want to see me and publicly declare their devotion. I want that to change. I want them to be able to perform that pledge of their allegiance to me from anywhere in the world at any time."

"Yes, my Lord" Francis grew excited at what he was about to share. "I have been working on something I think will please you," He ran out of the room and came back with something. It was unclear what it was because it was draped in a white sheet, but it was just slightly taller than Elyon himself. "Please, uncover it master" Francis spoke with glee.

Elyon walked over to the object and removed the white sheet. He was very pleased with what he saw. The only way he could describe it was that it was like a robot, but it was unlike any robot he had ever seen. It looked like a human in every way shape and form. It had arms and legs and a full body. It was slightly taller than himself.

It didn't just have the shape of a human, but it also had the appearance of one. It was covered in lifelike skin that made it almost impossible to tell you were looking at a robot. It looked more like you were looking at an actual lifeless person. It didn't look like some vague unrecognizable person, but it looked exactly like Elyon himself. Elyon walked around this image of himself in wonder at its lifelikeness. Everything seemed so real except that it was not alive. Its eyes were closed and head down unmoving, but otherwise, it was like staring into a mirror of himself.

Elyon noticed that it had what looked like skin, and hair. It was truly unbelievable. "Well done, Francis. It is a statue worthy of my honor."

Francis smirked like he held some kind of secret, "Oh it is more than a statue." He walked over to the image of Elyon, just as Elyon had done to him many months ago, Francis took a deep breath in and breathed out over the face of the object standing before them.

Instantly, the image became what appeared to be alive. It breathed out in a raspy voice, "Are you worthy of Elyon's love?"

Francis looked at the image and responded, "I, Benedetto Francis, worship Elyon alone and deny all others. He has my full devotion and allegiance."

The image again spoke in a voice that sounded like it was full of gravel, "You have been found worthy."

Francis turned his attention to actual Elyon, "I have thousands more of these made and ready to be shipped to every large city in the world. Before they leave, I will breathe life into each and every one of them. People won't have to travel to worship you, they will bow down to a living image of you in their very cities. They all pale in comparison to the one that I have prepared to place in the center of the Temple. It is ten times the height of the one you just saw. What shall I tell the cities that receive these smaller images of yourself?"

Elyon knew then what needed to happen, "We will tell the people that they must first bow down and pledge allegiance, love, and devotion to my image and forsake all others. Only after they have worshiped me, will they be allowed to receive a mark that will allow them to buy or sell anything."

Francis nodded in agreement, "Yes many people already have microchips for convenience of payments, it won't be hard to convince them to take the next step and get your microchip after they first make a public act of worship toward you."

Elyon continued, annoyed by Francis' interruption, "This will be different from any other microchip we have known. It will have a component that will alter their DNA forever once it is implanted. I want to make it impossible to ever reverse their decision once they decide to serve me. I want to be a part of the very blueprint of who they are. If someone tries to buy something and doesn't have my mark implanted in them, they are to be immediately rounded up and brought to one of the worship stations. If they refuse to worship me, kill them!"

Daily, more people joined Benjamin and his family in the cave. Almost all seemed to have the mark of the blue shield upon their forehead and all of those that were sealed used this time in the cave to study their newfound faith in Christ.

Even in his own family, his sister now bore the mark too. His mother had become a believer in Jesus as the Messiah, but she did not have the mark. At first, he was very confused by this. Was her confession of faith fake?

Then one of his new friends, Jonathan, explained to him. "The Bible prophesied that many would come to believe in Jesus Christ as the Messiah in the last days. However, only one hundred and forty-four thousand would be sealed with a mark upon their foreheads. Those that were sealed would be ethnic Jews that had never been intimate with anyone." Jonathan looked at him with intensity now, "Anyone who bears the seal will have supernatural protection on his life. The Antichrist army will not be able to harm him."

Benjamin sat back dumbfounded, "So, what. You're saying my sister and I are invincible?" He laughed nervously.

Jonathan smiled; he had the same thought at one time, "Only God knows. I do know this, if we are invincible as you say it's for a reason. It's so we can preach the truth without fear of anyone being able to shut us up."

Benjamin felt it then more than he ever had before. It felt like his very bones were on fire, and if he didn't get out of that cave and tell someone, he would explode. It was all making sense now. All the pieces were fitting together of why he was put on this earth, but then he looked over at his parents who were listening to their conversation. "They don't have the mark. What about them?"

"I don't know," Jonathan said. All I know is if you have the mark you are safe. My guess is they are relatively safe here in this cave.

They had lived a life of miracles every day since finding

this cave. Their people came in droves finding them and camping with them and others found nearby caves and did the same there. On this sheer mountainside, they should have run out of resources on the first day, but they always had more than enough.

Every cave in the mountain system had a clean and steady stream of water to drink from that never went dry. Every day they found a mountain goat or a ram caught in the thickets by the mouth of the cave. The bushes around the mountainside seemed to be ripe with a multitude of different kinds of berries. Almost all the newcomers that came mentioned finding abandoned cabins along their trek there where they loaded up on clothes, wheat, or shoes. They said it was miraculous. One minute they didn't see the cabin, the next it was there in front of them filled with exactly what they needed. It was like they were seeing the tangible hand of God providing for His people again like in the days of Moses.

His mother, Sarah, did not take long to believe in Jesus as the Messiah. It was clear to her that He was the one who rescued them and provided for them. His father was a harder case. Benjamin believed that his dad was hard to convince because he was afraid of being fooled again.

You could see on his face that he felt such shame that he had led his family so astray. First, he led them astray to be atheists and not believe in anything. Then, when Elyon came into the picture he encouraged all of them to follow after him wholeheartedly and was thoroughly duped yet again. Now, they were living in a cave as a result. He didn't want to be wrong again and have his family suffer as a result, so amid daily miracles, he sat, unbelieving.

Benjamin ached for his dad to know the peace he felt, but he had to begin to turn his thoughts to the others that he was called to help. He took out his little pocket Bible his friends had given him and began to study in earnest again as he had every day. He'd wait to tell his parents a few more days, giving him more time to study, but it was time for him to go out and tell the world what he had discovered here in this cave.

John came home from the food lines and told Katie, her parents, and Beth about his vision. Katie agreed instantly it was time to leave the city and head to John's parents' land. Katie's parents were not quite so convinced that it was the right move. They believed John, but at the same time, it seemed so far-fetched. To them, it seemed rash to leave the city on the word of the daydream of their 25-year-old son-in-law. They just wanted more time to think about it. They said, "Just give us one more day to think about it."

John packed up all their supplies and loaded the car so they would be ready to go first thing in the morning. He would find a way to convince her parents tomorrow and he wanted to be ready to hit the road as soon as that happened. He felt an urgency since his vision and didn't want to waste a single second. As soon as he had bags of food and water packed and loaded into the trunk of the car he crawled into bed next to his wife and slept until the sun woke him in the morning.

John thought he'd give Katie a few extra minutes to sleep

in and rest before she had to leave her childhood home. He did his normal morning ritual of drinking his coffee while he spent some time in the Word. When he finished, he turned on the TV in the living room to hear the latest developments on the news even though he felt the news had become hardly more than state-sanctioned propaganda.

The war had been ramping up daily. It seemed there was always something. The death toll rapidly rising and rumors of future wars of rebellion against the new government were just a few of the crises that were consuming everyone's thoughts.

He had watched for only a few minutes when the TV shut off on its own. He noticed the fan above him was slowing down and the lights had turned off as well. "Great, another power outage." He went to check his cell phone for updates to see when power was expected to be restored, but his cell was dead too. "That's strange," he thought knowing it had a full charge just a minute earlier. Both his in-laws and Katie's phone were all on the counter, so he checked all of their phones as well and they were all dead too.

John began to worry that this didn't seem like a normal power outage. He was regretting his decision to listen to Katie's parents and not leave the city last night like he originally wanted. He decided to run to his car and go to the gas station and fill up so he could have a full tank and he could get out of town right away. When he went into the garage and got in his car to turn it on, nothing happened.

That is when the pit in his stomach began to form. "Oh, God. Why didn't I listen and leave last night?" His car wouldn't turn on. It wasn't even making a sound like it was trying to. He ran into the house and got Katie's car keys off the hook by the front door and ran out to her car that was parked on the road. The same thing happened when he turned the key in the ignition, nothing.

He saw a neighbor across the street, dressed like he was ready to leave for work, getting out of his car. John ran across the street to him, "Hey, is your car working?"

The neighbor looked perplexed as he slammed his car door shut, "No! Piece of Junk won't even make a sound." Now, John knew. This was not a normal power outage. He didn't know why it happened. Maybe it was the latest in a series of counterattacks of the war. Maybe it was a solar flare. It didn't matter; The result was the same. His city had just had an electromagnetic pulse.

He didn't know how widespread the EMP was. Was it just his city or had other cities been attacked too? All he knew was that power was down everywhere and if they thought things were bad in the city now, they were only about to get worse. And fast!

He rushed in to wake Katie, "Katie, wake up. There's been an EMP. We have to get out of the city, now!" She rushed to get dressed and then woke up her parents and Beth. All the while he was throwing everything he could think of into every available backpack and bag.

They all gathered in the living room. You could still see a look of disbelief on the Williams' faces. They weren't sure if it really was an EMP, but between John's vision and then the events of the morning he wasn't taking any chances. He was leaving the city with his wife and Beth in the next five minutes with or without Robert and Beverly.

They reluctantly agreed to go with them but wanted more

time to grab some sentimental items. John became frustrated, "There is no time for pictures and trinkets. Things are about to get more real than you could ever imagine if even half of my vision was true. I have all the food and water we can carry, I have clothes, tents, and a first aid kid. That's all we have to have. We have to leave, now!"

His insistence wore them down, "But where will we go?" Their worry was becoming evident.

John thought for a minute. He had always assumed when things got bad he would head for his dad's house, but he also assumed he'd have a car to get there. Getting to his dad's house meant having to go through the center of the downtown district. Once more people figured out what was going on, the looting wouldn't be far behind. Things were already so violent, it just didn't feel wise to go through the downtown part of the city now.

Beth had been quiet the last two days regarding all of John's revelations and insistence on what they needed to do, but now as John was silent and unsure of their next move she spoke up, "I might have a place we can go."

CHAPTER TEN

"When He opened the fourth seal, I heard the voice of the fourth living creature saying, 'Come and see.' So I looked, and behold, a pale horse. And the name of him who sat on it was Death, and Hades followed with him. And power was given to them over a fourth of the earth, to kill with sword, with hunger, with death, and by beasts of the earth."
- Revelation 6:7-8

Benjamin and his fellow sealed brethren all felt called to go out to the nations. They heard that worship stations were being set up in every city where people were taking the mark. Benjamin had been studying scripture for hours each day and knew it was a matter of weeks, maybe days, before all buying and selling would be restricted to those with the mark.

So he and those like him all set out for nations around the world. He was shocked to learn that each person with the seal that he met felt called to a different nation. He did the math, and if God divided the sealed equally to each nation on the earth, then each nation could have over seven hundred believers preaching the gospel in it.

That's seven hundred untouchable people that the antichrist's army can't stop from telling people about God and His salvation. How exciting. Not everyone shared in his excitement though. His mother wept when he told her that he and his sister, Rachel, would be leaving, and his dad barely was able to hold in the emotion he tried so hard to hide.

They were worried about them, but it was more than that. Benjamin thought they were also scared. They weren't sealed. Harm could come to them, but he believed they would be safe where he left them and he made sure they had plenty of provisions before he set out with his sister on their journey.

They both felt called to stay in Israel and preach there. They began the long trek out of the mountains that they had fought so hard to hide within what felt like a short time ago. Their time passed quickly as they talked of fond memories of better times and dreamed of what the Lord was going to do when they reached the old city of Jerusalem.

They felt a supernatural strength as they continued on their journey. When they had previously run to the mountains, their feet ached, their lips were parched, and their stomachs growled. It was a hard journey. This time it felt full of joy and excitement and energy.

They arrived in the old city after just several days of walking. They had heard the stories, but they had never seen them firsthand. They marveled at the large ancient wall that surrounded the old city. They knew instinctively exactly where they felt led to go, so they walked to the Dome of the Rock. It was still present as it had always been, but it was now the Global Religion of Islam state worship center.

They stood in front of the doors and Rachel got down on

her knees and began to pray for open hearts for all who heard the message that day while Benjamin began to speak, "Everyone gather round! You will want to hear what I have to say."

Rachel never opened her eyes, but Benjamin looked around. So many people had already formed a circle around them. Many eyes eager for hope and eager for something more, but he saw a few eyes that looked black and empty inside. He had heard that Israel was the first nation to establish Elyon worship stations earlier that day and that people who visited those stations received a mark of allegiance to him. He wondered if those with dead eyes were the ones who had already visited the image of the beast.

Benjamin stood as straight as he could with his already tall frame so everyone could see him. "Friends! I have great news! Things are going to get better. Not right now on this earth. In fact, they might get harder here, but you can have hope of a life after this where you can be assured of no more pain and suffering. No more tears even."

Rachel tried to ignore the beginnings of grumbling she was hearing. People weren't sure yet, but were suspicious that they were hearing a contraband message. Rachel prayed that the people who were complaining wouldn't distract from those who needed to hear what her brother had to say. She was glad when he continued, "Jesus Christ is the way, the truth, and the life. He is the only way to heaven."

The crowd erupted into full yelling and threats at those last words and began throwing stones as large as a fist at the two of them. Each stone they threw missed. The stones went wide, they went high, and they hit other people in the crowd, but Benjamin watched in wonder as none went near them. "The Bible talks about ten virgins. Five were wise because they had plenty of oil in their lamps waiting for their groom. Five were foolish because they did not have enough oil in their lamps and when they went to get more oil they missed the coming of their groom."

Rachel heard the crowd begin to chant, "Kill them!" No matter what she heard, she kept her eyes closed and prayed. She didn't know that stones had been thrown at them and barely missed hitting her multiple times. She didn't know those same stones now lay neatly on the ground in front of them making a circle around them like some invisible force field stopped them from going any further. She also didn't see the man that took out a gun and walked right up to Benjamin stopping only five feet away from him.

The man put the gun against Benjamin's forehead and pulled the trigger, but it jammed. Nothing happened. Benjamin continued to preach, unfazed. He ignored the man a few inches away from him who was trying to unjam his gun so he could kill them.

"Storing up oil is cultivating a relationship with Jesus through prayer and studying his words so that when hard times come you have enough strength, enough oil, to keep the flame of your love for him alive."

The man in front of him gave up fixing his gun and decided to just bash Benjamin over the head with it. As the gun was raised to strike, the attacker inexplicably dropped it and grabbed his chest as he collapsed to the floor, dead. Everyone in the crowd fell silent and stopped their attempts to harm the siblings, staring in disbelief.

Benjamin looked from the man on the ground to those in the crowd, "There is a reason why Christians are not giving up Christ during such a hard time. It's because they know how real He is. Not everyone will be saved from death as I was here today, but still, they choose to believe. When you need food or you'll die will you sell your soul for a loaf of bread? When the gun is up to your head is not the time to get oil. Now is the time to get oil. Pray with me."

Benjamin prayed, "Jesus, forgive me of my sins. From this day forward I choose to serve you and you alone." As he prayed, he saw several in the crowd whispering the words as secretly as they could along with him and he thanked the Lord that at least some had been saved there that day. Even though most did not pray with him, he counted it a win that several had chosen the right path.

He tapped Rachel on the shoulder, and she looked up. Realizing now that he was done, she stopped praying and stood to her feet. The two of them walked past the angry mobs and police who wanted them dead without a scratch on them to a little quiet park in the distance where they rested until the next time the Lord called them to speak again.

Beth told John's family about her father who lived in a small little town in northern Arkansas. She said she hadn't seen him since she was a little girl, but he sent her a birthday card every year. When her mom died, she felt alone, so one of the things she did was keep his most recent card in her purse everywhere she went. She showed everyone the envelope with the return address. "I don't remember his house and if it is in the city or the country though."

John looked to her for permission as he asked her if he could see it, and when she nodded her head that he could, he took the card from her, "I know Jasper, Arkansas. My dad used to take me hiking there as a kid. It's just under three hundred miles south of here. Even if he lives in the center of this place, it's a very small town. We'd be much better off there than here. I want everyone to memorize this address. If we get split up, we meet up here. Once we get out of the city here, it is all national forests and small towns until we get there. It's the perfect place to head."

As they all memorized the address, Katie's mom, Beverly, looked at John with more than a little nervousness. "Three hundred miles... How long will that take us to walk?"

John looked at his mother-in-law with compassion. This was going to be a hard journey for her, he knew, "If we were all in perfect health and had unlimited resources we could walk it in about a week, but we are a large group. That will slow us down. Also, we don't have unlimited resources. We will have to find water along the way and I'm sure you guys might need some breaks. My goal is for us to walk at least two miles an hour for twelve hours a day, preferably three miles an hour." He took a minute to calculate the numbers in his head, "If we can get twenty to thirty miles in a day, we can be there in two weeks."

Robert and Beverly nodded their heads solemnly at the seriousness of the situation and the two week trek ahead of them. "We can do it. It won't be a problem" His father-in-law said reassuringly to his wife with his arm around her shoulders.

Within the first hour of them beginning the long walk from their home to their destination, John realized he had a hard situation on his hands. He and Katie often went hiking together, Beth was young and strong, but Katie's parents were a different story. They weren't old or weak, but they weren't young either. It became evident they also didn't seem to feel the urgency John felt when they started asking for frequent breaks. This time, John knew he couldn't give in to their requests.

He had listened to them once, instead of listening to the vision. He knew they had no ill intention in the advice they gave him. They were just scared. He thought to himself that it was his own fault that they were having to leave the city on foot rather than with the speed and safety of the car. Now, because he didn't listen to the urgency he felt, he was having to go further away from his parents instead of being safe with them right now.

Beverly and Robert's home was, luckily, fifteen minutes away from the heart of the downtown region of Kansas City; however, it was still in a highly populated area. Houses with a patch of grass in front you could hardly call a yard lined every street. They started their walk through their neighborhood.

At first, they stuck out like sore thumbs. It wasn't every day the neighborhood saw five people with backpacks on and tents attached to the backpacks hiking down a suburban sidewalk. They walked for an hour and made what felt like hardly any progress. They walked past people out with their car hoods open trying to repair whatever was causing them to not turn on. They saw families with their grills out cooking dinner since there was no power in their homes to cook. There were even a few children riding bikes in front of them.

"Bikes!" John whispered to the group. They didn't seem to comprehend his meaning so he drew them closer to him as he quietly explained, "If we can all get bikes, what would have taken us ten to fourteen days, gets cut down to three to five days!"

The light dawned in each one of their eyes. Katie was the first to ask, "But how? We only had a small amount of money to bring with us."

John thought it through for a moment as he looked around at the people in the neighborhood. "It's clear most of these people have no idea what they are facing and how valuable those bikes are about to become. We have to act now if we are going to be able to get them. Give me all the cash you have" He spoke to all of them and was discouraged when he realized it was only twenty dollars. "Not enough even to buy their daily rations." He looked up at them after he finished counting the money, "I need anything of value in your backpacks or on you."

Beverly and Katie took off their watches, earrings, and necklaces and handed them to John. It was a special matching set that they purchased together long before things got bad and was hard for them to hand over, but they did. John looked at the two women, "I need your rings too."

"Absolutely not!" Katie protested, stomping her foot like she was a little girl again.

John softened. He felt so sorry he had not listened immediately to the vision he had. He could have saved Katie this pain right now if he had only listened. "Sweetheart, I will only use it if I absolutely have to, but this is life and death. We have to get out of this city as quickly as possible."

With a heavy heart and tears silently slipping down her cheeks Katie agreed and slipped off the ring that she had only placed on her finger a year earlier. Her mother followed suit and John placed the rings in a separate pocket hoping to negotiate the bikes without needing to use the rings.

He walked up to the boys and asked where their parents were. The boys pointed to the open garage across the street at the husband and wife sitting in camping chairs watching their kids.

John walked across the street toward the man and woman giving a friendly wave, "Hi there! I see your power is out too."

"Yep," the man responded. "Nothing is working, not even our cars. Weirdest thing."

John felt an inner struggle. Should he warn this man what was actually happening as it was clear the couple in front of him had no idea what they were dealing with? He knew if he told them his suspicions that nothing worked because they had experienced an EMP they would never sell him the bikes and that would make it almost impossible to make such a long journey before things fell apart.

He said a quick prayer for wisdom and knew exactly what he was supposed to do. He would make the deal and then, afterward, warn the man of how to prepare. He just prayed the man didn't rescind the deal and take back the bikes when John told him they had experienced an EMP.

He couldn't think about that yet. The first thing he knew he had to do was get the bikes. "That's my family on the sidewalk across the street," he pointed toward where his wife, his in-laws, and Beth were standing. "We are on our way to visit family in the country, but our car isn't working either. I see your boys out there on those three bikes. Would you be interested in trading for them?"

The man laughed incredulously, "Trading? Why not just wait till the power comes back on and drive to the store and buy your own bike."

John thought long and hard about his answer, wanting to be truthful but not wanting to say too much, "I could wait, but I don't know how long that will take and we are eager to get to our destination. I have a little bit of cash and some Jewelry I could trade for all the bikes."

The man eyed the gold necklace, earrings, and watches, "How do I know these are even real?" He said even though it was obvious to John that he knew they were real and he was just playing the negotiating game.

"You have my word they're real, but you're welcome to inspect them closer if you want to be sure."

The man reached out and took the long gold chain that had a single diamond in the center of it and eyed it enviously as he glanced at the matching necklace still in John's hand. "I don't know. I might be willing to trade two bikes for all of this jewelry, but not all three."

John sighed, worried this would happen. "I have a diamond ring I can give you for the third bike." He took a single ring, his mother-in-law's, out of his pocket to show the man.

The man realized that John was desperate and so began to become increasingly stingy in his negotiations. He looked over at the three women on the sidewalk who were eagerly watching them, "I don't know. I'm guessing with those women over there that at least two of them are married and have rings. I'm thinking you are still holding on to at least one ring in that pocket of yours. I'll trade you the third bike for two rings."

John looked back at his wife with sadness and she immediately wilted into her mother's arms knowing what that look meant. He hated seeing her so sad, but it was about her safety. He cared more that he could keep her alive than he could keep her happy. With a heavy heart, he reached into his pocket and produced the final ring. "You have a deal."

The man smiled smugly as he yelled to his children, "Boys! Come over here right now!"

The boys rode their bikes over at the sound of their dad's voice and he sternly told them, "This gentleman has just purchased your bikes. Once he gives me that Jewelry in his hands, go ahead and hand him your bikes."

"Aw, dad!" they all whined in unison, but with one look from their father, they immediately obeyed and got off their bikes. John reluctantly handed the barter items to the man feeling both simultaneously taken advantage of and grateful. He took the bikes and in his anger didn't want to warn the man about anything like he had originally planned to do after the trade. But then he looked at the sad faces of the boys standing before him who had just lost their bikes.

He motioned for his family to come from across the street and get on the bikes and be ready to leave. They came over to the garage, took the bikes, and began to pile on as best they could. When they were ready, John turned back to the man, "Things are about to get really bad. I believe this isn't a power outage, but an EMP. Use all the jewelry you just got and barter for items to help you survive here.

Get as much food as you can. Barter for storage containers and then fill them up with water from the pond we passed on the way here. Make sure you have enough clothes and blankets to stay warm at night."

He quickly turned away and got on the bike. They all pedaled off quickly before the man had a chance to process what he had just been told and could rethink the trade he had just made.

John couldn't help but smile at the absurdity of the picture they made as they rode down the sidewalk out of their bustling community. They had three bikes for five people. Beth and Beverly both rode on the handlebars with their backpacks secured in front of them while John and his father-in-law pedaled the women with their backpacks on their backs. John thought it was grueling carrying the weight of another person on the bike alongside all their bags loaded down with supplies.

He looked over to his father-in-law who was red in the face and sweating more than he had ever seen someone sweat as he tried to pump the pedals carrying him and his wife up a steep hill. "How you doing over there?" John called to him at the top of the hill. Robert couldn't even speak. He just nodded his head that he was ok as he gasped for air. John was worried about him since he was older and out of shape, but he didn't have time to let that slow them down. They still had too much ground to cover before nightfall.

He glanced back at Katie, who was perhaps the most comical-looking of all among their trio. Her bike belonged to a little boy no more than five years old. She looked squished as she rode. Each time she pedaled, her knees came up almost to her cheeks and she also had a backpack on that kept dragging on the wheel behind her.

When they got to the top of the hill, he made a motion with his hand to follow him and led the way down the steep incline enjoying the few moments reprieve of pedaling while gravity did the work for him. Beth whooped like she was on a roller coaster enjoying every minute of being on the handlebars careering downhill at entirely unsafe speeds. He looked over at his mother-in-law and saw her face was one of terror and she held on to the handlebars with a vice grip as she and her husband raced down the hill. Katie used the downhill reprieve to stretch out her legs. She stuck them straight out like the letter 'V' and they extended several feet past the front wheel of the bike.

They continued to pedal past house after house until the terrain changed from houses into building after building. They were headed away from downtown, but there were still large cities to go through that surrounded the major metropolis they had just escaped.

As they rode down the highway, one after another, he saw abandoned fast food restaurants. When people began to barely be able to afford daily groceries, luxury and convenience food quickly became a thing of the past. He saw several people greedily eyeing their bikes, and he realized people might be starting to realize something more than a power outage was going on. He got off the main highway and took side streets for the final few miles to leave the large suburb city.

John was determined to get out of any big cities that night, but he looked over at his father-in-law and realized he couldn't push him anymore without risking a medical emergency. He saw a city park up in the distance and headed in that direction.

He saw that the park was abandoned and there were no nearby houses for people to see him ride into the park. He steered the bike into a hidden area in the trees behind the outhouses on the edge of the park. He kept pedaling and motioned to the others to do the same. They couldn't risk being seen entering the park and becoming a target of theft or worse.

He made it behind the outhouses and hid his bike behind them. He stood waiting for his exhausted family to catch up. They weren't far behind him, but you could see it took every bit of their strength for those final few pushes of the pedal. They made it to him and practically threw their bikes behind the outhouses as they got off of them. His father-in-law walked as if his legs had turned to Jello shaking as he stood. John raced over to him and helped him sit down as Beth brought him some water that she had in her backpack.

John saw his wife lying down on the ground at the tree line looking up at the sky trying to catch her breath. They made eye contact with each other and he mouthed the words, "Are you ok?"

She spoke between gulps of air "I'm fine. Just take care of daddy." That's what John did for the remainder of the night. He, along with Beth and his mother-in-law took care of the weary bicyclers and took shifts keeping watch through the night for people who wanted what they had.

---

* * *

Michael had never seen anything like it. The hatred toward full-gospel Christians and love for Elyon grew every day. Even as their world fell apart, the people seemed blind in their devotion to this evil man.

A cease-fire had been issued in the world war. It seemed Elyon had grown tired of waiting for the country's own governments to squash their rebellions. He set off EMPs in all the major cities that hosted mutinous forces.

In America, he set off an EMP in Houston, Texas; Jacksonville, Florida; and Kansas City, Missouri. In that one attack, he cut off all communication between the rebellious states that had seceded from the Union, squashing the uprising in a single maneuver. Michael was still shocked that it didn't stop there.

Elyon wanted to make sure no one dared to follow in those three states' footsteps. When the EMP took out their electrical grid, they were powerless to stop his officials from invading their state. Elyon sent in his men and used brutal force when he captured a large group of insurgents from Florida.

He televised to the world the public torture and then execution of every single member, both men and women, that had been captured. Michael had to turn away from the tv when they prepared to kill a thirty-year-old woman. They tied her hands to one horse and her feet to another. Michael didn't look when the man went to slap the rear ends of the horses, sending them in opposite directions and ripping the woman apart, but he heard the screams.

All the deaths were equally as gruesome and at the end of

the last execution, Elyon stared into the camera, and he promised any other future 'traitors' caught would face the same fate, plus all their innocent families at home.

It completely destroyed the willpower of almost everyone to continue to fight against what had become a seemingly undefeatable man. The organized military force within those three states stopped fighting, and the United States was freed from its internal conflict. They had already joined Elyon's one world government in name only, but now they were able to fully participate in Elyon's 'peacekeeping' strategies. The same thing happened in other countries around the world as well.

Michael cringed knowing that Elyon had his Alliance of Nations fully functioning. Ten nations joined together leading the world in a global economy and government. Every nation, either by force of a civil war or willing submission, was joined under the united banner of their supreme leader Elyon.

As he announced a cease-fire today, Elyon said that plans were underway to set up state-sanctioned worship centers in every country. These centers would not be for the unity of the global religions but would be a place to declare loyalty to him. Everyone would be required to visit their local worship center, and anyone who refused to publicly pledge their allegiance to Elyon would face consequences.

Michael knew exactly what he was talking about. It was the beginning of the enforcement of the mark of the beast. Michael had been in conversation with his unit precinct coordinator earlier that day, "I want to be ready when the Elyon worship centers come to our city to make sure it's well-received by our district and that my officers are ready to handle any rebellions that might arise."

She continued to smack her lips as she chewed her gum, barely looking up at him, "Oh you got time, hun. They just barely got it rolled out in Israel a couple of days ago and they are looking to establish it in the middle east and Europe first before bringing it to the states. Don't you worry your pretty little head about it. I'll let you know when it's coming to our district, but you should have a couple of weeks at least before that happens."

She seemed completely oblivious to his actual intention of getting that information from her as she never even looked up from her paperwork as he left her office. He breathed a sigh of relief. They had a little longer to prepare, to secretly preach the gospel, and figure out a plan.

He walked back to his desk to finish filing his paperwork for the day so he could go home. His day consisted mainly of the transportation of the dead lately. The amount of people who had died in the world was a sure sign they were in the fourth seal of Revelation.

Before Elyon declared himself a god, there were over eight billion people in the world. Then the war started and over a billion lives were lost. The highest estimates of the death toll of World War Two had been fifty to eighty million dead, which was a drop in the bucket compared to what they were dealing with now.

It was easier for America during the second world war because, other than Pearl Harbor, most of the deaths took place in other countries. That was not the case now because so much of the war involved a civil war within their own country. Before the EMP ever happened, cities were bombed and fighting had happened in the streets. Now, the dead were left in the streets in almost every major city in the United States; there were too many to remove in a timely manner.

As the dead bodies accumulated, there was a strange new disease that was starting to be reported worldwide. Every day the death toll rose from this disease that was being spread by the rats, vultures, and even the insects that fed on the dead bodies that littered the ground.

It seemed like every action of the antichrist led to a horrible natural consequence, but the world at large didn't see it that way. They laid the blame solely at the feet of Jews and of full-gospel Christians. The news reported regularly that extremist Christians were hoarding food and they were the reason for the shortages. Another common false report was that the Jews were the ones spreading the disease. It was like the propaganda days of the Holocaust.

When he saw signs of a plague that was rapidly engulfing the country along with the sharp rise in death, he suspected they were in the fourth seal prophesied in Revelation, but knowing it and seeing it come to pass were two entirely different things. The fourth seal said that a quarter of the whole earth would die.

He never imagined what that would mean practically. A quarter of the earth meant two billion people would die. A billion had already died and you couldn't step outside without being overpowered by the stench of decay on every street. He spent his days overseeing the collection of those bodies to the furnace to try and stop the progression of the diseases they were spreading, but people were dying faster than the workers could bury and burn them.

There were not enough workers for almost anything. There weren't enough police to keep people safe, not enough farmers to grow food, and not enough factory workers to distribute food. The city workers were drastically understaffed and couldn't keep the plumbing, electricity, and water working properly. The lack of access to clean water certainly did not help with stopping the spread of the disease in the world.

Every day was more death which meant every day there were fewer people to help society get back to normal. He couldn't even imagine the loss of life that would now be added from the EMPs that had just been set off. All those affected had just lost all access to medication, sanitation, and food preservation. His son was in one of those cities. He could only pray he got out in time.

CHAPTER ELEVEN

"And they worshiped the dragon, for he had given his authority to the beast, and they worshiped the beast, saying, 'Who is like the beast, and who can fight against it?'" - *Revelation 13:4*

In between his shifts keeping watch, John tried his best to sleep, but it was hard. Between the stench of the outhouse and the stench of the decaying bodies in the city around him, he had trouble finding enough peace to sleep. He looked over at Katie sleeping beside him and his heart lurched at the memories of how she cried when they finally rested for the night.

She tried to hide her tears from him as she spoke by laying her head on his chest, but he could still hear the pain in her voice, "It's so superficial of me crying over a ring. It doesn't matter. It's just a possession. It's our marriage that matters. So why am I so heartbroken?"

John didn't know what to say to make her feel better, so he simply stroked her hair as she lay against him until she fell asleep. He hoped that would give her some comfort. He wanted to do something. He hated that he couldn't fix things to take away her pain.

He looked at the woods behind him and noticed a tree with a portion of its bark exposed. He immediately thought back to the many outdoor survival training sessions his father had given him and his brother when they were teens. His dad wanted him to learn to make rope, so he taught him to make some from the bark of a tree.

John knew then what he could do to help his bride. He gently lifted her head off of his chest and placed it carefully onto the soft ground as he snuck to the tree line. He pulled off several fibers of the exposed bark and, instead of making a rope, went to work making a ring for her out of the twine-like substance he was creating.

It could hardly replace the diamond family heirloom that he had given to her when he asked her to marry him, but he would do his best to make sure she would feel his love for her every time she looked at it.

She lay sleeping peacefully, so he was able to easily measure her finger to get it to the right size without her stirring. He did an intricate design of twists and braids that made it more than a piece of wood, but something that was truly beautiful. Still sitting, he placed the ring in his pocket to give her at a later time. He looked up and noticed the sun had just barely begun to rise.

He didn't realize so much time had passed and was about to stand to wake the others when he saw a flash of light. He found himself suddenly standing behind the outhouses of the park. The sun was just a little higher in the sky than he remembered it being moments before. He looked in the distance and saw a gang of men holding bloody axes and machetes walking away from him. It looked like they were carrying the backpacks and bikes that belonged to John and his family.

He was going to run to stop them and get back his possessions, but he wanted to make sure Katie was safe first. Before he could turn to her, he tripped over something. He looked down and saw the dismembered bodies of his in-laws lying on top of one another. He had never seen such a horrific sight and had to turn away from them as he emptied the contents of last night's dinner from his stomach.

He thought to himself, "It must have been those men I just saw. I must have been so distracted making the ring, that I missed them coming to the camp and hurting Robert and Beverly. Poor Katie when she finds out."

He went to turn to the area where she slept to tell her about her parents when he saw his worst nightmare. She was covered in blood. She still lay on the ground, just like he left her, but her neck was now red instead of the creamy white it normally was, and all the life drained from her eyes. Before he could react there was another flash of light. This time it was accompanied by a loud thunderous crash that sounded eerily like the word "run" spoken in a low rumbling roar.

Instantly, he was no longer standing over his dead wife in the middle of the day. He was sitting next to her as she still slept soundly next to him. He saw that the sun was back to just beginning to peek over the horizon. In a panic, he rose from where he sat to where he remembered seeing his in-laws gruesomely laying. They too were perfectly peaceful and safe sleeping in each other's arms.

It had been another vision. He had to wake them up, "Wake up!" He ordered in a harsh whisper as he tried to shake the older couple awake. He didn't want to speak too loudly because he didn't know if that group of men were close by.

Katie's dad groaned, "Everything aches, let me sleep a little longer." Normally compassion for the older man would have overruled his logic, but not this time. He could not afford to ignore another vision.

"No. You have to get up. Now!" John spoke with a firmness that started Katie awake.

"John, what is it? Why the rush?"

"There is no time to explain, get on your bikes now! All of you!" It was taking too long, he thought. All the arguing and questions. He had to hurry them up. He started throwing backpacks at each of them, "Put this on."

His mother-in-law produced a slow yawn, "Slow down, John. We need energy if we are going to pedal all morning. Let's have breakfast and then we will get going." She started to unzip the backpack looking for protein bars for her husband.

John felt a frustration he had never felt before. No one was listening to him. He had to make them listen. He grabbed his father-in-law by the shoulders, led him to the bike, and pointed, "You, sit!" Then he pointed to Katie's mom and motioned toward the bike. He spoke with more sternness than he ever had before for her to get on the handlebars, "Now!"

Then he looked at Katie who stood back with her mouth agape taking in this strange, angry man that earlier that night had been stroking her hair. "Get on your backpack and get on your bike, Katie. We are leaving now!" Katie got on her bike.

Being newer to the group, Beth probably didn't know what to think and fearfully got on the handlebars of John's bike without any argument.

They all turned to leave the way they came when John stopped them, "Not that way. Follow me." They were about to protest that the path he suggested was less smooth and would be a harder ride when they saw coming in from the entrance of the park a group of ten men all with machetes and hatchets in their hands heading straight for them.

The official world war might have been over, but Tom felt like there were little battles all around him. He had been a prepper and stored food and everyone thought he was crazy. When he saw the prices and ration cards at the grocery store a few months back he knew that he had been right all along.

Since the EMP a few days ago things got drastically worse very quickly. Those who were sick began to die off quickly when they couldn't access vital medication. Overpriced ration-based grocery stores even became a luxurious memory of the past because with no vehicles running in this part of the country, no food was able to get in to restock the empty shelves. The hardest blow was probably the lack of sanitation and water for the city around him.

Tom would go out at night to gather information, so he could know what he was up against. When he snuck into a neighboring subdivision and apartment complex he smelled that the sewage had already backed up. The smell was offensive to him, but he could leave and go home. These people either had to choose to live in actual filth or leave, but where would they go? It wasn't like anyone had a lot of extra money laying around to go purchase a new home these days.

He realized they would probably go looking for abandoned homes, or places like his own home that could be overrun since he was the only one there to protect it. He went to inspect the water supply of the town by trying to turn on a hose on the side of one of the buildings. No water came out. He did this at several different locations confirming his suspicions that the city had no clean, running water.

Whatever disease that was infecting so many people around the world would only accelerate its spread as people had repulsive sanitation and no water due to the EMP. He shook his head in disgust thinking how this was just another catastrophe that could have been avoided if it weren't for the ego of Elyon.

Tom was luckier than those in town. No, not lucky. He was prepared. He had a well, but that had stopped pumping water to his trailer when the power went out. He anticipated that could happen eventually, so about five years back he had two different hand pump wells installed on his property. One was by his garden to water his plants and one by his mobile home for his own personal use. It might be more work to get water, but Tom smiled at the thought that he would not go thirsty and could keep clean.

His smile faded slightly at the thought that if anyone found out how prepared he was, they would want a piece of what he had created for himself as well. He had a fence around his property to keep his supplies safe, but that didn't seem to do much good. A few weeks ago, someone broke through his fence one day and stole his newly ripened apples off of his trees. He was so angry. He had plans for those apples!

When the EMP happened, he decided to put more protective measures in place. He put trip wires with bells all along his property to alert him. This only half worked. He heard the bells chiming at dusk one day and ran outside with his shotgun. He got there just in time to see a couple of teenagers running away with armfuls of fresh vegetables.

The final straw was earlier this morning. A group of men with guns entered his property. They didn't care if they hit the trip wire and rang the bells alerting Tom to their presence. They were going to take what they wanted by force.

Tom grabbed his gun and was ready to face them down to keep what was his, but when he looked out his window, before confronting them, he saw that there were at least ten men and they each were heavily armed. He was outmanned and outgunned.

He considered taking a stand anyway. How dare they come on his property and steal what was his, but then he glanced at all his food preps stacked against the walls of his living room. He had years worth of food for himself to survive inside the house. He wondered, "Is it really worth getting killed over a few tomato plants?"

He decided then to let them take what they wanted from the garden. He would stay inside and defend his home and the majority of his supplies. He only hoped the measures he had taken to make his house appear abandoned would fool the thieves on his property.

They knew someone was tending a garden, but they didn't know that there was more to the decrepit old trailer that had a busted-out window and broken glass on the stairs that led to the front door. It was not only inhabitable but also loaded with more supplies than Tom would ever be able to use by himself.

He watched from his window as he saw the group of men come and ravish his fruit trees and vegetable garden. They took every last thing in sight. It was too much to carry and left a trail of abandoned fruit behind them as they walked.

He was grateful that they ran out of arms to carry the supplies because that meant they wouldn't check if he had anything in his house of worth. That was one good thing about the EMP that had left him and everyone else without power a few days ago. Without vehicles, marauders were limited on how many items they could loot at a time.

He watched them get to the edge of his property line when he saw them being approached by another group that looked intent on taking the food that was not theirs. Within seconds, guns were drawn on both sides and there was a standoff, with all the beautiful fresh food dropped to their feet. Tom couldn't tell from his hidden spot in the corner of the window who fired the first shot, but he saw man after man drop to the ground in a shootout that would rival The Wild West.

That's what the world has become: The Wild West. People were dying of starvation everywhere and felt justified stealing from others to fill their stomachs. There may not be a world war anymore, but people are dying every day from small skirmishes in each city over things like stolen food.

When the shooting was done, most of the men lay dead on the ground, but a couple got up and hobbled off to tend to their wounds. As they walked away, one turned around and looked at the house. Tom tried to camouflage himself as best he could, but had been startled by the man's gaze and tried to move out of the line of sight. When Tom did this, he saw the curtain move. He couldn't be sure, but it was possible the man saw the curtain move as well.

If he saw it move, then all Tom's efforts to disguise his mobile home from the outside as decrepit and abandoned were for nothing. They would be back, with reinforcements. Tom needed to do more to prepare and protect his supplies from them. Next time, he would be ready.

Emma Johnson was back in her home in Omaha which held so many beautiful memories. She pulled quietly into her garage during the night and luckily all the neighbors had already been asleep and didn't see her arrive. She kept all the lights off as she got her boys settled on the oversized chairs and her husband situated on the couch while she went to the kitchen. She was going to do everything she could to help her family regain their strength.

It was a miracle, but no one had broken into her home or stolen any of her food while she was gone. She made them French toast with the bread and egg rations just like she used to do and she even found an unopened bottle of syrup in the pantry that she poured over the top of the food.

Her excitement at the meal was short-lived though. Her husband didn't have an appetite from whatever sickness still was wreaking havoc on his body. Her boy's eyes looked happy at the food in front of them, but they were too tired to eat it. Neither took a single bite. Her littlest boy just laid his head on the table and fell asleep. Her oldest son looked at her and asked if he could eat the meal tomorrow.

They were just so tired. Their stomachs had shrunk so much and they were weak. Her heart broke knowing how much they needed to eat but knowing that starvation was making them exhausted. She figured she could make sure they started eating again the next day after they got a good night's sleep.

She told her little ones that it was ok, the french toast would be waiting for them in the morning, and carried them one by one to the big master bed down the hall. As she carried the second little boy in her arms down the hall she heard her husband weakly call after her, "It's going to be ok. Don't forget. Trust God."

She laid them down and crawled in between the two of them, each one resting their head on her shoulder. She played with their hair as she sang them lullabies like she did when they were babies. She told them stories of how they used to crawl into bed with her every night and she would pretend like she was so squished, but really she loved it. The boys fell asleep laying on their mother feeling loved and safe. They thought of the hope of french toast in the morning as they floated off into dreams from which they would never wake.

Emma knew they had been hungry too long. She felt their breath shift away from the steady pace of slumber. She noticed their breathing was becoming weaker, more shallow and more infrequent and realized she was losing them as they slept in her arms.

She sat up and frantically tried to shake them awake, so she could force them to eat, "Wake up! Don't leave me! Please, wake up for mama!"

No matter how hard she tried, they wouldn't wake up. Their breathing was becoming thinner with each weak gasp and she realized it was only a matter of time until she lost them.

She laid back down between them and held them in her arms as the tears poured down her face. She wept realizing this was the last moment she would get to hold her sons.

She cried as she continued to sing all of their favorite songs and tell them their favorite stories. Even after she felt their bodies give up the fight, she continued to sing to them knowing that this was the last moment she would ever hold those sweet innocent little boys in her arms.

Her boys, who would never grow up to be men. Her boys who had never hurt anyone were laying lifeless in her arms.

She pulled them close to her and sobbed into their heads, "I'm so sorry boys. I'm so sorry I couldn't save you." She peppered their heads with kisses as she wept and told them how much she loved them and loved being their mom even though she knew they couldn't hear her.

Michael was running down a dark alley late at night. He was being pursued by something. He kept turning around to look behind him, but nothing was there. He got to a street corner and paused. There wasn't a car in sight. Everything was dark except for one window which had a light that was shining across the street from him.

He ran to the house that had the light on and banged on the door, "Let me in! You have to let me in!" A short old woman with hair as black as a raven except for a single white streak down the side opened up the door.

In a shaky voice that was tired from decades of use, she said, "May I help you?"

He looked at her with pleading eyes, "Please you have to let me in."

Even though she was old and frail, she opened the door wider for him to come in, shutting it behind him and locking the deadbolt.

"Thank you," he said between gulps of air as he struggled to catch his breath.

She simply nodded her head. "I have been waiting for you Michael."

He looked up, completely shocked at what she was saying. How could she have been waiting for him? He didn't even know he was coming this way. He had never been in this part of the town in his entire life.

She seemed to sense all his doubts and questions whirling around inside of him. "Sit down, please." He obeyed her instructions and sat on the flowered couch that was covered in plastic and looked like it could easily have been bought fifty years ago. When he sat on the uncomfortable squeaky cushion she began to speak, "I have a message for you and you must share every word of it with your wife. Do you understand?"

He nodded his head. She took a deep breath, "Soon, it will not be safe to stay in your home. You must find a man named Tom and go to him. Your son, John, will be there waiting for you." She handed him a slip of paper with an address written on it "Remember, Michael, not everything is bad. Christians are beginning to walk in supernatural power more than ever before showing the wonders of God."

Michael nodded solemnly. She placed a firm hand on his and looked at him with fire in her eyes, "Remember, no one can pluck you from his hand."

Instantly Michael's eyes shot open in his darkened room where he lay asleep seconds before. Another dream. He remembered every detail and raced to turn on the lights and write down the address to which he and Sophia should go. They were going to see John! He was so excited he could hardly take it.

Sophia yawned as she stretched on the bed, "Another dream?" She looked at the clock and realized it was still early. It was before midnight, they had just barely fallen asleep, so she propped herself up on her elbow. She looked at him writing rapidly on a piece of paper next to him. "What are you writing?"

He looked at her with excitement. "John's Ok. I just had a dream that told me where to find him! He's in Jasper, Arkansas!" He then told her every detail of the dream. He held her in his arms as they both went to sleep so excited that night. First, he would go to work in the morning so he could collect his last paycheck to help give them enough money for another week's worth of rations, and then they would leave to see John!

Benjamin and Rachel went to the Dome of the Rock the next day. They were so excited that they had been supernaturally protected and that several people gave their lives to the Lord, that they couldn't wait to do it again! It all started the same as the first time. They preached and some listened, but most yelled obscenities and unsuccessfully tried to stop them.

Where the experience differed from the first time Benjamin preached was toward the end. While Rachel prayed beside him, Benjamin asked if there were any who were willing to join with him as he said a prayer of salvation. He saw five people scattered throughout the crowd discretely close their eyes and mouth the words of the prayer along with him.

Benjamin was not the only person who noticed those five people praying. It seemed that Elyon's officers had been made aware that the last time they preached several people had joined him in his prayer. This time Elyon's men were determined to catch and detain any individuals who dared to accept the message Benjamin was sharing.

There were already a few officers stationed in the crowd, but as the people prayed with him, he saw more of Elyon's secret police emerging from the shadows and heading straight to the individuals that tried to hide their lips moving as they asked for forgiveness for their sins.

Benjamin saw several of the recent converts notice the police and escape before they were captured, but two were so engrossed in their prayers they didn't open their eyes in time. It looked to be a husband and wife standing side by side.

The secret police surrounded them but did not yet put their hands on them. The couple sensed that people were staring at them and opened their eyes to see police everywhere in front of them. One of the officers took a step forward from the line of his fellow enforcers "If you want to live you will say that you pledge your devotion to Elyon alone."

The married couple looked at each other, still holding hands. They gave a slight, sad smile to each other as they spoke to each other with only their eyes in a way only a couple deeply in love could. The husband stood a little straighter and mouthed the words, "I love you" to his wife and she wiped a tear with her free hand and mouthed the words back to him, "I love you too."

They both had determination on their face as they turned their attention back to the officers that were surrounding them. They knew there would be no escape. It was the husband that spoke first, "I will never deny Christ; He is my savior."

Benjamin had been so engrossed in the bravery of the brand new Christians that he hadn't noticed the officers behind them had taken out a sword. With the man's final word, the officer took the sword and decapitated the man as he stood still holding his wife's hand.

Benjamin saw the woman look away from her dismembered husband and look toward heaven with tears streaming down her face, "I'll see you soon" she quietly called out to the sky. She bowed her head and prayed which infuriated the men around her.

One officer sneered at her, "Do you care so little for your own life? Recant your faith or face the same fate as your husband."

She lifted her head looking at the man directly in the eyes. A resolve and boldness had replaced the tears that were in her eyes a moment earlier, "You only have the power to kill my body, you don't have the power to kill my soul. When I die today, I will be in heaven forever, but when you die, you will be in hell for all eternity."

The police all around her became full of rage and the crowd behind them who had been watching the whole altercation began to chant, "Kill her!"

The crowd began to pick up the stones that littered the street. They walked past the police line to throw the rocks at the woman who stood before them. The police did nothing to stop it. When they saw what was happening they broke their line allowing easier access for the mob to the woman. Stone after stone was thrown at her. Some were as big as a fist and hit her in the stomach, arms, and legs. She yelled out with a loud voice as the air was raining stones upon her, "I still choose Jesus!"

The throwing became more violent after that. The projectiles began landing on her head, knocking her to the ground. She was not unconscious and was fully aware as the mob pressed in closer to her so they could aim more precisely as they continued to pelt her with the large rocks.

Benjamin could just barely hear her whisper from her position on the ground as the strength was leaving her body, "I still choose Jesus."

The stones continued to be thrown long after she left this earth. The rage the crowd felt at being powerless to stop Benjamin's preaching was all being taken out on her. Benjamin wept as he saw what true devotion to Christ looks like played out in front of him and he prayed for God to avenge her death.

It seemed Miles grew further from his parents every day. He hadn't spoken to them in the last several months and he even asked his captain to put him on a different shift than his father so he wouldn't have to see him at work. Even though he still loved them, he just didn't believe the same as they did anymore and he didn't want to see the sadness in his dad's eyes each time he looked at him.

It had been a little over a year since Elyon declared himself as God in the temple and every day since then had been filled with more miracles. Miles started out skeptical. He supported the regime of Elyon because he believed in the goal of global unity and tolerance, not because he thought of him as a god. The more he saw, the more he began to believe that maybe it was possible that he could be god.

He just wished he could see it in person. Everything was on the news, but everyone knew that the news was not one hundred percent accurate. He wanted to see with his own eyes the miracles of Elyon. He stood around in the police station break room mesmerized by what he was watching. Elyon was on a platform in the middle of the stadium with the great prophet Francis at his side. Every seat was filled. It was like Miles was watching the Superbowl, except this was far better than any game he had ever seen.

Miles saw Elyon step up to the microphone, "You have seen me raise myself from the dead and many of you know that I am god." Cheers erupted from the stands as a deafening roar drowned out all other sounds. Francis motioned to everyone in the stands to quiet down. When the crowd calmed, Elyon continued, "I was able to unite the nations of the world into one global government. Because of me, this world has taken the first step to see paradise on earth!

With this statement, Francis led the way in cheering for Elyon. When the collective roar of the stadium would not stop, Francis spoke into a mic that stood empty next to Elyon, "Who is like Elyon and who can fight against him?"

The cheering in the stadium slowly transformed from an unintelligible roar to a clear chant spoken by all. Over and over the people present repeated Francis' words, "Who is like the Elyon, and who can fight against him?"

They only stopped their chant when Elyon raised his hands for silence after several minutes. "You have seen my miracle of defying death itself. Now prepare yourself to see more wonders I am capable of." The crowd of tens of thousands grew silent in anticipation. Even in the break room, miles could hear a pin drop. Everyone waited to see what would happen next.

Officials at the stadium began to drop something at the foot of the stage. What started as a few items turned into piles and piles of something Miles couldn't make out. Miles leaned over and whispered to his coworker, "What is that?" His coworker whispered back, "Original, unaltered Bibles." There were three large piles of Bibles that were stacked as high as the stage. They were placed in front of the stage where Elyon stood. The leader of the world remained silent until the last Bible was left on the ground in front of him.

Elyon then looked directly into the camera and Miles felt like there wasn't a gap of thousands of miles between them, but that he was in the very room with him, looking directly at him as he spoke.

"I understand some of you still doubt that I am God.

Today, I plan to remove all doubt so everyone can worship me as I deserve because when everyone worships me, only then will I bring utopia to our world."

"Before me stands the original unaltered Bibles of the Christian faith. These Bibles still contain hate-filled passages of intolerance to other religions and other lifestyle choices. They have been confiscated from Christians who were arrested all around the world just this week for practicing Christian extremism."

As the man spoke, Miles thought back to the Christians he had raided earlier this week. It had become easier to just kill them on the spot rather than try and arrest them. He wondered if the Bible he confiscated from their home was in the pile he now watched on the television. The thought filled him with excitement that he might be a part of that momentous day in some small way.

Elyon looked at the camera again, "For those of you who still doubt who I am, I want you to ask yourselves this question. If your version of religion were real and if your God were all-powerful, would he allow me to do this?" As he spoke that final word he raised his right hand into the air and looked up to the sky. He held his gaze and hands there for what seemed like an eternity, but it was probably only thirty seconds. Miles waited to see what he would do. Then, in one swift motion, he made a motion like he was grabbing something from the air and throwing it down into the middle of the first stack of Bibles. As his hand descended, so did a lightning bolt into the pile of books and they were consumed by fire.

The crowd who worshiped him earlier were now

uncontrollable in their praise of him. They were screaming with adoration about the power of Elyon and how God himself stood before them.

Elyon repeated the motion a second time raising his right fist into the air and with brute force bringing it down pointing in the direction of the second pile of books. This time it was not a lightning bolt that consumed the books, but a whirlwind of fire. It looked like a tornado that was ablaze with the light of the fire and, when the books were consumed, the tornado vaporized and disappeared as quickly as it had appeared.

He looked at the crowd again, leaving the final stack of books untouched before him. "I have heard reports of Christians faking miracles trying to win converts. I want you to know they are trying to counterfeit the real thing to trick you into missing out on all the power you could have by following me. Anyone who wants to have my spirit can walk in the same power I do."

Elyon smiled as he looked at the crowd, "I have given my spirit to my prophet. My spirit can be had by you too, but you must first worship me."

At that moment, Francis let out a scream, reached both of his hands to heaven and a series of lighting bolts came crashing from the cloudless sky into the remaining stack of Bibles. The lightning continued long after the books were burned to ash.

Francis slowly lowered his hands and the lighting stopped. He stepped up to the microphone once again. This time he spoke only three words, "Elyon is God." The chanting began in earnest then as the people cried in their devotion to him repeating those words over and over.

Miles realized he was repeating the words with the crowd on the television. "It is true " he said out loud to no one in particular. "Elyon is God." He looked around the room and saw many others repeating the same phrase as him, some with their hands raised to the air.

Miles thought then that he couldn't believe how much his parents had brainwashed him as a child to believe their religious fairy tales. He became filled with fury.

CHAPTER TWELVE

"When He opened the fifth seal, I saw under the altar the souls of those who had been slain for the word of God and for the testimony which they held. And they cried with a loud voice, saying, 'How long, O Lord, holy and true, until You judge and avenge our blood on those who dwell on the earth?'

Then a white robe was given to each of them; and it was said to them that they should rest a little while longer, until both the number of their fellow servants and their brethren, who would be killed as they were, was completed." - Revelation 6:9-11

John and his family pedaled like they never had before. If they thought they pushed themselves to the brink yesterday, they were sadly mistaken as they went with all their might through the rocky terrain on ill-fitting bikes while a gang of men with machetes and axes chased after them.

Riding on the rocky terrain with passengers on the handlebars was nearly impossible to do well. They had only been riding a couple of minutes and only recently lost their pursuers when Katie wiped out. She cried out as the tires skidded out on the gravel path throwing her to the ground.

John had Beth hop off of the handlebars and hold his bike while he ran back to help his wife up. He looked her over and saw that it was just cuts and scrapes, for the most part, so he ran to retrieve her bike for her.

When he was bringing it back he heard a twig snap in the direction they had just come from. Katie looked at John with fear in his eyes, "Did you hear that?"

John scanned the wood and saw a man with a hatchet in his hand emerging from where they had just escaped. The man clearly didn't think he was going to catch up with the group on bikes. Surprise and then excitement filled his eyes as he yelled to the rest of the gang that wasn't yet visible to John, "They're still here, come on!"

The man began to charge toward John. John yelled for Katie, Beverly, and Robert, "Get out of here! Don't wait for us. We'll catch up." Katie and her parents listened to John and left, but Beth couldn't leave without John. Beth was holding the bike with her hands shaking, watching John run toward her. The man was running behind him when Beth yelled, "John, Hurry! He's catching up to you!"

He made it back to Beth and the bike, but that gave the leader of the gang time to catch up as well. Before John could sit on the bike he was under attack. Beth screamed, "John, behind you!"

John turned around just in time to see a hatchet swinging at his head. He ducked and stayed bent at the waist as he charged the man head first into his stomach knocking him to the ground. The man's weapon went flying into the woods as the two of them wrestled on the ground. John heard Beth yell to him, "The rest of his men are coming, John, you have to hurry!"

John was about to tell Beth to leave without him while there was still time, but he managed to get on top of the man and land three well-placed blows in a row to his head. It was enough to disorient the man giving John the time he needed to race to the bike and hop on with Beth in front. They pedaled off with the gang only a few feet behind them. He felt a blade whir past his ear and saw it impale the ground in front of them.

Beth turned her face back toward John, "They're throwing axes at us, John. Hurry!"

John prayed with every pump of the pedal that he wouldn't wipe out. It would be over if he did. He pedaled for five minutes through the rough path and he finally saw a clearing to cut across and get back on a smooth sidewalk. Katie and her parents were waiting for them there. He didn't stop to talk to them but just kept on pedaling hoping that they realized to hop on their bikes and follow. The men were too close to take a break now. They all got on the sidewalk and continued to bike their way out of town.

No one spoke a word for hours as they continued to weave their way around the dead bodies and piles of garbage that littered the streets. They were trying to cover the final miles of the exit from the city. No one asked for a break or complained they were too tired to continue. Breakfast and even lunch were completely forgotten. They rode, grateful for the pain in their muscles at so much exertion because it meant they were alive.

Initially, they passed many groups of people. Some

families with sad eyes and some were groups of men like the one they had just escaped, but John and his family were all vigilant now and on high alert. When they saw anyone off in the distance, they went out of their way to find a different, more obscure route around people on the street no matter how innocent they might appear.

John was starting to feel safer as they had more and more miles between them and the city. The concrete jungle slowly turned into a spattering of houses and gas stations and then finally a forested road that was hardly traveled even in the best of times. He saw a trail in the middle of the forest and motioned for his group to follow him as they biked their way deeper into the woods. No one questioned him this time. He had proven that he was capable and also that he had their best interest at heart.

They rode deep into the heart of the forest until the underbrush wouldn't allow them to continue on the bikes anymore. John wasn't taking any chances of people finding where they rested for the night again. He had the group get off their bikes and walk their bikes an additional five minutes until he was sure they couldn't be found by anyone. "There. We should be safe here."

They all threw their bikes to the ground without saying a word, still stunned at the morning they had experienced. They all sat around their bikes, but it was Katie who spoke first, "How did you know, John?"

John looked at her, "I had another vision. I won't tell you what I saw, but I knew they were coming and were wanting to hurt all of us. They wanted what we had."

Robert put a protective hand around his wife as he looked

from his wife to his daughter, "Thank you, John. I can never repay you."

John nodded. "We should be safe here for the night. We are miles from the closest house and almost a whole day's bike ride from the park we just left. I haven't seen a car on the road the entire day. No one will find us here out in the middle of nowhere. We can set up camp and rest. I don't think we need a guard to keep watch. There's no one here and Beth said she can set up an alarm system just in case someone stumbles into our camp"

They all got to work, eager to be able to have some time where they were not working or riding a bike. John set up the tents. Robert used a stick to dig a hole far away from the tents. Then he started a fire in the hole as an added precaution to keep the flame from being spotted by anyone. The fire would keep them warm and they could cook with it later. Beth taught Katie how to set up tripwires around the property that would alert them if anyone or anything came near them during the night.

It didn't take long before they were ready to sit by the fire, eat some food and turn in for the night. Their bodies were all exhausted, but none of them wanted to go to sleep right away. The fear of their earlier near-death experience turned to excitement that the Lord had warned them and saved them from a gruesome death. How exciting that John was getting visions that were keeping them safe!

John shared in their excitement but wanted to also give some perspective, "Sometimes the Lord will intervene and keep us safe, but he doesn't promise that nothing bad will happen to us. He does promise to be with us when it does."

He reminded them. They all agreed of course, but tonight was one of the nights where they saw the hand of God tangibly save them and nothing could bring them down.

John saw the joy on everyone's faces and decided this would be the perfect time to give Katie the gift he had made her. He took her hands in his and looked into her eyes as they sat on a log by the fire together, "I'm so sorry we had to trade your ring for the bikes, baby, but I want you to know that you will always have my love."

The conversation between her parents and Beth quieted as they became interested in what John was saying. "I wanted to make you something so that you could always have a reminder of our love and our commitment. Something that would bring you joy."

He reached into his pocket, pulled out the ring made of twine, and slipped it on her finger just like he had when they took their vows. "I know it's not much and I know it may not be made from diamonds, but it was made from my love for you. When you look at it, remember that you matter more to me than any other person in the world."

Katie wiped her eyes which were filled with tears of joy and looked to those around her and saw there wasn't a single dry eye. "Oh, John. Thank you so much. I'll treasure it always." A morning of such turmoil and fear had turned into one of the sweetest and most joy-filled nights for Katie. She hugged John and the group continued to laugh together a little longer, not ready for the night to end quite yet. Soon, the night did end and everyone went to their tents: John and Katie in theirs, Her parents in their own, and Beth in hers. Everyone went to sleep with a smile on their face amazed at the joy that could be found in hard times.

Emma awoke the next morning as the sun began to peek into the room and she remembered what had happened the night before. She didn't want to believe it was true. She didn't want to believe her boys were gone, but there was no denying the truth as she felt their small lifeless bodies in her arms growing stiff as death was setting in.

She was numb from grief but sat up in the bed giving each boy a final kiss on their forehead. She crawled out and stood on the floor next to the bed looking at her precious angels who looked as though they were just sleeping. She pulled up the sheets and the comforter and tucked them in trying to pretend in her mind that they were really just resting and needed to be covered up to be warm and cozy in the bed.

In a daze, she walked to the bathroom and rummaged through her medicine cabinet grabbing every possible medicine that she could find that might help her husband. Her arms were loaded down with antibiotics, electrolyte supplements, and fever reducers. She walked down the hall, determined to save at least him.

She walked into the living room and her arms fell to her side. She dropped all the medicine and it all fell to the floor in a single motion. She saw her husband on the couch where she had left him, but his eyes were open in a vacant stare looking down the hallway to where her boys spent their final night on this earth. She ran to him and knelt beside him hoping her eyes were playing tricks on her, "Breathe Jerry. Please you can't leave me too!" But he was gone.

In a single day, she had lost her entire family: her boys to starvation and her husband to an illness that she wished would have claimed her life as well. She blamed God for their deaths. He had the power to stop their deaths and He chose not to. Without her husband around to encourage her to let go of the anger and blame and focus on eternity, her bitterness grew.

As she bent down on the floor next to her husband and laid him in a more natural position on the couch, she closed his eyes and kissed his cheek, "I'm sorry I couldn't save you or our boys. I'm so sorry." She cried until she had no more tears left to give. She stood up and decided she was leaving and was never looking back. She wasn't going to think about her family and she certainly wasn't going to think about God. She went to the garage and got in her car not caring which neighbors saw her. She welcomed death in many ways. All she knew is she had to leave and she didn't care where she ended up as long as it was far away from her home.

Michael woke up early before Sophia was awake. He wanted to get an early start, collect his last paycheck and be on his way to finally see his newly married son. He was eager to leave Nebraska City and head to the Ozarks where this Tom person was even though he would be leaving the convenience of electricity to head for an EMP-affected zone.

When he walked into the precinct, his captain came up to him and practically begged him to help with one quick Christian disturbance call that had just come in over dispatch before he picked up his check and left for the weekend.

A full-gospel Christian was being targeted for violence and his captain just wanted him to de-escalate the situation and bring the extremist Christian in for questioning. Michael tried to hide his frustration at having to postpone his plans for even a second, but if a Christian was in trouble, he wanted to help. So he went over to the state-run church where the disturbance was listed.

The first thing that he thought was that it was another hate crime against Christians. Of course, it wasn't called a hate crime. Michael got out of his car and walked into the church.

Instantly he felt evil surrounding him. This was no ordinary church. Sure it had once been a place where believers had gathered every Sunday and sang worship songs together, but it had been turned into something much more vile and evil.

The windows had all been darkened, so no light could get in. Candles were burning everywhere. There was a small group of singers on the stage singing to the tune of Amazing Grace,

"Oh bow to Elyon, the most high god. Worship him alone.
He once was dead, but now he lives, he is the king of all"

There was a line of people in front of Michael all waiting their turn for something. He tried to get a better look and that's when he saw what looked like a living statue of Elyon. It looked like the statue was talking, it seemed to be alive. At that moment, Michael realized there was no disturbance call he was supposed to respond to and he felt fear like he had never felt before. He was supposed to have weeks before the antichrist mark made its way to the states, but he had been told wrong. It was here before his eyes right now.

He had to get out of there. He turned to leave, but two guards were blocking the door. They were huge men; one with his arms crossed in front of him and one with a completely bald head, both equally terrifying. The one with his arms crossed across his chest spoke first, "You may not leave until you make your statement of faith to Elyon and receive his mark."

Michael tried to come up with an excuse. Anything to get him out of there, "Oh I'm coming right back, I just need to go grab my inhaler from my car." Michael didn't have asthma, it was just the only thing that came to his mind. He said a quick prayer for forgiveness to Jesus for lying, he just knew he had to find a way to get out of there.

The guard with a bald head took an imposing step forward, "You will get it after you have worshiped the image of Elyon. Back in line."

It was clear there was no way out of the building apart from a miracle from God himself. Michael knew this day was coming but thought he had more time. As he got closer to the front of the line, he was able to hear what everyone who approached the image was ordered to say. As each person approached the image of Elyon they did something physical to pay homage. Some laid down flat on the floor, some got on their knees with their hands raised in the air, and some went up to the image itself and kissed its feet. It didn't appear to matter what you did, as long as it was an act of worship.

After each person performed an act of worship, they each said something. Each person said something different, but they all had the same meaning. They all spoke of allegiance, devotion, and love for Elyon, some more emphatically than others.

None of this felt real. It felt like a dream. Michael watched, transfixed, as it was the turn of the teenage girl right in front of him. As she approached the statue, he was shocked as he heard the statue rasp out the words, "Are you worthy?"

With those words, the young girl got on her knees and said, "I am a devoted follower of Elyon."

Then the creature in front of her spoke again in a low voice that sounded more like a growl than a voice, "Do you understand that this decision can never be undone and you will forever belong to me."

Without hesitation, the girl looked up at the image and said, "I do."

Everything in Michael was filled with revulsion. It felt like a sick demon-possessed marriage ceremony as that thing in front of her spoke one final time in a voice that was far from human, "You have been found worthy."

With that, the girl arose and walked to the man waiting to the right of the stage. She held out her right hand and he injected something under her skin. Michael watched as it looked like her eyes turned from Green to black. She walked and talked like the same girl, but there was an increased evil inside her that was not there before she completed her act of worship to the image.

That was it. It was Michael's turn. There was nothing he could do to escape what was before him. He stepped up to the life-like idol in front of him and it asked, "Are you worthy?"

Michael experienced a momentary feeling of dread. His mind went through a thousand thoughts in what was probably only a few seconds. "What if he wasn't strong enough? What if he caved under the pressure? God, I'm scared, help me!" These were just a few of the many thoughts racing through his mind at that moment.

The demonic being in front of him asked the question again with increased volume, "Are you worthy?"

Michael knew his answer at that moment. "No one is worthy, but Jesus Christ the son of God." He saw stirring around him and knew most were getting angry, but some were listening. He thought to himself if he was tricked into coming here, maybe others here were tricked as well and this was his last chance to be a witness to them. "There is only one God and you are not Him! I will not kneel to you, but I kneel only to Jesus Christ the true king."

The beast roared with uncontrolled rage. It looked and acted like it was truly alive at that moment, fueled solely by hate "You are not found worthy! Kill him!"

He saw guards emerging from all corners of the room he had previously not seen. Michael's training kicked in and his hand went to his weapon. He would never hurt civilians, but he had no problem pointing his gun at one of Elyon's men who were coming to detain him. Before he was able to get his gun out of his holster, the two guards he encountered at the door were already upon him, cuffed his hands behind his back, and removed his weapon. Michael knew he couldn't win by force, so he yelled a final plea, "If you haven't taken the mark yet, it's not too late. Don't give in, this is Satan in disguise. Call out to Jesus. Turn to Him!"

The bald-headed guard reached him and struck him on his head with something large and heavy that he didn't see. It didn't knock him out, but it made all the fight leave his body. They dragged him over to a wooden table that used to hold the elements of communion but was now stained with blood. They laid him face down on the table with his head hanging off the edge.

As he lay on the table, heard the voice of the woman, who spoke to him in a dream just last night, saying "Remember, no one can pluck you from his hand." In a fraction of a second, those words took a whole new meaning for him. They might be able to kill his body, but they couldn't take his soul. As he lay face down on the table, he turned to look and saw the guard raise an ax high in the air above his neck. Michael braced for the blow. As he saw the man's arm swing down, he got out one final word. He yelled at the top of his lungs, "Jesus!"

Sophia screamed at the top of her lungs "No!" right as she saw the ax come down on Michael's neck. She was standing at the back of the church and saw her husband be killed, but she didn't know how that could be possible. The last thing she remembered was making plans to find a man named Tom and then falling asleep in her husband's arms.

This had to be a dream. She was dreaming just like her husband dreams. It still felt so real and she was having trouble keeping her emotions in check, but she had to. There was a reason she was dreaming this, and she had to figure out what it was.

She turned and saw a man standing next to her. He was tall and slender with brown hair and a trimmed brown beard. Even though she was surrounded by evil, she felt peace with him by her side. He reached out to take her hand and, as he did that, she saw a scar on the palm of his hand. She knew then she was looking at Jesus.

She grasped his hand in hers, "Why am I here? Why are you showing me this?!"

He looked at her with sadness and compassion in his eyes, "I wanted you to see with your own eyes that your husband didn't die in vain." He looked away from her then and looked towards a woman at the front of the line. She remembered this woman was fearful a moment ago but was now filled with boldness as she was being led to the same table her husband died on a few minutes earlier.

She was filled with pride that Michael had helped give someone the courage to take a stand for truth in his final moments. She looked around the room to see if there was anyone else that was about to defy the beast at the front of the room. That is when she saw him.

Her son was standing at the doorway with the same guard that had refused to let Michael out when he asked to go get something from the car. What was Miles doing there? She wondered to herself, but then she knew.

She heard him say to the guard, "So my father refused to pay his allegiance then."

The guard nodded his head yes, "It was exactly like you predicted. He was secretly a Christian extremist. It was a good thing you reported him to the chief."

Miles nodded with his eyes devoid of emotion, "If he's not with Elyon then he is against me. I had to know the truth."

Sophia saw her baby boy admit to orchestrating the murder of her husband. His father. Silent tears slipped down her face as she watched him cut to the head of the line. He placed himself in front of the image of the beast and got on his knees.

She turned frantically to Jesus beside her and begged, "Please, you have to stop him! He can't do this! Please don't let it end like this!"

Jesus was staring at Miles who was kneeling in front of the image of Elyon and she saw tears trailing down his cheeks, "I wish it weren't like this. I love him so much. I had so many plans for him. I wanted to be with him forever. I showed him my love over and over, but he kept rejecting me. Each time he rejected me his heart grew a little harder. It's too late now. His choice has been made."

She wanted to run away and hide. Anything instead of seeing her son reject any chance at ever being saved. She tried to cover her ears with her hands when Miles started to speak, but she heard every word as he pledged his allegiance and love to that creature on the stage.

He went above the bare minimum pledge of allegiance. Her heart broke into what felt like a thousand pieces as she heard him say, "I willingly give my soul over to you. I ask you now to fill me with the spirit of Elyon, I want no other god but you." He then walked eagerly over and had a chip implanted into the hairline of his forehead.

It couldn't be true. The child she had rocked to sleep as an infant and sang sweet lullabies to, the child she swung on the playground and cuddled in her lap, the child she prayed with at night laughed and cried with… Her baby boy had just sold his soul to the devil and had no chance at redemption. No chance of spending eternity in heaven with her.

She wept freely and turned to Jesus who looked more devastated than even she did, "It's just a dream, right? It's all a warning and I can wake up and save my husband and we can go find Miles before it's too late and make him believe in you again."

Jesus shook his head sorrowfully, "You are dreaming, but it is not just a dream. You have been shown your husband's death and that it was your son that betrayed him. It is a warning, but not because you can save them. It's a warning so you know to leave your house as soon as you wake up. You are not safe there, but you have more to do on earth before I call you home with me."

She was still in disbelief over Mile's decision. What was the point in even having him? What was the point of all those hours of prayer for him and those nighttime conversations on her bed as he shared his hopes and dreams? All those memories… for what?

She had to escape this dream. She had to wake up! She screamed it. "Wake up!" again and again she yelled, "Wake up!"

Jesus looked at her and said, "When you wake up you will see Michael gone from the bed beside you. When you call him on the phone, Miles will answer. That is your evidence that this was real and you must flee your home at once."

She woke up the next instant and was panting for air clawing at the sheets that were now soaked through with her sweat. It had been a dream. It was only a dream. There was still time. She had to warn Michael.

She reached over to his side of the bed and felt it empty. A pit fell in her stomach. She had to find him. She threw the covers off the bed and raced through the house looking for signs of him. He was nowhere to be found and his patrol car was not in the driveway.

She started to panic thinking of how to get ahold of her dear husband when she saw her cell phone sitting on the counter. She ran to it. She had to hear his voice. She called his cell phone, but it just kept ringing. On the last ring, Miles answered the phone. There was something sinister in his voice as he spoke to her, "Hi Mom. I'm with dad and we are coming to see you. Stay there, ok?" It was then that she knew... It was not just a dream.

CHAPTER THIRTEEN

"As in the days when you came out of the land of Egypt, I will show them wonders." - Micah 7:15

John was sleeping peacefully until he heard the jingle of a bell off in the distance. His eyes shot open in the dark and he listened closely. He heard again the unmistakable sound of alarm from his tripwire in the distance, but this time he heard twigs snappings as well. It sounded as if something large were headed toward their camp. It sounded too large to be human.

He shook Katie awake while putting his hand gently over her mouth so she wouldn't make a sound as she was startled awake in the middle of the night. He felt her breathing shift as she squirmed trying to get away from his hand, confused as to what was happening. John pulled her close and whispered as quietly into her ear as possible, "Did your parents and Beth keep all the food at the campfire? Did they tie it up in a tree like I showed them?"

He could feel realization flooding Katie at that moment as her shoulders raised in a shrug meaning she didn't know. John and Katie had been no strangers to camping. John was raised outdoors and knew what measures to take to keep hungry animals away from their food supplies. When he met Katie, she joined his family on many camping trips and outdoor hikes and quickly learned as well.

Her parents were another story. They were city folks through and through. If they went on vacation it always involved a hotel room. Fun for them had been Disney World or beach vacations. He doubted they had ever even been in the woods. John was silently kicking himself for not staying awake longer last night. He should have made sure they followed through on the basic camping safety protocols he taught them before he went to bed for the night.

The campfire where they ate was not very close to their tents. When they had finished eating yesterday, he took Katie's, Beth's, and his own backpack that contained their food and tied them together with a rope. Then he threw a part of that rope over a tall branch and hoisted up their possessions so that they were dangling in the air making it impossible for any predator to access.

Robert and Beverly weren't done eating at the same time as them last night. They assured him they would hang their backpack when they were done. He wondered now if they had done what they said they would or, worse if they brought any food back to their tent. He was kicking himself as he lay in the dark, feeling his wife shaking next to him, as the giant footfalls were getting closer. What was he thinking forgetting to tell the city folks who had never camped before not to bring any food with them into their tent?

They heard something with wide paws aggressively searching the area near their tents. It started sniffing and huffing in what felt like a low and very loud growl right behind them and John placed a single finger on Katie's lips to motion to her to stay quiet.

He doubted anyone in their campsite was still asleep after the growl they had just heard a few feet from them. Any doubt that they didn't hear their unwelcome visitor was removed when he heard Katie's mom loudly whisper from the tent next to them, "Oh Robert, I think it's a bear! What are we going to do?"

John wished he could somehow communicate to her to stay quiet without making him and his wife a target. His thoughts were soon interrupted by a ripping sound and a scream. It was the sound of her tent ripping and Beverly was screaming as the bear ripped through the material.

John didn't know what he was going to do. He had no weapons on him, but he knew he had to do something, so he ran out of the tent to see what was happening with Katie trailing behind him. It was a full moon and he could see clearly all around him as he got a glimpse of the bear. It struck him how much it reminded him of the animals he saw coming from the woods in his first vision. It looked so skinny. He guessed if humans were having trouble finding food, maybe the animals were too.

The bear no longer seemed interested in the smells of food that drew him to the tent. In its hunger, it had become aggressive toward the occupants of the tent. It raised its paw to strike at Robert.

Robert rolled out of the way of the giant claw that was striking the ground near where he lay a few seconds earlier. He seemed to be the object of the bear's attention, but before the animal could do any damage, Robert stood up and screamed as loudly as he could, startling the bear away.

John then saw Beverly jump to her feet and run as fast as she could in the opposite direction of the animal. That was the worst thing she could have done. His mother-in-law was making every camping mistake in the book as she ran as fast as she could trying to find safety. John started yelling with Robert trying to distract and scare the bear away from her.

It didn't work. The bear's attention had shifted away from Robert. A moment earlier, the animal was trying to figure out if the small man was a threat. Now the bear went down off of his two hind legs and went to all four legs as it sprinted after Beverly. It took only a few strides before it caught up to her and lunged on top of her.

It jumped on top of her back crushing her to the ground face down with its teeth sinking into the sides of her neck. It let go and got off, but then it swiped at her with massive force flipping her over so she was facing it. When she placed her hands up in the air trying to ward off the next attack from getting her in the face, the bear latched onto one of her arms. Its mouth engulfed her whole hand down to her elbow as it violently shook its head back and forth and her with it.

John heard Katie scream as they both watched in shock as all of this happened in a matter of seconds. John felt paralyzed in place. He didn't have any weapons; he was powerless.

The bear let go of the mangled arm out of its mouth and was about to lunge directly for her face. Before the bear had a chance to do that, he heard Katie pray beside him, "God give me strength. I'm scared. Be with me." Then he saw his wife take several confident strides toward the animal until she was right next to it.

The bear went off its two back legs and stood on the ground on all four paws. It was like a stare-down between the animal and Katie with her mom injured on the ground between them. John saw Katie's mouth move again in silent prayer before she spoke a single word to the creature. "Leave."

The bear quizzically turned its neck like he was asking a question and Katie repeated herself without ever raising her voice, "Leave."

To John's amazement, the bear, without hesitation, turned and walked out of the camp the same way it had come in. John couldn't believe his eyes. This was no ordinary bear encounter. This animal was far more aggressive than normal due to starvation. He had heard stories about scaring off a bear, but that was often from people making themselves appear big by waving their hands in the air and being extremely loud.

Katie did none of those things. She spoke so quietly and calmly that John could barely hear her, yet the bear obeyed her commands. He had just witnessed an actual miracle, but he realized there was no time to think of that as he saw Katie spring to action and run to her mother's side.

She bent down on her knees next to her mother and looked up to John with pleading eyes, "Help her, John!" He came over and joined Robert as they inspected the wounds. It was worse than he thought. There were three deep scratch wounds across her back and she probably had a few crushed ribs from when the bear first landed on her. Then there was her arm.

It was almost fully severed at the elbow and was only hanging on by a few tendons. John took off his belt and tied it as tightly as he possibly could well above the part of the arm that had been practically amputated.

It was then that he noticed her most serious injury. He remembered how when the bear first pounced on her it grabbed her with its teeth on the back of her neck. There were several very deep puncture wounds on her neck.

He saw that blood was gushing out from them faster than they knew was even possible. John sprang to action and ran to go get rags from his tent to shove into the wound to try and stop the bleeding. The clean rag was soaked with blood in seconds. He sent Robert to get one of his clean shirts and try again and the same thing happened. Within a few seconds, it was soaked through. Beverly was bleeding out in front of them and there was nothing they could do to stop it as she groaned in pain in front of them.

Maybe before the EMP they could have used their cell phones and called for a helicopter to fly them to a hospital. But they were in the middle of the woods with no vehicles. They certainly didn't have cell phones or helicopters or even hospitals. John sadly looked at his wife and shook his head 'no.' She knew what that meant. Her mom was dying.

Robert went and sat next to one side of her face with Katie on the other. Her mom looked at her husband first and gave him a weak smile, "You are the love of my life," she said.

Robert began to cry in earnest as he stroked her hair and leaned down and gave her a final kiss, "And you are mine, love. I'll see you soon."

Beverly turned her head to face Katie then and used all her

remaining strength to lift her one good hand and put it on her daughter's cheek, "Oh my precious girl. I am so proud of you." Each word she said came slower and harder for her to get out. "The woman of God you have become." Her voice was a mere whisper now, "I love you." Then her hand slipped off of Katie's cheek and fell to the ground and her eyes glazed over.

Katie reached down and closed her mom's eyes, "I love you too mom." Katie couldn't keep up her appearance of strength any longer. She bent down over the woman that had raised her and loved her and held her tight as she sobbed. She cried for hours.

While she and her dad mourned, John and Beth found two large sticks and flattened the end of them with his knife. They used the makeshift shovels they had created and began digging a hole. They had very little energy from their last two days of covering so many miles by bike, but they had to push a little harder and give Beverly the respect she deserved with a proper burial.

When they had finished the hole, Beth went to find some fresh flowers while John went over to his wife, "It's time," he told her gently as he lifted her off of her mother. Katie stayed in place as her dad came over to her and they embraced.

While the father and daughter cried in each other's arms, John bent down, picked up Beverly, carried her over to the freshly dug hole, and placed her gently inside. He used his wooden branch shovel and began to refill the hole looking for the last time upon the face that was so precious to him: the face that welcomed him as a son. He thought back to all the sweet memories he had made with her with each shovelful of dirt he tossed into the hole.

When he was done, Beth had come back and she laid the wildflowers she had picked on top of the grave. She had also gotten a large branch and carved 'Beverly' into it, which she stuck into the ground at the head of the grave as a grave marker.

Katie's dad helped his daughter to her feet and supported her as they walked over to the grave. John knew they needed closure so as they all stood around the gravesite he spoke of the fond memories he had of Beverly and of her character. He quoted psalms thirty-one that spoke of everything a woman should be and said her mom was all those things and more. He ended with a prayer. No one talked about continuing their journey that day. They needed time to just grieve together.

Sophia still didn't want to believe it was more than a dream, but deep down she knew it was real. God had given her the gift of seeing her husband's final moments. It was a gift to see him stand up and boldly proclaim the name of Jesus even though it meant his death. She remembered the promise she made him make at the beginning of this that he wouldn't take any unnecessary risks. He had kept his word. Their son had tricked him and he was left with no choice. He either could sell his soul to the devil or he could stand up for truth in his final moments. Her heart filled with pride that she was married to such a man as she remembered Michael's final moments.

Her heart ached that she wouldn't see him again in this life, but she comforted herself with the knowledge that she would see him soon as it had already been a year since Elyon had declared himself to be God.

If she allowed herself to think about her son Miles her heart would ache. He was unsavable now that he had taken the mark. She didn't have the hope of one day soon seeing him in heaven. She vacillated from feeling like a failure as a mother to realizing that God gives each of us free will and Miles had chosen to turn his back on what he knew to be true.

At first, she questioned what was the point of it all, but as she quickly packed her bags to leave she realized the point was she obeyed God. She obeyed God by bringing a precious little boy into the world and she obeyed Him when she raised him to follow Christ. That was the point.

She also had over two decades of memories that she would cherish 'til the day she died. Memories of happier times and a boy with a softer, kinder heart. As she put the last of her clothes and food into a suitcase, she vowed to only think of the good memories with Miles. She would only think of Miles as who he used to be. She wouldn't think of who her son was now: an evil man who betrayed his father and orchestrated his murder.

Sophia lived in Nebraska City, which was not affected by the EMPs that had hit three major cities and their outlying areas in the United States. They still had power and running water, although not daily, since the rolling power outages due to labor shortages. She threw her suitcase in her car and got ready to leave for the address Michael wrote down the night before his execution.

She was determined to get to this stranger's house as quickly as possible. Sophia was so grateful that Michael had told her so many details about his dream. He normally would just share the highlights of each dream, but this time was different. He told her everything he could remember, left nothing out, and left the sheet of paper with Tom's address on the nightstand next to his side of the bed.

She knew from the dream that she was going to see her son, John. Oh, how she had missed him since he moved to the city. To hear that not only was John still alive but that she would see him again, made her heart burst with hope. "If only Michael were with me to see him too," She thought, trying to fight off the sadness that would consume her if she let it.

Tom's house was a half-day drive away. Normally, she would just go the fastest route, but that meant going through at least one big city, Kansas City, and it had been affected by the EMP. No, she couldn't risk that. She would be too big a target with a working vehicle in a city with no modern conveniences.

She was worried GPS might not work in every city if it was close to the EMP-affected zone. So she mapped out her route using an old school map that Michael made sure she always kept in her car for emergencies. She made sure to use only lightly traveled back roads. She sighed. It would take her at least twice as long on the back roads as on the highway.

She didn't have much choice. She threw the map in the passenger seat as well as all the remaining food in the house. She knew she had to leave quickly. She believed the dream was more than just comfort to see her husband stand strong in his final moments and have some closure. She believed the dream was so she could see that her son Miles had fully given himself to evil and was not to be trusted. She was sure if she stayed any longer in the house that he had grown up in, he would come for her next to pledge her allegiance to Elyon. As much as she wanted to see Miles one last time, hug him, and tell him she loved him anyway, she couldn't let that happen.

"I have to get out of the house right away before it is too late," she said to herself as she got in her car, opened the garage door, turned on the car, and pulled out of her driveway. For the last time, she looked at the house that held so many memories of her son's childhood and her marriage to Michael. She gave the house a long glance and said goodbye in her heart as she pulled out onto the street and began to drive away.

The next morning, John didn't have the heart to make them leave. Katie had cried through the night and was finally sleeping peacefully, so he let their group stay one more day at the campsite even though it was making the resources they had carried with them dangerously low. He did the math and realized the next morning they would only have one water bottle apiece as they started their journey. They would have to find a clean water source first thing tomorrow. He would worry about that then. For now, he just had to help his wife regain her strength. He knew half the battle of overcoming hard circumstances was staying positive. His wife's mental health was worth the risk he was taking with their water.

When the next morning came, he made the announcement it was time to pack up camp. Everyone was quiet as they put away the tents that they would carry on their backs above their backpacks and got ready to leave. Beth still rode on John's handlebars, and Katie pedaled the miniature kid bike. When they looked at Robert on his bike without his wife on the handlebars in front of him a lump formed in John's throat. "Time to go."

He led the pack with Katie in the rear. They went back through the rough terrain through the woods that they encountered on their way into the forest. The ride seemed harder this time. Maybe that was because last time they knew when they finished they would get to rest together. This time, all that would be waiting for them was at least one more grueling day on the road before they would reach their destination.

When he finally got off the rocky path and reached the highway he stopped and waited for everyone to catch up. Beth used the time to get off the handlebars and stretch her legs. Just as Katie had caught up to the group, John noticed a pack of dogs headed their way.

At first, he didn't think anything of it. They were clearly dogs, not wolves. There were some smaller dogs that were once someone's pet and some larger dogs that were probably guard dogs for someone's home once. He saw mainly German Shepherds and Pit Bulls with a few smaller mutts in the mix. They were all abandoned it seemed and stayed together as if they had formed a pack.

As the pack of dogs grew closer, he saw that they, too, were skinny. They were probably all pets at one point and then as resources for humans became harder to find, they were dumped. John understood it: if people can't afford to feed their children they certainly weren't going to spend money feeding dogs, but it was still sad.

Not only were they too skinny, but they were all growling. They weren't just on a leisurely walk together enjoying the sunshine, they were hunting. In packs. And they were headed straight towards them.

In the dog's effort to survive, they had become feral, and more like wolves than the loving pets they once were. John saw them pick up speed as the entire pack of almost twenty dogs started to race toward them all. John was filled with anger and not fear. His family had lost enough this week; they would lose no more. He remembered how when Katie prayed, they had a miracle in the woods. So, he told everyone with him to pray for another miracle.

John prayed as well as he laid down the bike and walked toward the animals that had stopped running and were standing a few feet from him while snarling with their fangs showing. He stopped and didn't know what to do next, they still looked angry and menacing like they wanted to tear him apart. Without warning, a cat raced in between him and where the dogs stood and ran past him into the woods. As one, the dogs all turned their aggression toward the cat as they chased after it until they couldn't be seen. Their earlier mission of attacking the group on the bikes was forgotten. It seemed his group had experienced another miracle.

As they continued to ride in the quiet countryside, he thought it over. He saw that there were times when God protected them from danger and supernaturally allowed them to escape harm. There were other times, like the night with Beverly, when bad things happened to them. "Just because they were walking in the power of God like never before, did not mean they had immunity from the pain of life," he thought as he grew thirsty, his water bottle long emptied.

He had been looking for hours but never saw a single sign of a water source as they biked. The sun was unrelenting as it beat down on their backs exacerbating the problem of their dehydration. They should have been at their destination by nightfall, but it was becoming impossible as their pace crawled to that of a snail due to their thirst.

It was Robert who first collapsed off of his bike, physically incapable of going any further until his body had the water it so desperately needed. John wondered if this was one of those moments of feeling the pain of life and if there was going to be another death.

As he thought of his wife potentially losing another parent in the same week he realized they hadn't prayed together about their lack of water. In their quest for survival, they didn't take time to speak with the one that could actually help them survive.

John helped Beth off the bike and gathered the group of four into a circle. As they joined hands, John led the prayer, "Father we are in desperate need of you. You have our unending devotion and even in times of pain, we say You are good! Even when we are hurting we say we trust You. If right now, You choose to call us all home, that is ok. We are eager for the day that we can be with You always, but we are asking for a miracle. Please, God, make a way for us to find something to drink. Amen."

As he said the word, 'amen' he thought he heard someone say, "Take out your water bottle from your backpack." When John opened his eyes after hearing that he was half expecting to see a lake suddenly appear in front of them to fill up the bottle with, but that didn't happen. He must not have heard what he thought he did.

He asked Robert if he was able to continue and when he assured him he was feeling better they got back on their bikes. Within a few moments, he heard it again, "Take out your water bottle from your backpack." He looked around and there were trees as far as the eye could see in every direction. Not lush and green trees full of life, but most of them were dead or dying. It looked like this area was experiencing a drought.

He was thinking that he must have been experiencing the beginning stages of hallucinations that are often associated with severe dehydration when he heard a crash behind him. This time it was Katie on the ground who collapsed off of her bike. He heard the voice a third time, "Take out your water bottle from your backpack." Still thinking he was crazy, he reached into his backpack instead of rushing straight to Katie's side.

To his amazement, it was filled with fresh, clean sparkling water. It had been empty when he put it in his backpack last. He rushed over to Katie's side, lifted her head, and began to slowly pour water down her parched throat. Robert and Beth looked on with wonder and excitedly checked their backpacks too. John heard a holler and smiled as he saw Robert lift a full water bottle from his backpack and begin to gulp it down in its entirety.

Katie was able to sit up and continued to take sips passing it back and forth between her and John. Beth was all smiles as she watched this take place and said, "That was amazing!"

Katie saw Beth was about to do something stupid and tried to call out to stop her, but her voice was too slow. Beth looked at them and playfully said, "I want to try something." She then proceeded to empty the entirety of the contents of her newly filled water bottle over her head, relishing the relief from the heat of the sun on her head.

Katie shakily stood to her feet, "Why did you do that Beth? We need to conserve the water as much as possible" she said as she handed Beth what remained of hers and John's water and put Beth's now empty bottle back in her backpack.

Beth just smiled as she refused John and Katie's remaining water and reached into her backpack to retrieve the empty bottle Katie had just put in there. Katie gasped, "It's full again!" Beth laughed and this time she drank the water.

The whole group started laughing and began putting the empty bottles in the backpacks, taking them out full and pouring them on their heads. Putting them back in the backpacks again, taking them out, and drinking them. Over and over they repeated this process laughing and smiling as they threw water at each other like a little kid's water fight, the sadness they felt earlier, momentarily forgotten.

CHAPTER FOURTEEN

"And it shall come to pass afterward, that I will pour out my Spirit on all flesh; your sons and your daughters shall prophesy, your old men shall dream dreams, and your young men shall see visions. Even on the male and female servants in those days, I will pour out my Spirit. And I will show wonders in the heavens and on the earth, blood and fire and columns of smoke. The sun shall be turned to darkness, and the moon to blood, before the great and awesome day of the Lord, comes"
- Joel 2:28-31

John and his crew didn't make it as far as they had hoped. He had planned to be there by now, but because of their slow pace throughout the day from lack of water, they still had another couple of hours to go before sunset. They were forced to rest for the night and they made another campsite far from the road.

There was no food left to worry about bears smelling. All they had was the unending water supply they carried with them in their backpacks. They were resting around the campfire singing "How Great Thou Art" when Katie suddenly saw a flash of light. When the light dissipated it was as if she were suddenly transported to another place.

She looked around and saw a grassy field filled with wildflowers of every color she had ever known and even some colors she had not seen before. There were children playing. She saw a waterfall far away, and, around it, was a large group of people all wearing white robes. She did a double take when she thought she saw John's father wearing a white robe among the group.

Before she had time to process what that meant, she saw her mom walking toward her. Her mom was radiant. She was more like Katie's age and less like the age she was just a few days ago before she passed away. The wrinkles and sunspots were gone, her body was strong and sleek, and her hair was full and thicker than Katie had ever seen. It was a face of youth and a face of joy.

Her mom saw her, broke into a run, and swept her up in her arms. She swung her around as she used to when she was a little girl, "Oh Katie girl, how good it is to see you!"

Katie began to cry and her mom pulled away from the embrace and wiped away her tears, "Why are you crying sweetie?" Her mom seemed genuinely confused by Katie's tears.

"Mom, you died. It was horrible. You were in so much pain." Katie paused, struggling to get the remaining words out, "And I miss you."

Beverly laughed with a voice that filled the air around it and Katie's heart with joy, "Oh honey, I don't feel any of that now. Can't you see how wonderful it is here?"

Katie looked around at the paradise all around her and

was beginning to feel a little better, but still was struggling with a small lingering sadness, "Don't you miss me too?"

Her mom took her by her hand and they walked hand in hand through the field of flowers toward a waterfall and stream up ahead. It was no ordinary waterfall. It looked like the cliff that the water was falling from was miles in the air. The cliff made a 'U' shape around the pool of water at the bottom and children were running behind the waterfall. They were having fun hiding behind the cascading water and then jumping through it into the sparkling pool below.

Beverly brought Katie's thoughts back to her mother who was walking beside her, "Oh, Katie, you don't realize that where you live time is so fleeting. It's like a vapor and will be gone before you know it." Her mom paused, "Plus I know a secret."

Her mom had a twinkle in her eyes that made it impossible for Katie to resist asking, "What? What's the secret?"

Her mom paused for a moment before pointing to the group of people all wearing white robes resting by the water. Katie looked to where she was pointing and saw the man who she earlier thought was John's father. The man began to wave excitedly at her and when she waved back she saw his smile. She was sure of it then, "Mom! Is that John's dad?"

Katie's mom smiled at her daughter, "Those are the saints who have given up their lives for Christ. Michael joined them very recently." Her voice became a whisper as though she were sharing some delightful secret, "Their number grows every day. It won't be long at all now till Jesus comes for the rest of you and we can be together always." Her voice returned to her normal volume, "So, you see, how could I be sad and miss you? We will be together, forever, sooner than you could imagine. And this time," She wrapped her arm around her daughter's shoulders, "nothing will ever separate us again."

Her mom suddenly let go and broke into a run and headed toward the stream in the opposite direction of the waterfall and saints in robes, "Follow me, I want you to meet someone!"

Katie struggled to keep up. Her mom seemed to have a stamina and speed Katie had never seen. As she was running through the field, she couldn't help but think her mom was right. It was so good to be with her right now, but even though she couldn't stay with her, it wouldn't be long until they were together forever. "How had she become so consumed with grief that she had forgotten that?" She wondered.

When she finally caught up with her mom at the water she saw her mother was not alone: a man was standing next to her. She gasped as she looked at his face and instantly knew who it was. In a breathy, awestruck voice she whispered his name, "Jesus."

Jesus smiled at her and as he held open his arms, she raced into them and squeezed him as tight as she could. He laughed as he wrapped his arms around her as well and the force of her hug almost knocked them both down. She let go and wiped the happy tears from her eyes, "I can't believe it's you."

He put both hands on her shoulders and looked at her with a fierceness in his eyes. The way he looked at her made her not doubt a word he said when he spoke, "I have loved you since the beginning of time. I have watched you grow up. I have seen when you laugh and when you cry. It won't be long, my precious Katie, 'til I'm going to come and get you and we will be together like this forever."

Katie, still so full of joy, asked him what he meant by him coming to get her. She wondered if she were about to die.

He motioned for her to sit by the stream and he sat next to her as they both let their bare feet rest in the coolness of the water. She watched as the water seemed to race over the rocks as if the water itself were alive and had a mind of its own. His voice shook her from her thoughts, "No, you're not going to die, Katie. I am coming back to the earth, but this time it will be very different from the first time I came.

The first time, I was a baby in a manger and I died on the cross. All of that had to happen so you could be with me forever, but next time I come to earth it won't be anything like that."

Katie did not understand. "How will it be different? What will it be like?"

She saw sadness in his eyes as he spoke of those who rejected him, "I have waited as long as I could. I've allowed men to have whatever they desire and fulfill the evil in their hearts. I have permitted the antichrist to think that he has power, but only for a short time. All of this was so that as many people as possible would have a chance to choose me and to choose heaven. Some people need to clearly see the difference between good and evil before they would ever choose me."

With the words of Jesus echoing in her mind, Katie remembered a message she heard preached once many years ago. It said the reason for God's judgment is so that he can use the least severe means possible to reach the greatest number of people all without violating their free will.

Jesus seemed to know exactly what she was thinking, "For some people, the only time they can hear me is in the midst of turmoil. They don't hear me calling them when everything is good. I am pursuing them in the midst of the storm telling them they are wanted and loved, but the time left to make a decision is short."

She saw his eyes shift from a loving blue that reflected the clear water in front of them to a fiery amber as he continued to speak, "But the time of waiting is quickly coming to a close. I will not allow my people to suffer much longer at the hands of these evil men in the antichrist regime. I didn't stay in the grave and I will not stay in heaven forever. I'm alive and soon the whole world will know it. I am coming back very soon."

She saw the passion in his eyes as he spoke and she could feel his love for her in the air around her. It was like the air itself was alive in this place and washing over her with his love. "It's time to go back, Katie."

Katie couldn't help herself as a little whine snuck into her voice, "Oh please no. I don't want to leave you. Please let me stay with you."

Jesus smiled and playfully nudged his shoulder against hers, "It won't be long" He stood up and reached down to help her to her feet, "You have to go back. You still have a job to do, your time hasn't come yet, but it will soon."

Katie nodded eagerly excited to fulfill the mission she had been given. "I will do what you want, I promise"

They began to walk back toward the direction of where

she first arrived. She saw in the distance giant gates taller than any skyscraper she had ever seen on earth. The gates sparkled and reflected the light that was all around her. Every inch of the gate was covered in shiny white droplets. Each spindle looked like an extremely long pearl necklace suspended between a thicker pearl strand above and below it.

The gates were connected to a wall that went as far as the eye could see in both directions. The wall itself was like an unclimbable mountain built with a stone that shimmered on every surface.

Where the gates started, there was a road that led around the city paved with pure gold. Beyond that was an ocean so clear and so still and calm it looked like glass. She saw a giant mansion that looked like it was almost finished being built, except the word mansion hardly could describe what she saw. It was a home that went beyond the edges of her sight.

She was trying to soak in every sight as they continued their walk. She didn't know when it happened, but at some point, she realized Jesus was not walking right beside her any longer, she was walking alone. She frantically looked around wanting to get a glimpse of him one last time. She saw him a little distance away. His eyes locked with hers and there was silence between them for a few moments before he said, "Tell as many as you can."

Benjamin and Rachel had been preaching in front of the Dome of the Rock every day since they first arrived in the city. It was always the same with Benjamin preaching and Leah on her knees praying beside him for their safety and for softened receptive hearts of those still able to be reached with the truth.

Each day more people filled the street with dead, angry eyes and fewer people listened with eyes filled with hope and hunger for truth, but still, they preached. Many times people had tried to arrest, hurt or kill them and every time those people either failed or were injured themselves.

This particular morning when they woke up, they both knew their time of publicly sharing the gospel had come to an end for a season. It had been much shorter than they expected, but they felt something telling them that they needed to go back to the mountain and check on their parents.

They began their long journey back to the mountains. To pass the time, they sang hymns, recount the miracles God had done keeping them safe while they preached, and remembered the many stories of salvation they had seen over the last several weeks.

They also passed the days walking by praying for their father. They hoped he would be more open to receiving the truth about Jesus from them. He had been so worried about making another mistake in what he believed that he stopped making any decisions. The brother and sister hoped that when they told him everything they had seen as they preached in the old city, perhaps it would help him to finally believe in Jesus.

The next thing Katie saw after she heard those final words in heaven, "Tell as many as you can," was another flash of light. She no longer looked at the crystal clear stream in front of her or the fiery eyes of her king, but at the campfire and her husband sitting beside her. She was in shock. This felt like more than just a vision. This felt like she had actually been in heaven and talked with Jesus.

She was trying to process what had happened. It seemed that no one was surprised to see her sitting next to John. She must not have physically left her body, but her spirit was transported up to heaven. She couldn't believe it. She had seen, talked with, and even touched Jesus! It was the most amazing thing she ever experienced!

She wasn't doing a good job of hiding the joy, surprise, and even shock on her face because while John was still singing the final words of the hymn, he looked over at his wife and stopped singing, "Katie, are you ok?"

Her smile grew larger, "Oh, I'm more than ok, John. I have so much to tell you."

She told him everything she saw, but she was careful to leave out the one detail about his father. The joy bubbling out of her was contagious. No one at the campfire could wipe the smile off his or her face as they heard Katie talk about heaven and Jesus.

The sadness of losing Beverely was still there, but it was different. There was perspective now at how temporary it all was and how soon the trials they were facing would be over. John reminded them that it had been a little over a year since the antichrist revealed himself in the temple and the Bible was very clear that once that occurs the countdown has begun. No one knows exactly when it will happen other than it's at the seventh trumpet. All that can be known for sure is there are no more than three and a half years from the incident in the temple before Jesus returns.

Robert began to have many questions for John. His eagerness to learn was restored as he heard that his sweet wife was laughing and running in heaven, "Will we be here all the way until the end of the three and a half years?"

John explained that they would not. "Right now we are probably in the fifth seal judgment which is when martyrdom increases. There are seven seals, then seven trumpets and lastly there are seven bowl judgments. On the very last trumpet is when all the Christians will be raptured and leave the trials of this earth."

Robert nodded his head in understanding, "I've heard the verse that says, 'We will not all sleep, but we will all be changed, in a moment, in the twinkling of an eye, at the last trumpet; for the trumpet will sound, and the dead will be raised imperishable, and we will be changed.' I always thought that verse meant a secret rapture before the antichrist came, but it makes sense. When it says the last trumpet sounds it means the literal last trumpet of the seven trumpet judgments."

John became excited talking about this. It was more than just talking about theology in the Bible, they were seeing actual Bible prophecy come to life before their eyes. "If a little over a year has already passed, we know it absolutely can't be longer than three years left until we all see Jesus. My guess is that it's even less than that because we leave this earth on the seventh trumpet. The timeline shows that after the seventh trumpet, there are still seven bowls of God's wrath to be poured out before the three and a half years are complete."

Robert was getting excited, "I was always taught that no man can know the day or the hour, but I guess that doesn't mean we can't know when the season is coming close."

The air in their group had shifted. They were filled with hope and excitement. The last year had been extremely difficult, but now they knew something that made it all worthwhile.

When Miles saw his father's final display of rebellion toward the great Elyon all doubt was erased. He knew he had made the right move in turning his father in to the authorities as a suspected Christian extremist. After Miles went forward and took his mark of allegiance, several others in line behind him copied his father's example and refused to bow their knee. Miles was angry because he felt like even in death, his dad led people astray.

Miles was ashamed to call such a man his father who would knowingly lead people to choose a path that would lead to their deaths. "The man was heartless," he thought to himself. He could only hope that his mother was not corrupted by his father's ideologies as well.

After Miles watched his dad's execution as a traitor, his father's cell phone rang. He saw on the caller ID that it was his mother. He picked it up and told her that he was with his dad and to stay put. He couldn't leave right away though. He had to finish dealing with the remaining Christian rebels in Elyon's sanctuary. Once they all received the same fate as his father, he got in his car and headed to his childhood home.

He saw it was empty and the car was not in the garage. He was angry she didn't listen to him, so he went to wait inside until she returned. He wanted to have a little chat with his mother and escort her to the church so she could have the privilege of pledging her allegiance with her son by her side. As the minutes ticked on, he noticed some items out of place and disheveled which was unlike her. He investigated further and saw that all her clothes were missing and the pantry emptied of all food.

He roared in anger that she had run away, "So she is an extremist after all. She has heard that the mark stations are up and running and has left the city." As his anger burned inside of him, he stormed from room to room destroying everything in his presence. He threw lamps against the walls. He dragged his hand along the countertop in the kitchen with such force that every plate and every appliance went crashing to the floor. He went to the bedroom and took a knife to the bed.

When his energy was spent, he sat on the bed, panting. In the corner of his eye, he noticed an odd piece of paper on the nightstand. It looked like someone had written on top of it and the ink from the pen bled through. It was written in his dad's handwriting and he couldn't make out most of what it said. There were only two legible words: Jasper, Arkansas.

Miles picked it up and studied it. It was far away. Definitely out of his jurisdiction as an officer. It might be nothing, but he couldn't shake the feeling that it was important. He put the note in his back pocket hoping that this obscure find would help lead him to his traitorous mother.

He left the house with no love, remorse, or fond memories in his heart. He was consumed with only anger and vengeance.

CHAPTER FIFTEEN

"But mark this: There will be terrible times in the last days.
People will be lovers of themselves, lovers of money, boastful,
proud, abusive, disobedient to their parents, ungrateful,
unholy, without love, unforgiving, slanderous, without self-
control, brutal, not lovers of the good, treacherous, rash,
conceited, lovers of pleasure rather than lovers of God" - 2
Timothy 3:1-4

John, Robert, Katie, and Beth got an early start the next morning to bike the final thirty miles to Tom. He figured it should take them no more than three hours. "We will be there by lunch," His excitement was contagious to the rest of the group.

They put their weary bodies back on the bikes and set off. The water in their backpacks continued to replenish for the ride. They were an hour into the journey when the rain began. The weather outside was warm, so they kept riding in the rain, determined to finish as quickly as possible. As they went down a large hill, John and Beth rode into a large puddle. He lost control of his bike. It skidded as the tire lost all traction.

The wheel seemed to have a mind of its own. It skidded straight for a rock and John and Beth went flying off of the bike and slid across the rough pavement.

Katie and Robert went to John and Beth to check their injuries. They were both very scraped up with road rash all along their arms and legs, but neither had serious injuries. The bike was another story. The rock the bike hit destroyed it. A giant hole in the tire let all the air escape and the metal frame was bent. The third bike was useless.

What would have been a two-hour bike ride just turned into a seven-hour walk in the rain. Their bellies were all growling as they hadn't eaten anything the previous day, but at least they had water. Robert gave up his bike for Beth and he and John both walked as the ladies biked next to them. Beth and Katie pedaled slowly in step with the walkers beside them.

The slower pace allowed time for conversation. Katie slowed her pace and she and John fell out of earshot of the other two, "John, I have something to tell you."

John looked at her expectantly and she continued not wanting to make eye contact, "I didn't tell you everything about my experience in heaven. I saw something else there you should know."

She paused trying to figure out the right words, clearly uncomfortable. John tried his best to put her mind at ease, "It's ok Katie. Whatever it is, just tell me."

She took a deep breath before continuing to speak, "I saw your dad, John. He was in heaven." She looked over at John and saw he had stopped walking and just stood there with his mouth open. She spoke quickly then wanting to get it over with, "He was wearing a white robe. There were so many people with him wearing white robes. My mom pointed to all of them and told me they were the martyrs who had recently died for Christ."

John began walking again, continuing on in silence. Katie left him alone with his thoughts. She knew he processed information best internally. She rode in silence next to him for over an hour waiting for him to speak. He finally asked her a question, "Are you sure it was him?"

Katie's heart broke that her husband was hurting and tried to share the good things she saw hoping to make him feel better, "Yes, I'm sure. He waved at me, John. He recognized me and I waved back. He looked so happy, he had the biggest smile on his face I have ever seen. There was the most beautiful waterfall and he and everyone around him looked to be resting there waiting for something. He seemed content, John."

John nodded his head in understanding as they continued on in silence a little further. He turned to Katie and shocked her as he smiled at her. "Katie, my dad is one of the martyrs in a white robe that is crying out to Jesus to avenge their blood! My dad is a hero!"

John beamed with pride and joy. She had expected tears or anger or both. That's what she had felt when her mom died, "John aren't you sad?"

John's smile lessened just a little, "Yes, I'm sad, but the joy I feel is so much stronger. Your vision makes so much sense. Time is so short here. We will be in heaven with him and with Jesus soon, and he's not in heaven because he died of natural causes, he's there because he died a hero's death! That's who my father is. A hero! That's what I'm choosing to think of. I don't want to think about how I won't see him for the next year or two here on earth."

Katie felt like a giant weight had been lifted off of her shoulders at his reaction. She had been so scared to tell him and hurt him after all they had been through. She should have known how strong her husband was, "John, I'm so happy to hear that!"

They continued in thoughtful silence, "My only concern is really for my mom. Did you see her in your vision? Was she there too?" Katie shook her head 'no' that she wasn't.

John wasn't sure what he felt. It was a strange mixture of joy that she was still alive and worry that she was in danger. "Then that means she's still here and she's alone without her husband. She hasn't been without him since she was sixteen. I have to find her. I have to make sure she's safe."

Katie understood his worry. Once a loved one was in heaven, there was no more pain. Until then, no one wants to know someone you love might be suffering. "We will find her, John, but first we have to get to safety. I'm so tired."

John understood that his wife came first, but as soon as he got her settled and safe, he planned to find his mom and bring her to them. He prayed for his mom for the rest of their journey.

Sophia had left in a hurry from her home late in the morning and drove the back roads she had mapped out for almost ten hours before her eyes became too heavy and she had to pull over for the night. She saw an old abandoned gas station and pulled in behind it, hiding her car from anyone who might pass by and see her car.

As she slept, she dreamed. She dreamed that she was in the back row of her vehicle looking at herself in the front seat driving the car. She saw that she was driving down a long stretch of road. Next to her was a woman sitting in her passenger seat. The woman had golden brown skin with short, dark, curly hair. She looked to be in her early thirties and was extremely skinny like she hadn't eaten in days, maybe weeks. As she watched herself drive, she seemed like she knew the person sitting next to her and was comfortable with her there.

As she was driving along the road she drove over a railroad track. This railroad track stuck out to her as being different from the many others she had driven over on the last day. This one had tents lining both sides of it like people had made this area their home. Sophia and the woman beside her continued on the road for a quarter-mile past the tracks before noticing that there was a blockade up ahead.

People were trying to block her from going any further. She quickly put the car in reverse and started to go backward, but the large group in the tent city had all rushed into the road and formed a human barricade which included women and children. There was no way to get past them without running over little kids. They were trapped. She saw herself turn to this woman in the passenger seat and say, "We should have stopped the car and abandoned it before the railroad track. Now they will take the car and us."

Her eyes popped open and she knew right away she had just dreamed all that. She replayed the strange dream over and over in her mind. "Who was that woman?" She wondered. She tried to shake off all the questions and confusion it left her with because she saw that the sun was rising and she needed to get going. She reached behind her to take out a granola bar and a bottle of water for her breakfast.

As she reached for her supplies scattered in the backseat she thought of her dream again. Maybe she should shove as much of it into her backpack as possible, just in case she had to abandon her car. She filled her backpack until it was overflowing with water bottles and food. She grabbed her quick breakfast and began to eat it as she began her drive again. She was eager to get going and only had a couple of hours left before she arrived at the address her husband had received in his dream.

Up until this point, she had been driving in areas that were not affected by the EMP, but as she got closer to her destination she saw more and more signs that she was now in an area that had devastation wreaked upon it from the sudden blow of losing all technological advances overnight. Before now, she had seen the occasional car driving on the road. Now the roads were completely desolate except for the occasional person walking. The houses she passed all had their windows open even though it was almost a hundred degrees. Very few people would voluntarily choose the stifling fresh air over air conditioning in such extreme heat.

The most telling signs were the stoplights and pedestrians. In the first little town she passed through that had been affected by the EMP, none of the stoplights were working. Several people out on the sidewalks were looking at her working vehicle greedily as she passed by them.

Suddenly, a man jumped in front of her car making her screech to a halt to avoid running him over. She was yelling at the man she nearly missed hitting, wondering why in the world he was standing in front of her, "Get out of my way!"

While she was shooing the man in front of her with her hands and yelling at him to move, another man rushed up to her door and tried to open it. Her door was locked out of habit, so he picked up a rock from beside him on the road and reached back ready to strike the window. This man had every intention of taking the car for himself by force. Before he followed through on his strike, she jerked the wheel to the right and pressed the gas narrowly missing the man standing in front of her car who was trying to block her escape. Her tires squealed as she sped away.

Her heart was beating fast as she drove off realizing she was now driving a giant red moving bullseye. She left the little town and was traveling down a seemingly deserted canopied road. She was trying to think of how best to keep her car while finishing the final leg of her drive when she passed by a woman walking on the side of the road. As she sped past her she did a double-take. It was the woman from her dream.

She pulled her car over to the shoulder of the road and put it in park. The woman stopped walking and eyed her suspiciously. Sophia got out of the car and realized she probably scared the woman half to death. "I'm sorry if I scared you. I just saw you walking and felt like God was telling me to help you."

The woman scoffed, "Ha, God. Some help he's been for me. Plus, why should I trust you? Maybe you have a gang of men in that car waiting to hurt me as soon as I get close."

Sophia realized this was going to be harder than she first thought. The woman had no way to know Sophia wasn't dangerous. She didn't blame her for her apprehension, "I promise I just want to help." She opened the side doors of her vehicle showing that no one was inside, showing the woman piles of food and water bottles in the car, "I thought you might be hungry or thirsty, can I get you something?"

The woman looked around wondering if it was a trap and if someone was lurking in the woods ready to pounce, but they were completely alone. She walked up to the car and grabbed a drink and some trail mix. She started eating slowly at first, but then faster not realizing how hungry she was. She finished her bag and threw it on the ground and grabbed another without asking.

Sophia wished she were more like Michael at that moment. Michael would have been fine with the woman's rudeness in response to his generosity. Sophia, on the other hand, struggled to contain her impatient self from rearing its ugly head. She held in the comments that she wanted to make. She wanted to tell the woman next to her that it would be nice to say thank you or please before taking more of someone else's food.

Sophia kept all that to herself and asked Jesus to make her more like Him in her responses. She let the woman eat while she told her story trying to make the woman feel more at ease. She didn't leave out anything. She told her about Michael's dreams, her dreams, and even about Michael's death. She ended by sharing her most recent dream about the railroad and her sitting in the car next to her as they drove like they knew each other.

The emaciated woman stared at her like she had lost her mind, "I think you're crazy, but I have nowhere else to go, so what the heck. It beats walking."

Sophia stuck out her hand to shake "Good I'm glad! I'm Sophia."

The woman ignored the outstretched hand, "I'm Emma" She said as she headed to the passenger seat and got in unceremoniously.

Sophia awkwardly lowered the rejected hand and took a deep breath. She wanted to launch into a lecture about manners, but she thought back to Miles and guilt consumed her. She didn't know if she would ever be able to let go of the feelings that her son's failures were her fault. She wondered if it was her constant lecturing that led him to have such hatred for her and all she held dear. She vowed to try and handle tough situations differently and said a prayer as she closed the back doors "Lord help me to reach her heart for you and not react in anger to her rudeness." She got into the driver's seat and they set off driving again.

Sophia started off the drive asking questions, but each thing she asked was met with a shrug of the shoulders. It was clear her new friend did not want to talk, so they sat in silence watching the trees whizz past them in a blur. They hadn't driven for more than fifteen minutes when Emma spoke up for the first time since they had gotten in the car, "Look!" She sounded skeptical, but with a hint of fear lacing her words. She pointed out a railroad crossing sign up ahead on the side of the road.

Sophia pulled over to the side of the road and they both sat in silence trying to figure out if they should keep going.

Emma was the first to speak up, "There are so many railroad tracks. How would you even know if this is the same one as your dream? We should keep going."

Just then though, they both saw two children run from the tree line at the railroad tracks and two men raced after them and dragged them out of view, back into the trees. If they hadn't been staring intently in that direction they would have missed it, but there was no denying what they saw. Children and men were hiding among the trees at the railroad track up ahead.

Sophia began to think about her next move. She could reverse the car around and head the way she came, but there were no other side streets from here to the town she just left where the man had just tried to carjack her only a little earlier. It wasn't just the thief that worried her. It seemed the whole town she just left wanted her car.

She was still thinking over her options when she noticed movement in the trees up ahead. When she looked closer, she could see many people trying to stealthily make their way through the trees toward the two women in the car. They had made good progress before Sophia noticed them. They were closer than she would have liked. She would just have to risk going back to the town she just left.

"Hold on!" Sophia put the car in reverse and punched the gas as hard as she could. She looked over and saw Emma with one hand on the roof, the other hand on the window, and her foot on the ground desperately trying to push an imaginary brake pedal.

She went in reverse at top speeds until the people were half a football field away. Without warning, she stopped, put the car in drive, and did a u-turn that practically made the car go up on two wheels.

Emma started yelling, "Ok. Ok. It's official. I was right. You're crazy."

Sophia nervously chucked as she continued to drive away. She looked in the rearview mirror and saw that the group was much larger than she first thought. They all stood still on the road as they stared angrily at the retreating car. She took a deep breath and briefly closed her eyes as she felt a sense of relief wash over her. In that brief moment of gathering her composure, she missed seeing a pile of glass on the road. All of a sudden, she felt her tire blow out.

She struggled to maintain control of the wheel as they were skidding sideways down the road before they came to a sudden stop. They both just stared at each other in stunned silence. Sophia saw the group at the train tracks start running toward the disabled car.

Sophia thought to herself that at least they had more of a head start now. She grabbed the packed backpack from the backseat as she told Emma: "We have to go! Now!" Emma seemed to shake from a daze and grabbed a couple of items and raced out of the car joining Sophia.

They ran away from the car into the tree line opposite where everyone was approaching. Instead of heading straight toward their destination, they went the opposite way deep into the trees as far as they could. They didn't stop running until they were sure they weren't being pursued.

Sophia looked behind her and didn't see any sign of anyone following them. Everything was quiet. They both stopped to catch their breath. It appeared the people wanted the car and what was in it more than they wanted the ladies. Although, Sophia had a suspicion that, if they would have been captured, the people from the tracks would have considered it a bonus. She shuddered at what could have been and sent up a silent prayer of thanks for God's hand of protection.

Sophia looked at Emma, "I'm not sure what to do now. I have the address memorized where we are headed, but I don't have my map."

Emma reached into her back pocket and unfolded the map she snatched as she ran out of the car, "You mean this? I guess it's a good thing you brought me along then, huh?" It was the first time Sophia had seen her smile and it was beautiful, "I figured it was important."

Sophia hugged her fiercely. She was so grateful not to be alone and to have the map. She was overwhelmed with emotion. Emma laughed and peeled Sophia's arms off from around her neck, "Come on, Let's go. I'm guessing we have a long walk ahead of us."

Miles' bosses took notice that he reported his own father to the cause of Elyon and he received a promotion. He was the new "Enforcement Director of the Midwestern Region." This region was extended to include every city in the central time zone. He was in charge of making sure each city in his jurisdiction was properly enforcing the requirement of Elyon's mark for all its population.

He smiled inwardly knowing this would give him the access he needed to thoroughly investigate the city of Jasper that his dad had scribbled on the pad next to his bed so Miles could locate his mom. He couldn't let himself become consumed by that yet. One thing at a time. Right now, he had to focus on his hometown of Nebraska City as well as Omaha where his headquarters were located. His orders to ensure those two cities were in complete compliance took priority. Had his orders been just for the town of Nebraska City, he could have been on the road to Jasper by morning, but enforcing the edicts for the city of Omaha would take significantly longer.

The more quickly he finished, the more quickly he could turn his attention to Jasper where he expected to find his mom. Even if he had to search for her in his time off, he didn't care. Whatever it took, he would see to it that every knee, including his mother's, bowed to Elyon.

Robert and Beth were the first to arrive at Tom's land that evening with John and Katie trailing a little ways behind. They were all soaking wet and covered in mud. It had rained almost the whole way and the last hour was all dirt roads. They could hardly recognize one another when they finally arrived. They were almost there. Only the ascending driveway leading to Tom's house remained, then their almost weeklong ordeal would finally be over.

The driveway seemed unsafe even for walking. Shards of glass, down trees, and old lumber with rusty nails blocked it's entire length. Beth wondered if her dad still lived here, or if their traveling was for nought.

John and Katie caught up to them and Beth thought to

herself, "Oh well, no turning back now," as she led the group to the land just a little to the side of the driveway. Parts of the land were overgrown with weeds and grass as high as their waist and other parts appeared barren and covered with nothing more than dead grass and leaves. Robert walked beside her and in a few moments, she was able to see the outline of the house. "There it is!" she pointed excitedly.

As everyone followed the direction that her hand was pointing they saw the outline of a house in the distance. It looked abandoned but they didn't care. It was a shelter. Everyone quickened their pace eager to finally be able to rest for a little while.

It was Beth who first heard the groaning crack of old wood splintering. She looked next to her. Robert was there walking the fastest she had seen him walk all day out of excitement to almost be done. He suddenly stopped walking as he gave her a look of surprise before he looked down to his feet and then disappeared, "Robert!" She screamed and ran over to him followed closely behind by Katie and John.

When Beth reached the area where she last saw Robert, she saw that the hole in the ground that had swallowed him was only about eight feet deep. It had been covered by old deteriorated plywood. She looked at the remaining plywood that did not fall into the hole with Robert and saw it had been camouflaged by dry dead leaves and grass. It was a trap.

She looked into the hole and saw Robert bleeding and unconscious. Bamboo spikes were sticking up from the ground all around the trap. His leg was suspended from the pointed stick, which was protruding from his shin just above his ankle where it had impaled him. The rest of his body lay at an awkward angle. His body was hanging down from his suspended leg and resting on the ground below the spike. It was a miracle he had not been impaled by any other of the spikes protruding all around him. He was not hit in any vital organs, but he was still severely injured.

John jumped into action and scaled down the side of the pit to the bottom. He surveyed the damage to his father-in-law and saw that the blood was only coming from his leg. John surmised that he probably hit his head hard enough to knock him unconscious when his leg got impaled. He would have to lift the injured leg off the spike, then treat it quickly before he bled too much. There was no guarantee he wouldn't still bleed out. They had no modern medicine. As he was weighing all his options he heard the unmistakable sound of a pump-action shotgun being cocked and ready to fire above him.

John felt like a caged animal wanting to strike, but being powerless at the bottom of the hole while his wife was at the top with a gun pointed at her. He heard a man speak in a strong southern drawl, "I don' know what ya'll thank you're doin' here on m' property, but you lil ladies have 'til the coun' o' three to leave 'fore I start shootin'.

Beth took a step forward timidly and the man moved the aim of his gun from Katie over to Beth. He was clearly agitated at aiming his weapon at a young girl, "I ain't never shot no woman, but I will if I have to if you take one step closer.

Beth stopped, "Daddy?" She asked in a voice that sounded like a little girl

Tom began to slowly lower his weapon to the ground in disbelief. Then his common sense got the better of him and he raised his weapon again to the girl in front of him, "You won't be foolin' me, playin' to my soft side! Get off my property whoe'er y' are.

Beth put her hand over her heart, "It's me, Beth. Mama and Davie are dead. I've been all alone. But then I remembered the card you sent me for my birthday." She pulled out the birthday card from her back pocket that she had carried throughout the trip to help them remember the address, "and I thought maybe you could help me.

Tom lowered the gun, he was completely convinced that she was who she claimed to be. He stood as still as a statue in complete shock. Beth spoke to him again: "Please daddy, these are my friends. You have to help him!" She pointed down into the trap where Robert lay injured.

Tom shook off the stupor temporarily paralyzing him and sprang into action. He carefully laid down the loaded shotgun, pointing it away from all of them, and he climbed down into the pit. When he saw the injured man, he took off his belt. He tied it tightly around the leg above the point of impalement, "This is so he doesn't bleed out when we take the leg off of the spike" He explained to John.

Tom asked John, "You got a knife?" John shook his head no and Tom just rolled his eyes at the unpreparedness of city-folk. He then took out the longest pocket knife John had ever seen and a lighter. He held the blade of the knife over the flame until it faintly glowed red. He handed it to John, "Here, when we take his leg off you gonna put this directly on the wound to help stop the bleedin'. Put the handle in your teeth when you're done."

To John's amazement, the man then reached up to John's

shoulder, "You don' mind if I use yur shirt to tie up the wound when yure done cauterizing it?" He didn't even wait for an answer before he ripped off the sleeve of John's shirt. He stuck the top of the sleeve into his mouth and began ripping it from top to bottom making it one long sheet that he planned to tie around the man's leg. John was shocked, it was like the man was some sort of cowboy superhero.

Tom turned to John, "Ya genna stand there starin' with your mouth open or ya genna help me?" He reached over to Robert's foot and put his hand underneath it, "On the count of three I'm genna lift his foot and you're genna lift his body so we even until he off the spike." The man didn't pause for air, John thought. "One, two, three!"

The two men lifted Robert well over their heads until he was free of the spike. The hole in the leg instantly started gushing blood that had previously been stopped up by the wood sticking through the hole. John sprang into action and took the handle of the still hot knife out of his mouth and held it in his hands. He took a deep breath hesitating for just a second before he placed the blade on Robert's leg.

That woke Robert up from his unconscious slumber. Robert screamed as John smelled the odor of burning flesh. He heard Tom's voice say, "Again, the other side of his leg" and John realized he wasn't done. He had to hear his poor father-in-law suffer yet again. He turned the blade over to the other side that was still burning hot and placed it against the other bleeding hole. Robert screamed like John had never heard a human scream before, then passed out from the pain.

The wound oozed, so Tom took John's shredded sleeve, wrapped it around the wound, and tied the cloth tightly in case the bleeding started again. He then scaled his way up out of the hole and looked at the women, "Any you ladies got a rope in them bags of yurs?"

With shaky hands, Beth reached into her backpack and took out the rope that they used to hang the food from the trees when they camped and handed it to her dad.

Tom nodded his head in thanks as he took the rope and threw one end over the edge and yelled down into the hole, "Tie it underneath his arms. Then you push while I pull."

John tied the rope around Robert, "Ok pull!" He got underneath Robert and helped by pushing him up as Tom yanked on the rope from up top. Finally, Robert was out of the hole and lying unconscious on the ground. John climbed out of the pit behind him and collapsed on the ground catching his breath.

Tom looked at the weary travelers and said, "Ain't no time to stop now. You got yourselves an injured man that needs tendin." He hooked his hands underneath Robert's arms and looked impatiently at John. John had never felt such exhaustion, but he had to push himself just a little bit further. He stood up and took Robert's feet and the two men carried him back to the house.

As they walked carrying their patient between them, Tom yelled out, "Would one of you ladies make sure to get my gun right quick?" So, Katie and Beth followed behind them, wrangling the two bikes, the backpacks, and Tom's gun.

They all set off toward the house and Tom gave them one final warning, "Make sure you follow the path I set real careful-like. I got a lot more traps like that one we just left."

CHAPTER SIXTEEN

"I looked when he opened the sixth seal, and behold, there was a great earthquake; and the sun became black as sackcloth of hair, and the moon became like blood." - Revelation 6:12

Sophia and Emma made their way through the woods over the course of the next day. They stayed far away from any signs of life, either animal or human. They stayed off all the roads and traveled in the woods beside the highways they were supposed to be on to get to Tom's house.

It was going to take them a full day to get to where they were going and to pass the time Sophia kept talking to Emma trying to learn more about her. She saw a sad faraway look in Emma's eyes when she asked the question, "Do you have any family?"

When Emma didn't answer, Sophia assumed she asked a sensitive question, and they walked together in silence. After a little while, Emma spoke up, "I used to have a family." Sophia stayed quiet and just listened, giving Emma a chance to share what was weighing her down. "I had a perfect family. A husband and two kids.

We went to church every Sunday and I served God with everything I had. I sang on the worship team, I volunteered in the Sunday school classroom and I even participated in the once-a-month homeless outreach. God was everything to me."

She turned to Sophia with anger burning behind her glassy eyes, "We aren't supposed to be here for this you know. We were supposed to escape all of this. How could a God who loved us leave us here like this?" Sophia nodded in understanding, but not in agreement.

She saw so much of Miles in Emma. She saw all the same questions and the same anger. She had heard arguments against God many times from Miles. She would share the truth with Emma soon but now was not the time. Now was the time to just listen. She prayed that God would redeem her failures to reach her son by allowing her to do a better job with this woman beside her.

Emma turned her face back to the path ahead of them, "When Elyon declared himself as God, I knew I had gotten it wrong about being raptured before the end-times began. It was then I started to get so mad at God. My husband kept me from letting my bitterness grow though. He kept reminding me to trust God. Even when he was arrested and tortured for preaching the Gospel he still encouraged me to have faith in God."

Emma continued to share the story with Sophia of how her husband couldn't find work and, as a result, there wasn't enough money most weeks to buy their rations. "I was mad at God already and us all having empty stomachs didn't help that. One time I scraped enough money together and waited in line all day. I got to the front and was so excited to finally have food to feed my babies.

When I left the store, it was raining and I slipped and fell. The groceries went everywhere, spoiling half of them. The other half thieves ran away with. I begged for them to let me go through again and buy some more, but the workers refused. I had already used my ration allotment for the week.

There was a kind man in the line who gave me his ration for the week which I tried to feed to my babies... but it was too little too late. They died of starvation. The very next day, my husband died from the disease so many had. I left and drove until I ran out of gas. Then I walked not knowing where I was going. I was just trying to get as far as I could from the memories."

Emma turned to look at Sophia, "Tell me, how can a loving and good God stand by and watch as little children starve to death? How can a kind God allow us to stay here and suffer instead of rapturing us up before all this happened?"

Sophia took a deep breath and prayed knowing her words would never fully ease this woman's pain. Only the peace that God could bring would provide the comfort she truly needed, but she would try, "All of those things are so horrible. I am so sorry, Emma. Your family sounded beautiful. You know God didn't do any of those things right? People did.

An evil man started us down a path that led to death and disease. It was desperate people who stole your food while you laid on the pavement outside the store. You're angry at the wrong person."

Emma angrily wiped away a tear from her eye, frustrated with herself that she was crying, "Yeah, but if God is so powerful he could have stopped it."

Sophia agreed, "Yes, he could have stopped it, but then what of those thieves' free will? He wanted to give them a chance to repent to come to him. He has had a protective hand on our world restraining the evil in men's hearts for so long. He has only recently removed that hand. We are seeing the evil that really lurks in people if they don't have God. All of this is so that as many as possible can be saved and live forever in heaven. Sometimes He does stop evil. Like he did with us on the train tracks."

Emma picked up her pace now, the stride of her walk matching the frustration she felt, "He shouldn't have dont that! Why did he save me and not them? I would have sacrificed myself a thousand times if my boys would still be alive!"

Sophia's short legs struggled to keep up with her, "I know. You sound like you are a good mother."

Emma interrupted, "Was. I was a good mother."

Sophia nodded sadly before continuing, "God must have some purpose left for you here on this earth before you get to enjoy a life of no more pain. Think of it like this. You've been in church, so you know what's prophesied that's yet to come. It's going to get a lot worse before it gets better. Your precious boys don't have to experience any of that. They get to rest in heaven with their daddy. They're probably playing tag in some field of flowers with their dad right now. They are laughing and happy. It'll be your turn to play with them there soon, but not yet. First, you have work to do."

Emma kicked at a rock in front of her with each step, "It just doesn't make sense. We shouldn't have to suffer at all.

What's the point of life!"

Sophia was struggling to find the right words. She knew that suffering was just a part of life. God wasn't some Santa Claus that just gave presents and granted wishes. She thought of the questions that had gone through her mind years ago as she watched Miles begin his descent away from Christ. It used to make her so mad when Miles questioned God's goodness. She would tell him, "How can we say we trust and follow God if we only do so when everything is good? Isn't that conditional love? Do we only love God when he gives us exactly what we want, but the second things get tough we bolt?" They were all valid points, but she still lost her son. Maybe if she had prayed more about how to reach him he wouldn't be lost forever.

Sophia shook herself out of her self-incriminating thoughts and tried to be fully present hearing Emma's questions. She tried to be patient with Emma and prayed that she would only give answers that would draw Emma's heart closer to God and not push it further away from Him. The young woman beside her was hurting. She probably had a wrong mindset about God before all this which made it harder for her to accept the curve balls life threw at her, "I guess the point of all of this is that God wants us to trust Him. There will be good, but there will be bad. He wants us to trust Him both on the mountains and in the valleys. Only he can see the end from the beginning and he has a plan that we can't see. We are supposed to know that, if we love Him, he promises that He will work together on all of these hard things for our good. It will turn out ok in the end."

Emma slowed down her walk allowing Sophia to catch up

and catch her breath as she mulled all that over. Sadness was still in her voice, but less angry "I still wish the Christians escaped all this."

"If I'm going to be honest, so do I. That would have been easier no doubt. I think about my son, Miles. I believe he was pulling away, but still loved the Lord before Elyon came onto the scene. If the rapture would have happened before the tribulation he could be in heaven with me, but instead, he is lost forever. I guess this whole thing revealed what was truly in his heart that was unseen."

Sophia had to stop as emotion stopped her voice. She took a minute to compose herself before continuing, "Think of how many people would have been left confused without anyone to guide them to the truth if all the Christians were gone. We have seen so many deceived by Elyon, I can't imagine how much higher the number would have been if true Christians weren't here to badly speak the Biblical truth they had been studying their whole life.

Plus think of it. We get to be like the Christians in the book of Acts! We are living in a time of Christian history that neither has been nor will ever be again. We are seeing miracles. Just look at the dreams that saved our lives. Could you have imagined those dreams even just three years ago?

I know the pain of loss. I miss my husband. When the pain overwhelms you remember to trust in Jesus. We only have a very short time until we will all be together again."

Emma's face showed a warring of pain and hope. They had passed the day talking and didn't realize they had reached Tom's home.

They started up the driveway and saw that it was

impassable. It was littered with so much debris. They decided to walk on the land going around it when the ground began to shake and they both looked at each other with wide eyes as Emma spoke in a voice filled with exasperation as she rolled her eyes, "What now?"

Benjamin and Rachel made it back to the mountain where they had lived until recently. They stood at the opening of the cave that had been home for many months scanning their faces and looking for their parents. They saw their mom sitting and talking with their dad. She somehow sensed their gaze and suddenly looked up from her conversation and looked straight at them.

She let out a squeal, jumped up, and raced to greet them. The three of them embraced, held each other, and cried. The world had changed so much. A short absence felt so long because everything was life or death. They didn't know if they'd see each other again before heaven. When they finished hugging, their mother stood between her two children, her arms around both of them as they walked over to where Jacob sat. Jacob was one of many people in the cave hiding from the antichrist army.

Jacob was standing waiting for his kids to get close and when they did he took them into his arms one by one in a fiercely strong hug. His two grown children stood in front of him and placed one firm hand on each of their shoulders as he looked at them with moist eyes, "I have been worried. How have you been?"

Benjamin sat down and motioned for his father to do the

same next to him. The family sat in a circle as Benjamin and Rachel took turns sharing everything that had happened to them since they had left their parents.

They told their parents about all the miracles they witnessed, and how many people surrendered to Jesus even though it had meant certain death for them. They shared the stories of the mark of the beast and how many people were becoming consumed by hate and choosing to worship Elyon.

When Rachel finished the last of the details of what they experienced, Benjamin turned to his dad, "Do you believe us dad that it all happened like we said it did?"

Jacob thought long before answering. "Yes, son. I trust you. If you say that's what happened, then I take you at your word."

Benjamin smiled, "Then are you ready to give your life to Jesus?"

Jacob took it all in, "You present a convincing story children, but I'm just not ready yet."

Benjamin nodded sadly. He didn't understand why he could preach and strangers would have their hearts softened, but he couldn't convince the person he loved most in the world. He said a silent prayer that the Lord would continue to work on his dad as they moved on to different topics and started their dinner.

Not long after they started eating, they heard a low rumbling begin in the mountain. They and everyone around them began to stand looking to see what was happening. That's when it all clicked for Benjamin, "It's the sixth seal. This must be the beginning of the great earthquake prophesied in Revelation."

Those who had the seal of protection on their forehead agreed. Benjamin ran to the mouth of the cave. As he looked out, he saw the land beyond the mountain looked odd. It looked like the hills in the distance weren't stationary. They looked like waves you might see in an ocean, but instead of blue and watery, they were green and grassy as they moved up and down.

Benjamin yelled back to everyone behind him in the cave who were waiting for a report of what he was seeing, "It looks like the earth is rolling and rippling as far as I can see." As he spoke, rocks started falling inside the cave as the earth continued to shake.

Benjamin ran back to his parents and yelled out, "Quickly, everyone that has the mark of the Lord, protect those that are not sealed." So all of those with the blue shield of protection engraved on their forehead became a human shield over those that had no seal protecting them. As rocks rained down all around them, those that took shelter under those that were sealed were not harmed.

John and Tom had no sooner got Robert in the house, resting on a bed, when then the shaking began. It was a violent shaking that seemed to rattle the whole house. Picture frames fell from the walls and the dishes came crashing out of the cabinets onto the floor. John saw Katie and Beth struggle to stand as they staggered their way to an open doorway to brace for support from the falling objects all around them.

They got into the doorway just as a large gun cabinet in the living room crashed to the floor behind them. John felt like the ground was rolling underneath him and he was starting to feel seasick as the shaking just wouldn't seem to stop. They all looked up as a large crack formed in the roof from one end of the house to the other.

Each minute that the quake continued, the house seemed to get destroyed a little more. At five minutes, the earthquake was still going strong. John yelled over the noise of the shaking and crashing toward Tom, "Do earthquakes normally last this long in this part of the country?"

The previously invincible mountain man was white as a ghost afraid as he shook his head, "Ain't never heard about no earthquakes in these parts."

Every day Miles had a quota to fill. He had to visit a certain number of houses that had residents who hadn't been registered as receiving the mark. Miles was in a high-rise building in the city finishing his daily quota when he felt the building he was in begin to sway.

He walked to the large glass window of the second floor and saw the tall buildings surrounding him looked like they were swaying like a tree might in a windy storm. As he stood at the window, he saw the glass shatter from the building across from him. The building next to that one suddenly buckled from the intensity of the shaking and crashed to the ground with all its occupants still inside.

He realized standing next to the window was not smart and ran to try and get out of the building, but just at that moment, something crashed blocking his exit so he instead, on wobbly feet, ran underneath a desk, praying to Elyon that it would stop and he would be spared death.

Elyon was busy working at his desk when the first tremors shook his building. It was such a jarring jolt, that he momentarily lost the cool and calm demeanor that he had at all times. Francis came running into the room frantically, "It's an earthquake. I just got a call that it's the biggest one they have ever seen. We have to get you out of the city. Follow me to the chopper on the roof."

Francis fled the room and ran up the stairs to the rooftop access where his private helicopter was waiting, already running with its blades spinning ready to deliver the leader of the world to safety.

He and Francis climbed in quickly. Two other staff workers filed onto the rooftop right before the chopper lifted off. They were running toward him begging to be included in the chopper and escape the earthquake.

Elyon put on his headphones and spoke into the mic to the pilot, "Don't you dare pick them up. There is no time, get me out of here. Now!" The pilot obeyed his orders and lifted off. They were in the air for a minute hovering above the rooftop as the pilot was configuring the GPS. Elyon looked below him and saw the people he had left disappear into a dust cloud as the building he just left collapsed.

The pilot veered the chopper quickly out of the way of the rising dust pile from the destroyed building and quickly adjusted to gain altitude. Elyon looked around him and saw devastation everywhere. He saw the ground look like it was rolling as if it were the ocean and not solid ground. He saw the mountains in the distance shaking so much it appeared they were shifting locations just a little with each shake. He saw the buildings below him in piles of rubble with fires breaking out everywhere. Even the forest had been decimated as trees were strewn all over the ground from cracking and the strain of the sustained shaking.

He was filled with rage because he knew this was no ordinary earthquake. He angrily thought to himself that it was the God of heaven wreaking havoc on his kingdom. He took his headset off as he looked out the window, "God has all of heaven, how dare he try to insert himself into my domain!"

Francis looked at him and mouthed the words, "What'd you say?" Elyon just shook his head 'no' to Francis letting him know he wasn't talking to him. He looked out the window and saw that the earthquake was not stopping. It had been ten minutes and still, the earth shook. He put back on his headset and looked at Francis, "How far away are the reports saying this earthquake is reaching."

Francis looked at him and was full of fear, "Initial reports have just been reported to me; its current reach is seven thousand miles. Every minute the quake continues, its reach widens. The whole world is feeling this quake to some degree.

Elyon looked down and saw the rolling of the ground slowly begin to subside. It was finally dying down. He was about to ask the pilot to put him down somewhere safe when he looked out to the ocean in the far distance and saw what looked like a giant wall heading directly for them. He spoke urgently to the pilot "Get me inland now! A tsunami is coming!"

When the quake ended, Benjamin stopped shielding his father from falling debris and looked around. Not a single person was harmed. As he took in the faces around him he saw many new faces he had never seen before. It seemed newcomers had decided to join them in hiding in the cave. Benjamin walked up to someone in a military uniform, "Hi, I'm Benjamin. You are?"

The man looked up at him with the dead eyes that had become all too familiar to Benjamin by now, "I'm Major Wallace. I'm part of an operational team searching for insurgents in the area." He paused and looked around the room at the people praying and reading Bibles as they recovered from surviving such an ordeal. "It seems as though I found some when I stumbled into this cave seeking shelter from the quake. You will all be coming with me before the day is over."

The Major walked over to the mouth of the cave to look out and it was then he saw a wall of water headed toward them. Looking at his fearful face, Benjamin and Rachel walked over to see what he was looking at. They saw the water coming, but they were high in the mountain so the water hit well below the mouth of the cave before rushing past. The water raced by like a rapid against the base of the cave and continued its path of destruction heading toward the city. Benjamin tried to wrack his brain if he had ever seen a tsunami travel that far inland as he walked back to his parents with Rachel.

The Major was mesmerized by the tsunami that had surrounded their cave. It was several minutes before he took his eyes off their new landscape and turned to face the insurgents behind him. When he finally turned around he saw a wall of young people all with a blue shield on their foreheads. Those without a shield were standing behind them. Benjamin stepped forward from his place on the wall, "You are welcome to try and arrest those here without the seal of protection." He paused as he took one more step closer to the Major, "But I don't recommend it."

The major and his men stood in anger. They were not outmanned, but they knew they didn't have a chance against so many that had the seal of protection on their head. He had seen others preaching with the blue shield on their forehead. He remembered how all his men were completely unable to stop them. All their attempts failed and some of his men had even died unexplainable sudden deaths when they attacked someone with a blue shield. So, he backed off and sat at the mouth of the cave with his men waiting for the water to recede enough for them to be able to leave.

When the trembling finally stopped, John heard the faint ringing of bells. "That's odd, what's that sound?" John asked Tom.

Something clicked with Tom and he said, "That's my perimeter alarm I rigged up. It's how I knew y'all were here. Sheesh, it's one thing after another!" He grabbed his shotgun the girls had brought back to the house and ran out with John following close behind him, careful to not step anywhere Tom didn't step.

When they got to the front of the property they spied from a hidden spot who it was that was approaching uninvited. John sprang up from out of their hiding spot, surprising Tom, "That's my mom! That's my mom! Tom, quick, go to her, make sure she doesn't fall into one of your traps."

Tom looked at him surprised, "Ya brought a whole party with ya didn't ya?" He said as he raced to catch up to the women before they hit the first booby trap. When he stood before them a tired Sophia said, "Are you Tom?"

Tom laughed surprised and said, "Well how'd ya know that?"

She smiled weakly, "It's a long story. Can we go sit inside and I'll tell you all about it?"

Tom agreed and they followed him up to where John had stayed hidden. Tom left so quickly that John wasn't able to follow in the path behind him making sure to not fall into any of the traps, so he stayed where he was, out of sight, anxiously waiting. When his mom got close to the spot where he sat, he jumped out, startling her just like he used to love to do when he was a boy, "Mom!"

She fell backward from fright and Tom caught her in his arms before she hit the ground. It didn't take her long to recover and when she did she ran to her son's arms, "My boy!" They held each other for such a long time and just wept in each other's arms before Tom said, "Why don' we bring this reunion back to the house?"

Sophia and John followed behind Tom and Emma, catching up on all that had happened since he last saw her. He had his arm protectively around her shoulders and she leaned her head against his shoulder as they walked. In the relatively short walk to the house, they talked about so many things. John told her the details of his wedding, about the visions he started having, and about how Beverly was now waiting for them in Heaven, but John knew he had to get to the most important topic, "I know about dad, mom."

Sophia stopped, shocked. What do you mean? How can you know?

"Katie saw him in a dream in heaven in a white robe resting by the water. He was happy and waving, mom."

Sophia was taking in every word he said. Emma was trying not to eavesdrop on such a personal conversation, but couldn't help herself. Something about the man, John, looked so familiar to her. She slowed to walk a little closer to them, so she wouldn't miss any details. Sophia didn't care who heard their conversation. She wanted to know every detail, "Are you sure John? He was happy?"

John gave his mom a little squeeze, "Yes mom. Katie said she never saw a smile so big."

His mom with her little short legs was practically skipping now, "Hurry up John. I can't wait to see my new daughter and have her tell me everything!"

On the walk to the house, John's attention shifted to Emma and he did a double take. It was the woman from the grocery store who lost all her food.

Emma saw him staring at her and became annoyed at his perusal, "Can I help you with something?"

John shook himself out of his stupor, "I'm sorry to stare. It's just I think we've met before. At the grocery store. In the rain."

John saw her hardened expression turn to soft and then sad at the memory. He saw tears well up in her eyes that she was unable to stop. He realized then he made a terrible mistake bringing up that encounter. She was alone. Those two boys he saw at the store weren't with her anymore. He wished he realized sooner that something terrible must have happened to those two severely malnourished boys he saw with her.

He felt stupid and apologized, "I'm so sorry. I didn't mean to bring up something painful."

Emma angrily wiped away her tears that she was powerless to stop, "Not your fault. Thanks for the food. You were about the only kind person I've met these last few months. Now can we change the subject?"

Emma walked briskly past all of them toward the house, ending the conversation. John looked toward his mom and she gave him a sad smile.

Sophia said, "She's been through a lot, John. Poor thing. Why am I not surprised that you found a way to help someone in need?"

His mom smiled a proud smile and gave him a hug as they walked the last few steps to the house.

When they got to the house, Sophia hugged Katie as if she had been her daughter from birth and she introduced herself to Beth. Other than Robert who still laid unconscious on the bed, it was a joyous reunion filled with laughter and tears.

When everyone had finished greeting Sophia, Tom asked to speak to Beth privately. They walked outside to the back porch and sat on two rocking chairs in awkward silence. Tom didn't know how to start a conversation with the daughter he hadn't seen in almost a decade. "I'd ask how ya been, but I spect it's the same as we've all been. Rotten."

Beth laughed at how cute her dad was. He was obviously trying to connect with her, but he was failing miserably. He needed some help, so she decided to steer the topic to something more positive than how rotten everything had been. "Thank you for all the birthday cards. I should have written back."

Tom stopped rocking and looked at her sadly. The big mountain man suddenly appeared vulnerable and small, "Why didn't you?"

Beth kept rocking and looked off in the distance as she spoke, "I had so much anger. I regret it now."

Tom shrugged his shoulders trying to act tough, "Don't blame you. There's no time in life for people that do you wrong."

With his words, Beth realized how wrong she had been for not forgiving her father sooner. She realized how much she had been forgiven by Christ. "No, Daddy. I don't think that's right. I was wrong to not forgive you for everything. I missed so much time I could've had with you."

Tom shook his head and looked away from her off into the distance, "Nah, weren't your fault. I wun't the best dad to ya when you were with me. I didn't spend enough time with ya or treat your mom that good. You had every right to be mad."

They continued to rock in silence when John turned away from looking off into nothing and, instead, looked back at his daughter as he stopped rocking again, "I have missed ya Bethy."

Beth smiled, she had completely forgotten the nickname,

'Bethy' that he called her when she was little. She had hated him so much for so long for not loving them enough. She felt abandoned when he didn't fight to see her more. She was so focused on the fact that he wasn't the dad she wished she had, that she had missed out on enjoying the love he could give her. She took his hand in hers, "I'm glad I'm here with you, daddy."

He looked at his little girl's hands and felt tears sting his eyes. He stood up from his rocking chair trying to fight the emotion welling up inside of him. He wanted to lean down and kiss her on the top of her head like he did when she was a little girl, but he stopped himself. He had this weird feeling of not knowing how to be a dad to this almost grown-up girl in front of him. So, instead, he smiled a goofy big smile, "Me too Bethy, me too."

He reached out his hand to her and she took it as he helped her up from the rocking chair. All of them had spent a lot of time catching up on old times and new trials. There would be more time in the future to try and make up for lost time, but right now they needed to find out more information if they were going to survive all the craziness happening around them.

The EMP took out all electronics, but Tom was prepared. He kept a few essential electronics in a faraday cage that protected items from the effects of an EMP. Tom went to get the ham radio that he had kept in the EMP-proof box and put it in the middle of the living room of the coffee table.

It was like a scene out of the Waltons television show. The radio was in the middle of the room and a group of people were crowded around it in a circle. No longer was it an option to have some of them sitting on the couches watching TV while others in the same room were on their phones and laptops. The days of everyone being physically together while, emotionally, being simultaneously miles apart was a thing of the past for this group. Instead, they listened together to the radio and every detail of news from the outside world was more interesting than any social media app had ever been.

As they listened to the radio they were shocked to hear that the entire earth had felt the earthquake, some places more than others. The epicenter was in Israel at the temple. There were reports of massive casualties and tsunamis and aftershocks that were continuing to increase the death toll. The government was saying that because of the prolonged disruption of the earthquake, all of the mountains and islands of the earth were on a slightly shifted latitudinal and longitudinal plane.

John looked at the group that had gathered in the small house, "I guess we just entered the sixth seal."

Katie looked up at John with so much hope and life in her eyes, "John, we are getting so close now to His coming. I can hardly wait."

Sophia spoke then, "This was different from all the other seal judgments so far. All the other ones have been caused by man's selfish and evil decisions. The food withheld caused starvation, the wars caused death and disease. All of it was from the actions of man. This is the first time we are seeing a judgment from God himself on the decisions these evil men are making."

John agreed, "This validates everything Christians have been saying all along. This is the end of time and Elyon is the antichrist. Those that have not sold their soul to the devil yet will maybe now see the truth, that it is God who is in control!"

Miles emerged from under his desk when the last of the tremors had stopped. He had to pick his way through the piles just to get to the exit. The exit was completely blocked with fallen pieces of roof and concrete walls. His hands bled as he picked up large chunks of concrete and rebar over and over until his hands became raw.

It took him hours, but he finally made his way outside and was able to take in his first deep breath of semi-clean air. There were still dust clouds all around him from the recently fallen buildings that made it hard to take in a full deep breath.

He looked up to the sky at a patch of the sun peeking through the dust cloud and saw something strange. He didn't think he remembered hearing any reports of a solar eclipse happening that day, but that is exactly what he saw. The moon was moving in front of the sun and the sky suddenly shifted to total darkness. He had seen solar eclipses before. This felt different. It shouldn't last very long, but it seemed like the moon was stuck in place and the darkness seemed to permeate the air all around him.

He looked back up to the sky and saw a bit of the sun peeking out around the edges of the moon. He had to do a double take as he looked at the moon which was blocking the majority of all the light. The moon started to take on a glow of its own. It started black as it blocked the sun, but then turned a yellow color that morphed its way into red. The moon was as red as blood, but it didn't just look like the color red, the moon looked like it was covered in a thick blood paste and was stuck in the middle of the sky.

Miles knew then that the earthquake he just survived and now the sun turning black in the middle of the day and being stuck in a state of a solar eclipse was not just a natural disaster. It was one of the judgments of God his dad and brother used to talk about eventually coming and he was filled with rage. He was filled with rage because he knew then that there was a battle between the God in heaven he always heard about and Elyon. He was filled with hatred that God would dare to judge him.

CHAPTER SEVENTEEN

"And the stars of heaven fell to the earth, as a fig tree drops its late figs when it is shaken by a mighty wind. Then the sky receded as a scroll when it is rolled up, and every mountain and island was moved out of its place. And the kings of the earth, the great men, the rich men, the commanders, the mighty men, every slave and every free man, hid themselves in the caves and in the rocks of the mountains, and said to the mountains and rocks, 'Fall on us and hide us from the face of Him who sits on the throne and from the wrath of the Lamb! For the great day of His wrath has come, and who is able to stand?'" - Revelation 6:13-17

It had been four days of pitch blackness at Tom's house. He did his best to listen to the Ham radio for updates, but it seemed like the disturbance in the sky was messing up his radio frequencies and reception. He was only able to get bits and pieces of the news. From what he could gather, there was an unexpected solar eclipse that occurred about six hours from his home and the sun and the moon had stood still in that same location for four days now.

The whole world had been thrown into darkness and it was messing everything up. He never realized how much he relied on the sun for everything. Even something as simple as telling time had become incredibly difficult. None of them had old-school watches on. Most of them used to rely on their phones to know what time it was.

When the EMP came that put an end to that for all of them, but Sophia. It had been alright though because they still had the sun. They had a good general estimate of when they should wake up, eat, and go to bed. Now, their bodies felt completely disoriented and they didn't know when it was day or when it was night. Some of them were suffering from insomnia, while others would fall asleep often, but never sleep well. They felt like they were in a state of perpetual jetlag.

The scientists were trying to explain this cosmic disturbance away as the earth was temporarily being off of its axis and it had stopped its normal rotation. They were still struggling to come up with a reason why. Many were trying to theorize that the prolonged earthquake had resulted in a disturbance to the rotational pattern of the earth causing it to appear that the sun and moon stood still. That explanation seemed to make more sense to Tom than that it was a judgment from God as John and Sophia were trying to tell him.

Another thing he didn't expect when he first saw that the sun wasn't coming back right away was how cold it got. It didn't take long at all for the temperatures to drop and without the sun to warm things up during the day, they continued to get colder. He was rummaging in his attic for old clothes and they were all wearing layers six and seven deep trying to stay warm.

On one of the many cold nights, or days there was no way to tell, that they huddled together on the couch Sophia turned to her son in the dark room lit only by the fire in the fireplace, "John, there's something you don't know."

She had not just John's full attention, but everyone else's as well. There was no option to go talk privately. The only room that had any warmth was the room with the fire, so they all had to stay there. She continued on, not bothering to whisper as she felt the eyes of everyone in the room on her, "I know that Katie saw your father in heaven and told you that he had died a hero's death as a martyr. What you don't know is that it was your brother, Miles, that turned him in."

John heard the audible gasp of his wife next to him and felt emotion threatening to choke out his words, "Are you sure? You can't know that!"

Sophia sadly bowed her head trying to hide the shame she felt at what her youngest son had become. She was trying to hide the devastation that his choices brought her, "Yes I am sure. I saw it in the same dream that showed me your father had died. It was his idea to test your father's allegiance to Elyon. After your father died, I saw, in my dream, your brother go up and take the mark of the beast for himself."

John jumped off the couch, "No! He took the mark?!"

Sophia raised her head and looked up at John, the sadness in her eyes gave John the answer he needed. He sank back on the couch next to his wife. This, in many ways, was a harder loss than the loss of his father. He knew his father had died a hero's death. He would see his father again in heaven very soon.

This was different. This meant the little boy that he played baseball with, built legos with, and went on camping trips with had grown into an evil man. They were best friends until the last several years... That same little boy who was once his best friend betrayed his dad. He wouldn't get to spend eternity with his brother. His, once sweet, brother and best friend would suffer for eternity. Knowing that felt worse than death for John.

He sat silently in his wife's arms for hours processing all the information. It was hard to know how long without the sun to track the time, but the whole time he prayed. As he prayed, he felt strength returning to him. He felt ready to face whatever was coming next.

John, Katie, and Sophia had been warning Tom that there was more to seal six and they needed to prepare. They told him what was next and said they needed to dig out a small cave in the hillside to keep them safe. They were about to get to work on this project when Tom stopped them.

He was hesitant to tell a bunch of strangers all of his secrets, but if they were right they needed to hide. He didn't want to waste time digging small holes when he had an underground shelter he could take them all to. Also, if they were right it seemed like they had the inside scoop of what was going to happen next and they'd be handy to have around. He stopped them as they all got up to go get shovels so they could get to work, "I might got somewhere we can be safe."

So, Tom showed them his secret underground bunker. He really hated it down there and would much rather ride out any storm in his home, cracked roof and all, but they said this was no storm he would want to ride out. He made a makeshift stretcher for Robert, who was healing very slowly and still slept much of the day and they all went down to his barn that was a hundred yards from the house. John and Tom laid the stretcher, with Robert on it, down on the ground, then Tom went to the very middle of the barn.

It really wasn't much of a barn. It was just four large poles with a metal roof on top and the floor was covered in thousands of tiny rocks. As Tom stood in the middle of the barn he started moving some of the rocks to the side. The more rocks he moved the more John was able to see a shape emerge. "It's a handle to a door hatch!" John rushed over to Tom to help him remove the remaining rocks clearing up the space around the hatch. The hatch had been hidden by the thousands of rocks, but even now that it was more visible it still was well camouflaged. There were rocks glued everywhere to the door and the handle so you could hardly tell what you were seeing.

After Tom opened the hatch to the vertical tunnel that led into an underground shelter, he and John went over to the stretcher and brought him first to the opening. He was the hardest to get down because he was too weak to leave the stretcher and access to the shelter was straight down. They debated several ways to get him down, but in the end, they decided to first secure him to the stretcher. They had rope tying him down every which way. He looked more like a mummy than a very injured man on a stretcher.

John went down the ladder first to help guide the stretcher which would be lowered by rope. Tom then slowly pushed the stretcher down into the hole as it dangled by the rope. John held the bottom of it with his hand to make sure it didn't bang on the walls and further injure Robert. Every two steps down the ladder, John would yell up to lower Robert just a little more from the rope. They did this the entire way down until they reached the bottom where John was able to gently lay his father-in-law flat on the ground. Robert looked grateful that the ordeal was over, but was too weak to say so.

John raced back up the ladder just in time to see everyone staring at the sky. He looked up as well and saw that the darkness was slowly starting to fade. The earth must have started its rotation again and that meant there may not be much time until the next part of seal six begins. He looked at his family and friends, "I don't know how much time we have, ladies hurry and get in the hatch."

Sophia, Beth, Emma, and then Katie all ran over to the vertical stairwell and began the climb down. As Tom and John went to take their turn to go down, they saw something in the sky. It looked like a shooting star at first, but then there wasn't just one, but thousands of shooting stars. They were coming into the atmosphere as the size of houses, but then they began to burn up as they got closer to earth and ended by landing like small bombs on the surrounding land. Tom and John looked at each other and closed the hatch behind them as they climbed down the stairs into the safety of the underground shelter from whatever was falling from the sky.

Benjamin and Rachel heard the explosions before they saw them. They were deep in the cave with their parents when they started hearing bombs going off all around them.

Benjamin raced to the mouth of the cave with Rachel and stood in awe as he saw the darkness had left the sky. There was light again, but it was more than light. It was blinding as it streaked across the sky.

It looked like a massive meteor shower was hitting the earth. None of the asteroids seemed to be abnormally large to cause an extinction-level event, but there were thousands of them. They started huge with massive plums of smoke trailing behind their path. Their reduced size upon landing were still causing massive amounts of damage. The sheer volume of the small meteors crashing into the earth and exploding with fire and craters were causing devastation everywhere he looked.

Trees were catching on fire and burning on the mountainside, there were giant holes in the earth in the valley below him. Off in the distance, in the direction of the city, he saw a giant plume of smoke. There was so much smoke it looked like it was possible the whole city was burning.

He turned around and looked at those in his cave and realized how many of them didn't have the seal of the one hundred and forty-four thousand on their head. They looked afraid. How many among those might be like his father and still fighting against surrendering to the Lord with their life?

Benjamin stood on a boulder at the mouth of the cave and faced toward the inside. Everyone looked at him as the stars continued to shoot behind him explosively hitting the earth. "What you are seeing was foretold thousands of years ago. We knew this was coming. It is a judgment of God. It is not a judgment on believers but on those who have chosen not to believe. God is not pouring His wrath out on the Christians. In fact, I believe that though Christians aren't necessarily protected from the evil acts of men during this time, they will be protected from the wrath God pours out on evil men."

He pointed to the fire literally raining down from heaven, "This is not God trying to hurt those that love Him. This is Him doing everything he can to let unbelievers know that He is real and give them another opportunity to choose Him. It is also God giving justice by destroying the works of the antichrist."

The front of the cave was packed and everyone's attention was on him. The shooting stars had slowed down to a trickle by this point, their fury burned out. As Benjamin spoke the last of his message, his eyes were focused only on his father, Jacob, at that moment, "If you haven't made a decision for Christ, commit your life to Him. Now is the time, not later. This is the sixth seal judgment. We are almost to the trumpet judgments and those will be so much more intense than anything you have seen so far. Be on the right side of history. Choose today whom you will serve."

At that moment the blue sky that was the backdrop behind Benjamin split. It was like someone took a knife and sliced it down the middle and as it was cut, the edges rolled back like a scroll on either side revealing the black universe beyond the sky. It wasn't just the black universe though. As everyone's eyes adjusted to what they were seeing they realized they were getting a glimpse into the invisible realm.

They saw angels and demons having a battle in the air. It was like watching ancient combat take place. Swords were clashing as grotesque creatures were trying to encroach upon the angel's territory and the angels were holding them back. Just beyond the war between good and evil above them, they saw heaven.

The first thing that caught Benjamin's eye was a giant throne chair. The edges of the entire seat were done in pure gold with intricate designs. Benjamin was able to focus on any detail he wanted even though it seemed to be thousands of miles away.

He looked at the designs on the chair closer and saw that it looked like the history of the earth was etched into the gold. He saw Noah's ark and Noah preaching. He saw David throwing a stone at Goliath. He was shocked when he looked closer and saw himself standing in front of the mouth of the cave preaching as the fire rained down around him. It seemed like the throne itself was telling a story of the world.

Benjamin's gaze shifted off the design of the chair. He was now trying to see who was in it. He couldn't see who was in the throne chair because it was so large. It was taller than the scope of his vision allowed him to see, but you could see the bottom of the chair and the feet of someone that was sitting in it. He instinctively knew that it was God and looked around him and saw everyone also drawing the same conclusion. The throne was surrounded by a sea that was as clear as glass.

More people than could be counted in white robes were bowing down to a man, of average height, who stood at the right side of the throne. These people were all of different colors and ethnicities and they all had palm branches in their hands that they waved at the man, Jesus, as they would bow down. Everyone in the cave could hear them clearly saying, "Salvation belongs to our God who sits on the throne, and to the Lamb!

And as quickly as it all began it was over. The sky was no

longer cut and everything was back to normal. If you wanted to, you could probably convince yourself you had imagined the whole thing because it all had only lasted probably five seconds, but everyone in the cave saw the same thing. There was no denying that everyone had just got a glimpse into heaven.

———————————

Elyon and Francis were hidden safely in a government underground bunker when the meteors started falling from the sky. He was in no danger, nor were any of his men. So why did he find three of his top aides cowering in a corner crying "We've made him angry. We have to hide from God!"

He had become so angry that he ordered his bodyguard to shoot them. Before the shot rang out in the tiny underground facility, he looked at them and said, "You dared to doubt I am god. Now, I will show you who you should really fear." Then he motioned with his head to his bodyguard that he was finished and three shots echoed in the crowded room.

If anyone was afraid of God, they didn't mention it after that. The communications officer did not know when it was safe to return to the surface as the meteors had knocked out almost all the satellites from the sky. All normal modes of communication were completely disrupted, but there was a moment when everyone could just feel that it was time to head back up.

They had reached the top as the last meteorite struck the ground in the distance. It was over, or so they thought. When the last person exited the bunker and stood on the ground, the sky in front of them split down the middle.

Everyone then had their eyes opened to see the spirit realm that was hidden from them before. They saw heaven and God just like those in the cave did, but they saw more than that too. They only briefly had their attention on God in heaven because their focus was almost immediately shifted to what was around them.

They weren't just seeing the spirit realm that was in the sky, but what had previously been hidden on the earth was now revealed to them as well. Every one of them had snake-like small humans slithering all over them. They saw the creatures sinking their fangs into them before slinking to a new part of their body and again striking them. All of Elyon's people were consumed with fear at the grotesque and disfigured creatures crawling all over them. Elyon's top officials were clawing at themselves trying to rid themselves of the beings that seemed to be slithering all around them, but each time they picked one off of them, two more would take its place.

For Elyon's men, the five-second vision felt like hours of torture, but as suddenly as it had begun, it was over. Even Elyon looked shaken, but he tried to hide it, "It is a trick of our enemy. We have just experienced hallucinations common with chemical warfare. Don't let their mind games win. We are stronger than them!"

John was the first to go up from the bunker to make sure everything was safe. He saw that so much around him was destroyed, but the rain of fire had stopped. He called down the hatch that it was safe to come up and they came up one by one. They had to pull Robert out by the rope the same way they had brought him down and it was slow going, but they all made it out and to the barn's rocky floor.

As they stood together and surveyed the damage, they all saw the sky split down the middle in front of them and they all saw heaven.

They all saw God on his throne and Jesus beside Him. It filled the hearts of the saved with hope and joy, but it filled Tom and Emma's hearts with fear. The entire group began to focus on the details around the throne when they all started noticing something that brought so much joy where there had once been pain.

Sophia looked at John and took a step forward toward the scene, "John! It's your dad. I see him bowing down to Jesus!

John saw his dad then. His dad got up from bowing before Jesus and turned toward him. It appeared like his dad was looking right at him. John grabbed Katie's hand with one hand and waved to his dad with the other, "I see him! I see him!" Everyone gasped when they saw Michael wave back to his son from heaven.

John couldn't believe it. He had hoped that his dad was watching him from heaven looking down at him and proud, but now he knew for sure that it was true. His dad turned away from waving at John and looked at his mom. Michael held her eyes for a moment before he put his hand to his heart and tapped his chest three times. The love was still evident in his eyes even across the distance between heaven and earth.

Katie and Robert saw the beautiful encounter of their friends beside them and they started scanning the scene in heaven eagerly. It was Katie who first saw her mom, "Dad, I see mom! She's there!"

Robert smiled for the first time since his injury, "I see her honey, I see her!"

Katie and Robert had tears running down their cheeks as they saw Beverly in heaven turn to them both and put her hands to her lips and extend her hand out to them like she was blowing them a kiss.

Beth joined in the excitement and nudged Tom next to her, "Do you see her dad? There she is! There's mom! She's in that white robe… and there's Davie off to the side. Doesn't he look happy dad?"

Emma saw Tom wipe a tear from his eye and turn his face away from his family above him in what looked like shame. Emma didn't have time to think about why Tom did that. She wanted to see if she could see her family too. She searched the scene in front of her and then she saw it.

She saw her husband holding the hands of their two sons. They all looked so healthy and so happy. The emaciated bodies that she last saw were gone. Her little boy's cheeks were full of life and her husband looked like he did before the reeducation camp had ravaged his body. The little boys were jumping up and down in excitement as Jesus was coming close to the three of them. As Jesus got closer, the boys ran to him and jumped into his arms as he spun them in a circle, all of them laughing. Never had she seen her husband and children so happy.

Emma ran several steps and fell to her knees looking up at her family. They saw her then. Jesus placed the boys on the ground and pointed down to Emma who was crying on the earth. Her boys both jumped up and down as they saw their mom and waved excitedly with big smiles on their faces. They started running and pointing at all of their favorite things trying to show her how happy they were.

When the two boys had finished running around showing her all their favorite things they ran to each grab one of Jesus' hands as their father stood behind them. Jesus and her family all looked at Emma with such love. There was no doubt that her children and husband felt no pain and were happier than they had ever been.

Then it was over. The sky was back to a blue and cloudless sunny day. It had happened as fast as looking at a streak of lightning across the sky. During that time, they had all seen something different and it felt like so much longer than a few seconds. It felt like a glimpse into a paradise that none of them wanted it to end.

Emma, on her knees, sobbed. "I have been so wrong to blame God. They all looked so happy. All I could focus on was what I lost that I couldn't see what they gained. I was so worried about giving them the perfect life here on earth that I forgot we're all living for a great life in heaven, not here."

She wept as Sophia and Katie went to comfort her and pray with her.

Tom stood shell shocked. Up until even a minute ago, he hadn't believed in God. It was much easier to explain away all the fulfilled prophecies he was seeing as coincidence, but now there was no denying what he had seen. If it had been just him that saw it, maybe he could explain it away that he was just going crazy, but they had all seen it. He wasn't crazy. That really just happened and if that did just happen, then that meant God was real. He wasn't sure he was ready to deal with that fact yet. He didn't know how he could ever measure up to what he just saw. He would never be good enough after all the mistakes in his past. It felt pointless to even try, so he decided to just ignore it and pretend like it never happened.

CHAPTER EIGHTEEN

"When He opened the seventh seal, there was silence in heaven for about half an hour. And I saw the seven angels who stand before God, and to them were given seven trumpets. Then another angel, having a golden censer, came and stood at the altar. He was given much incense, that he should offer it with the prayers of all the saints upon the golden altar which was before the throne. And the smoke of the incense, with the prayers of the saints, ascended before God from the angel's hand. Then the angel took the censer, filled it with fire from the altar, and threw it to the earth. And there were noises, thunderings, lightnings, and an earthquake. So the seven angels who had the seven trumpets prepared themselves to sound." - Revelation 8:1-6

Miles had seen what everyone else had. His coworkers and he had all seen the scene of heaven and then instantly been distracted by the disgusting beings that seemed to make their home inside and all around them. While it was happening, he felt like he was going crazy. He clawed at his body trying to yank the creatures off of him, but each time he'd rip one off, two would take its place.

The news had reports of chemical warfare agents that had been released that made everyone see hallucinations and every person's hallucination was different. The news anchors said that the Christians' latest attack was a release of a pathogen that made everyone hallucinate one of two potential scenes. Some people saw heaven and others saw demons. Miles was furious thinking that the Christians were messing with his mind and it was the last straw for Miles. The hallucination had left him with both physical and emotional scars.

When he saw the slithering creatures crawling all over him he went crazy trying to get them off of himself. They didn't come off easily. He had to dig his nails deep into his skin and rip them off of him. He remembered how as soon as he'd removed one, two more would take its place. His efforts became frantic and left him with physical scars all over his body from where he tried to claw at himself to get them off.

His psychological wounds ran deeper. He had nightmares every night that replayed that incident in vivid detail. Sometimes when he would first wake up from those nightmares he could swear that he saw the same grotesque beings crawling around at the foot of his bed and on top of him, but then in an instant, they would disappear and he would be alone with his thoughts and fears. The terror he felt from those creatures was unlike anything he had ever felt. He just wanted to forget it ever happened, but the nightmares kept it fresh in his mind.

The nightmares made Miles so angry because it was the Christians' fault he was suffering and they weren't suffering at all. The news said they had received some sort of antidote prior to the attack and that was why they all had peaceful and beautiful hallucinations of heaven and God in the sky. The news said it was a direct attack on those with Elyon's mark as they were the only ones who saw a living nightmare.

Every day he hunted down and found more Christians to arrest. He was on a personal crusade to track down anyone evading the mark and each one he'd arrest he'd send immediately to the Elyon worship stations. Miles thought that every time, with boring predictability, they would always refuse the mark and subsequently be beheaded.

He fumed to his coworker one day, "It is crazy to me that the Christians who are so full of hate and intolerance didn't see what we saw. That just shows what we saw was an attack from the Christians, just like Elyon said at his press conference."

His coworker agreed, but before he could speak Miles continued with venom in his voice, "You know my mom is one of them." He spoke with disgust dripping from every syllable, "A Christian. I'm embarrassed by my whole family. I think I know where she went to hide and I'm going to find her and when I do she will either willingly and joyfully take the mark... Or I will be the one to personally see that her head no longer stays attached to her body."

Tom was grateful for all the help from his new guests. He never would have been able to clean up such a mess on his own, but he wondered if he had enough food to keep all of them alive. He had enough supplies for three people for two years. There were seven of them. He guessed he could make that supply work for all of them for a year, but even with strict rationing, he didn't think that would be enough.

Tom thought to himself, "John claimed that since it had been just over a year since Elyon lost his dadgum mind in the temple that there were no more than two and a half years left of this mess before it was all over."

He still thought John was a bit crazy, but if he was right then he figured if they rationed they might be able to get by for at least half of that time. Technically it wasn't nearly enough, but some fruit trees survived for this year's harvest and next year there would be tons of fruit on the trees. He also still knew how to plant a garden for next year. They'd get by, he figured.

As Tom helped John repair the cracked roof from the earthquake that let in every drop of water, he was grateful. He was grateful to see his daughter who he never thought he'd see again. He was grateful for so many helping hands and people that seemed genuinely good-hearted.

Tom worried about Robert, he wasn't healing as fast as he would have liked to see. He was still unable to walk and a fever kept him in bed most of the day. He probably just needed some time to heal. Lost in his thoughts, he suddenly realized everything had become deathly quiet. He never heard such quiet in his entire life. The birds had stopped chirping, the annoying dog in the distance had stopped barking and even the wind wasn't blowing. With each second that passed where the wind continued to be completely non-existent, the air grew thicker and began to feel alive in a way it never had before.

Each breath suddenly felt like he was breathing in through a mouth filled with cotton balls. Any sound that he could possibly want to make was choked out from the effort of simply trying to breathe through the thickness of the air. It wasn't painful. It was just a very odd feeling to suddenly have breathing take concentration as he adjusted to the dense air in his lungs.

He looked at the trees and saw that not a single leaf was quivering in the wind. His gaze continued upward to the sky that, moments before, had large, puffy clouds that you could see being pushed westward by a steady breeze. Now the clouds looked frozen in place. When the wind had stopped moving, everything stopped moving with it. The silence around him felt alive like it had a mind of its own and was silencing everything around it.

As Tom was trying to comprehend what was happening, he dropped the hammer in his hand onto the roof. He was shocked as he watched it fall much slower than it should. It was like the dense air was decelerating its descent. When the hammer finally made contact, it didn't make a sound. He would have expected it to make a thud as it landed or a scraping sound as it slid down the shingles, but instead, all he heard was silence.

Tom was starting to think that there was more to the thickness of the air. It felt oppressive like it was stopping the very sound waves themselves. Tom tested out this theory and tried to clap his hands to see if he could make them make a sound. He watched his hands move in slow motion in front of him. His hands looked like they might if he were underwater and trying to clap them together. They moved slowly as if the ripples of the air were slowing them down. When they finally did make contact with one another there was no sound. The dense air around him was muting all sound.

It was such a stark contrast to the noise of the last several weeks. He remembered the noise of the entire earth-shaking and rumbling, his daughter, Sophia and Emma screaming, and explosions as satellites and meteors hit the ground. His head is still ringing from the sound of it all and now this. The polar opposite. His ears started to feel pressure from the quiet that silenced even the wind.

He looked around and saw that everyone around him also sensed the change in the environment and that none of them were speaking either.

Elyon remembered how his advisors panicked when they saw the vision of heaven followed by the slithering demons crawling around and inside of themselves. He had to think quickly to come up with an explanation that would show he was still in control. He told them it was the latest in a series of attacks from the Christians and Jews. He told them that his top scientists had run tests and found trace elements proving that it was chemical warfare.

He assured them it was nothing more than a trick of the enemy that made them see demonic creatures slithering around them. They all believed his story because they didn't want to believe the truth. To believe that what they saw was real, was to accept they had chosen the wrong side. None of them wanted to be wrong, so instead, they all willingly embraced Elyon's explanation and grew in their rage toward

Christians and Jews.

Elyon was blind to the truth. He knew the prophecies all said that his days were numbered, but he believed it was more lies from God. Elyon didn't understand how, but it was as if the spirit inside of him that guided him gave him knowledge of God himself. Elyon somehow knew that God has a deep deep love for humans and it causes God profound sadness when someone turns from him and heads toward hell.

He believed that God had no intention of letting people go to hell. All Elyon had to do was get enough people going there and God would relent in his judgments. Once that was accomplished, Elyon believed God would leave him alone to rule the earth.

Right now, God was not leaving him alone. He was raining judgments out from heaven on him and, with that knowledge, his fury grew. When he had seen the vision in the sky for those few seconds, his hatred of God consumed every part of him like it never had before and he continued to feel it every second of every day since then.

If the God of heaven thought he judged him, then he would make God sorry. He would wound him the best way he knew how, by hurting people. To his current enforcement officers of the mark he offered promotions and pay raises based on the number of rebels apprehended. For civilians, he gave incentives for them to report on their neighbors any suspicious activity that would lead to the capture of someone who did not have his mark. Free food, government-funded financial stipends, and free housing were just a few of the many rewards for neighbors turning on their neighbors. Elyon was determined to kill as many people as possible who refused his mark.

If he couldn't destroy their soul, then he would destroy their body. Elyon smiled a sick smile as he thought that he would enjoy every second of it. That thought lingered in his mind as silence enveloped his office. The secretary stopped typing on the keyboard, the sound of the air conditioner whirring died down and the sound of the traffic in the street completely stopped.

He looked outside and saw the stillness that filled the countryside. It seemed even the wind had stopped blowing. The ocean in the distance, which had moments earlier had large waves, now was completely still and flat.

It was a deafening silence that had a thickness to it. Elyon went to open his mouth in defiance to God to scream of his hatred for him, but no sound came out. He was mute and powerless to say a word. His hatred grew as every second passed in silence.

During the silence, Tom's mind wandered. His house was far out in the middle of nowhere and was still without any power. Sophia shared earlier with him that she and Michael had power where they lived. In fact, the majority of America was not affected by the EMP, but three large regions had been brought back to a more primitive way of living overnight.

With so much death in the world, manpower was at an all-time low and it was common to have rolling power outages from a lack of workers within the fully functional electrical grid. There was just not the manpower needed to rebuild the entire electrical infrastructure that had been knocked out by the EMP. Tom didn't expect that would change anytime soon either.

Tom told everyone of his encounter with the thieves earlier in the year, but that they hadn't been back since they had an all-out skirmish in his front yard. Tom didn't expect that to last forever. He had fruit trees and those people saw a garden. They would know this place was somewhere they could steal resources from and they would be back. Tom was sure of it. When Tom's houseguests found that out, they all prayed for strength for when even more trials might come to their doorstep, but Tom did something far more practical. He prepared more traps to keep his supplies secure from looters.

While Tom used the silence to think about future defensive maneuvers to keep his home secure, Katie, Beth, Emma, Sophia, and John used the time to pray. They prayed for Robert who was in the house sleeping yet again with a fever that made them suspicious that infection had set in. They prayed for Tom that his heart would be softened to the truth and he would accept Christ.

Most of all they prayed for Christ to return. Katie had seen heaven twice now and was so eager to be there forever. Her prayers every day spurred everyone on to pray, "Even so Lord Jesus come quickly." Right now they prayed that prayer in silence. They prayed that God would give justice to the many that were being rounded up and killed daily for their faith.

After thirty minutes, they started to hear faint sounds gradually begin again. The air was becoming less thick around them and they were no longer surrounded by only silence. They heard a bird chirping in the distance and that annoying dog was back barking. They never appreciated the mundane everyday sounds of life more than they did right then, but then the sounds grew. It started as a low rumbling and then the ground started to shake again similar to what it had done during the great earthquake but without the same intensity this time.

Katie yelled up to John from the bottom of the ladder in front of the house, "John. Tom. Get down, it's another earthquake."

The two men hurried off of the ridge pole of the roof and carefully headed toward the ladder as they felt the house begin to shake beneath them. It was Tom who noticed the change around them first, "Look!" He pointed up to the sky above them. What had been a clear sky, had turned to dark filled with ominous-looking clouds.

There was no rain, but there were flashes of lightning all around them as the thunder roared continuously. One crash of lightning was followed by another with a constant, deafening roar of thunder. There were no breaks for silence in between each new crack of lighting. They piled on one after another. A few minutes ago there had been complete silence, and now it was so loud with terrifying sounds that they could barely think straight. Each subsequent thunderclap lasted longer than the previous and the lightning streaked across the sky like a million glowing fingers stretching the length of the sky around them. All of the sights and sounds before them happened while the earth shook around them.

John made it to the edge of the roof and took a moment to steady himself and secure the ladder. Before climbing down, he looked at Tom, " That was the seventh seal, my friend. The trumpets are next. Are you ready?"

Tom didn't have time to answer as the lightning started striking the ground all around them. The earth itself seemed to be catching on fire as much of the green grass started burning and spreading. The grass started burning with a lightning strike in front of the house. Once a few blades caught on fire it spread like a controlled burn in front of the house to the treeline to the west charing half of all the vegetation in sight to black.

With the lightning and fire came hail, but it was not like any hail John had ever seen or heard about in his life. John saw hail pelting the ground in the distance as the storm was heading toward them. It looked like each ice rock falling from the sky was almost two feet in diameter. It didn't look like it was falling gently from the sky either. It was coming down with such force that it had to be falling at a rate of at least several hundred miles per hour.

John raced down the ladder first. He had planned to go into the house for shelter when a hailstone that had to weigh at least seventy-five pounds crashed right through a portion of the roof on the mobile home. The home was being demolished by the storm like it was nothing more than a house of cards.

Tom was trying to make his way down the ladder as everyone was yelling for him to hurry. On his final step of the ladder, a lightning bolt struck the top step. John was able to see the electrical currents pulse down the metal ladder and through Tom's hands. Tom was thrown off the ladder from the force of the currents and landed with a thud twenty feet behind them. Beth shrieked, "Daddy!"

Everyone raced over to him and John was the first to notice that he wasn't breathing. He immediately began doing chest compressions on him praying with every pump of his chest, "Please God, don't let him die!" There was such an urgency to save Tom. He didn't know the Lord yet, he wouldn't go to heaven if he died at that moment.

John let out an audible sigh of relief when Tom took a series of shallow breaths and whispered with what little strength he had, "Bunker." John looked around him and saw the lightning continue to hit the ground at random. Now each strike was accompanied by hail stones so large it was less like hail and more like a boulder from an ancient Roman catapult.

John realized Tom was right, they had to get to the bunker as fast as they could. The trumpets weren't coming. They were already there. He tried to help Tom to his feet, but the countryman had barely any strength. It took both John and Katie to help him up as the strong mountain man draped his arms around their shoulders and limped with them as they walked as fast as they could to the underground shelter.

Tom's extra two-hundred pounds made each movement seem slow motion and took all their strength. Katie stopped suddenly and looked at her mother-in-law, "My dad! He's still in the house! Can you take my spot helping Tom, I have to go back and get my dad!"

Sophia switched places with Katie without hesitation, but before Katie could leave, John yelled out to his wife, "Stop! Katie, you can't go." John looked at the hail as it fell all around them. Trees were being stripped bare. He saw a deer running from the storm in the woods. As it ran, a large piece of hail hurled straight towards its head and John saw it knocked to the ground and looked to be instantly dead from the impact. The orchard that Tom boasted would be full of fresh fruit next season was on fire from the lightning that seemed to pulverize everything in its path.

John realized then, they'd be lucky if they even made it to the shelter. There was no way Katie could carry her father by herself on the stretcher through this storm. "Katie, your dad's on a stretcher and can't walk at all, you'll need help."

Beth chimed in wanting to be useful, "I can help her carry him."

John shook his head, "It's too dangerous and he's too heavy for even the two of you to carry him. Katie, help me get Tom and everyone to the shelter, and then you and I can go back for him. It's a suicide mission if you try to do it on your own."

The rain was so intense that John couldn't see the tears that he knew were streaming down her face, "I can't leave my dad, John. He's all alone. I won't leave him!"

Each step was agony for John as they were practically dragging the mostly immobile Tom with them to the bunker. "We aren't leaving him. You and I will go back for him. I promise."

Katie became defiant to the man she loved, "No, John. Take Tom and the rest to the bunker. I'll be right behind you." She paused for a moment, "I love you."

With those three words, Katie turned and rushed into the home full of holes in the roof from the rapidly falling hail around them. John didn't have a choice. If he went after his wife, he would be leaving four people in the elements to die.

There was no way Sophia and Beth could carry Tom alone. Emma wasn't able to help them, she was still fighting to put weight back on her and just the act of walking was exhausting her. She certainly didn't have the strength to help carry an injured man. If he went with his wife, they would all die. He had to keep going and just pray that the Lord would protect his stubborn, beautiful wife.

They finally made it to the pole barn at the edge of the pasture and John carefully sat Tom down on the rocky floor. He ran over to the hatch to open it so they could all go in. There was no time to set up a rope pulley system for Tom and the barn seemed moments away from collapsing around them. He had to find a way to get Tom, who could barely stand for more than a minute on his own, down a vertical staircase.

John looked at the women with him, "Emma go in first. Mom and Beth, you guys help me get him to the opening and then you both go down, ok?"

The ladies nodded and did their best to get Tom situated with his legs dangling at the edge of the stairs before they climbed down. They climbed over his legs and once they made it to the bottom, it was time for John to go down with Tom. John took one last look at the house where his wife had run into. He could barely see through the pouring rain and smoke from the fire all around, but he was able to make out the outline of the house.

It seemed like hail was falling everywhere now. There was nowhere left in the open that was safe. He saw the beams start to give way on the barn roof above them and he looked at the house where his wife was. He was wondering, after he got Tom safely to the bunker floor, how he would get to her and get her and her father safely back to the bunker.

He hadn't even finished his thought when he saw the house in the distance completely crumble. A giant series of hailstones pelted at it and it crumbled like a pile of sticks. One second he saw the outline and the next it was gone and his wife with it.

John let out a roar, "NO!"

John had never felt such a primal urge to protect someone. His wife. His beloved. She needed him. There was a chance he could still save her.

He left the stairs and Tom and was about to rush into the hail to go pull his wife from the rubble when he turned back to see a large piece of hail hit the roof behind him. A piece of metal shrapnel from the metal roof went flying and embedded itself deep in Tom's arm. Tom yelled out in pain and looked at him. Tom didn't want to ask John to stay and help him because he knew that helping him meant not helping Katie. Tom felt his own lack of strength though. He knew was not strong enough to make it down the stairs alone. He would die if John didn't help and for the first time in his life, he was truly scared. In a faint voice begged, "Please, help me John."

John held back tears as he ran back to the stairs and began to climb the first few steps down it. He yelled for Tom, "I'll get you down, but then I'm leaving for Katie. You're going to have to help me out. Scoot back until you are sitting on my shoulders."

Tom had very little strength, but was able to scoot backward toward John. He scraped the entire underside of his body against the rocks doing so until he was sitting on John's shoulders as a child would. Except he was no child. He was a large man and John was struggling to hold him, "Steady yourself on the stairs."

Tom was about to reach out to the steps to steady himself,

but first summoned all his strength and pulled down the hatch door closing them into the bunker. John climbed down the first two steps feeling like his legs were going to buckle underneath him with the weight of each step. Even though Tom tried to hold on to the ladder to give some support and steady them, it barely helped ease the burden on John's shoulders. They were almost to the bottom step when they heard a deafening boom above them. It sounded like the entire barn had just collapsed on top of the entrance they just came in.

John took the final step and turned to his mom and yelled with no patience in his voice, "Get him off of me, now!"

Sophia and Beth all tried to hold up Tom while John wriggled out from underneath him. He immediately started racing back up the steps.

His mom called out to him, "John, come back! Where are you going?"

John just ignored her. He had to get to his wife. Katie needed him.

His mom was becoming frantic, "John, come back it's too dangerous! John!"

John refused to listen. He made it to the top and tried to push open the hatch door. Normally it flung right open, but this time it wouldn't budge. He tried again pushing with all his might, "Open you stupid piece of metal!"

Nothing happened. He hit it with his fists, but they quickly became bloody, so he switched to trying to ram his whole shoulder into the door jam. He was on a ladder below the hatch, so he couldn't get the leverage he needed when using his shoulder. He went back to using his bloodied hand, but this time he tried to hit it with the base of his palm. Every attempt and every angle was fruitless.

He knew he was no match for the bomb-proof bunker, but he had so much frustration and felt powerless. He beat on the door hoping with each bloodied knuckle a miracle would happen and the door would fly open, but that never happened.

He heard his mom crying at the bottom of the stairs feeling his pain with him. He thought to himself that it was so easy in the moment of a vision to have hope and believe it was all going to be ok. He thought to himself how proud he had been that he had such a good perspective about his dad dying.

He laughed as he thought, "I'll see him soon, right?" It was all meaningless words to him at that moment. When it came to his wife, all positive outlooks went flying out the window. He didn't want to think positively; he just wanted her.

He didn't care if he was going to die tomorrow and be with her in heaven forever then. It was too long. A single second away from her was too long. She couldn't die. He had to get to her. But each time he beat the metal that refused to budge his strength became a little less and he knew he wasn't getting out of there. He was trapped.

He stopped fighting and hung onto the top rung of the ladder and screamed as loud as he could like a caged animal desperate to escape. He had no words. It was just a guttural war cry of desperation to save his wife that came from the depths of his soul.

His screams of frustration turned into cries of despair as he repeated over and over, "I'm so sorry Katie."

He sat there as the minutes turned into hours shutting out the world around him. He thought only of his wife who he was powerless to save.

Made in the USA
Columbia, SC
30 November 2022

72219900R00190